TERRESTRIAL HISTORY

ALSO BY JOE MUNGO REED

Hammer

We Begin Our Ascent

TERRESTRIAL HISTORY

A NOVEL

JOE MUNGO REED

W. W. NORTON & COMPANY
Independent Publishers Since 1923

This is a work of fiction. Names, characters, places, and incidents are the products of the author's imagination or are used fictitiously. Any resemblance to actual events, locales, or persons, living or dead, is entirely coincidental.

Printed in the United States of America
First Edition

For information about permission to reproduce selections from this book, write to Permissions, W. W. Norton & Company, Inc., 500 Fifth Avenue, New York, NY 10110

For information about special discounts for bulk purchases, please contact W. W. Norton Special Sales at specialsales@wwnorton.com or 800-233-4830

Manufacturing by Lakeside Book Company
Production manager: Devon Zahn

ISBN 978-1-324-07937-8

W. W. Norton & Company, Inc.
500 Fifth Avenue, New York, NY 10110
www.wwnorton.com

W. W. Norton & Company Ltd.
15 Carlisle Street, London W1D 3BS

10 9 8 7 6 5 4 3 2 1

In memory of Will Reed
(1954–2016)

TERRESTRIAL HISTORY

1

HANNAH

He came out of the ocean. He walked up the seabed until the seabed became a beach, strode through the waves as if the water weren't even there. He stopped only when he stood before me.

But first, of course, I should explain.

I'm not the kind of person to tell a story like this. I've always been irritated by mysticism, by blithe statements about inexplicable phenomena. At dinner parties, say, when people start to recount spooky, inexplicable events, I'm the one with their teeth gritted, calculating privately the way in which the experience being spoken of could be accounted for by suggestion, by mist, by a bird loose in the attic, by strong painkillers or carbon monoxide poisoning.

I'm irked by the way such stories are told so lightly, as if visits from spirits or aliens should have no implications for our rule-governed world, for the forces that underpin our grids of GPS and radio, our steady certainty that our cars will drive, and our planes will stay in the sky. *If you really have had a premonition*, I have wanted to ask these friends, *how do you think that works, in terms of the flow of time, in terms of chains of cause and effect? Or what substance do you think a ghostly soul is made of, that it may pertain after death and still reflect light as it moves flittingly across a moonlit garden? Where does the essence of old Uncle Toby, whom you believe to be haunting you, reside?*

Don't get me wrong, I don't deny mystery. Science is driven, after all, by what is unknown. Newton spoke of himself as a boy playing on the seashore, whilst the great ocean of truth lay undiscovered. Yet the mysteries of the supernatural have always seemed so facile, so simple in the way that they posit forces that flatter our sentimental views of ourselves. Existence at a quantum level is stranger than the strangest ghost story. But it isn't built around *our* everlasting existence, the echoing of *our* own little human dramas across time and space. In all its complexity and strange elegance, is the universe really built to allow us glimpses of our dead? Forewarnings of small instances of bad luck? I know it is a poor thing to say about others' beliefs, but it seems so childish.

Which is all to say—at too great a length, as is my way—that I understand. I realise that you may be doubting, that you might think my own story is so much familiar anthropocentrism.

If this is the case, then I can say only that I was once wary like this, like you.

I came to the house to finish a review paper on computing challenges in confinement models, which I had spent almost two years putting off. My husband Ruaraidh suggested I come out for two weeks over the university's summer break. He would take care of our four-year-old son, Andrew, on his own for the time I was away.

I was grateful for the gesture, and I resented the gesture. I was in a hole, and for some reason I didn't want to be dragged out. My work, my research, had always been the thing I needed no encouragement with. Yet, since they'd let my contract expire at the fusion lab down in Oxford (because I wouldn't reconcile myself with their approach to turbulence modelling), and since I had returned to Edinburgh, to boring, piecemeal work and reviews of the findings of others, I had been making no real progress. "You don't know how to work," Ruaraidh told me. "You only know how to play."

He was an academic too, but his research was different. He wrote doggedly about neoliberalism in the Western novel. "Isn't that a bit outdated?" I asked him back when I first met him. "Why are you still stuck on that?"

He had frowned and said, "The effects of the ideology are still with us, and anyway, couldn't I say the same thing about fusion?"

Touché, I thought. He was exciting then, different from all the physicists I worked with in the way that he was so broadly educated and interested, not hidebound and literal, as my colleagues were.

I had vainly thought that I was also different from the other researchers in my lab. I had been a wunderkind, it's true. I had been horribly indulged. I didn't want to be like the other physicists, and I liked Ruaraidh for all the ways that he wasn't like a physicist.

Yet, alone at the white cottage, I was no longer a wunderkind; not a *kind* at all, in fact. And probably Ruaraidh was right; I'd been reliant on intuition and simple childish curiosity. I felt neither impulse now.

I walked around the creaking house and thought of the paper I was supposed to write. But I moved to do nothing. The first day on the island, arriving off the ferry, I'd spent time making the cottage habitable: opening the shutters, turning on the hot water, vacuuming up the dust that had accumulated on sills. After that, I'd gone to the shops in town to buy provisions, and then I allowed myself to take things slowly, assuring myself that I needed to acclimatise. I made a coffee and then another. My drafts and data sat untouched on the black hard drive on the kitchen table. The weather was blissful. I walked along the coast for hours. (Because what was the point of coming all the way out here, to this landscape, if I wasn't going to permit myself to explore it?) Like this, I found that I had been at the cottage for over a week and done none of the work that I had come with the intention of completing.

We had bought the house with the money that my father left me in his will. He collapsed with a heart attack at sixty-eight, just before the pandemic. He wasn't young, I suppose, but it was still a jarring death. He had been such a fit man, a jogging grandfather: the kind one sees out on country roads on a Sunday morning, clad in a fluorescent rain jacket and baggy leggings, grimacing gamely into the rain. The summer after his death, on a holiday on Lewis, Ruaraidh and I, exploring the west side of the island, drove down a road as far as it would go, until it became a rutted track, and there was a pretty white cottage with a FOR SALE sign nailed to the gate.

Ruaraidh was more doubtful than I was. His own father was an islander, born and raised on Mull. He was wary of these rural communities with their gossip, their hostility to outsiders. He thought, with justification, that we should be leaving the property for locals who would use it year-round. (But surely it would have been other city dwellers who would have bought it if we hadn't.)

He said, "Do you know what you're getting yourself into?"

"Not really," I said. But that was the point.

As a young researcher, I had been told that I was a natural, that my mind was built for the work that I did. I'd first written on shear effects in magnatised plasmas. The logic had somehow felt easy to me. I'd seen a way to synthesise a couple of ideas. It just seemed to click, though I worked day and night, I'll admit. I didn't dwell on the labour I did, however, because it felt better to think my small successes the result of some innate property of mine, evidence of a capability I held within myself. I loved the idea that I had an edge on all the other Ph.D.s who laboured at the same task. But now, in the house, one cause of my reluctance to do my work was the worry that I might not *be able* to complete it as I once had. I was forty. (*Only forty*, I tried to reassure myself.) Things had fallen into place before, resolved for me as they hadn't for others. But recently such clarity had been harder to come by. What if I was losing my edge?

Once, everything had felt so close to hand. But life had been so much simpler. There was just the work. There was not our flat, not Ruaraidh, not Andrew needing to be taken down to school with his lunch, his gym kit, his art project, the permission form for the trip next week, and Jasper to be dropped at the dog walker with a bag of food for the day. Loading the car on such days, when it was my turn, I was up and down the stairs to the flat, having forgotten so many things, and I still left without something I should have taken. I felt that my mind was fractured by it all.

Also, I thought of my mother, confined for the last five years to a nursing home in East Kilbride. She drifted, lucid sometimes and able to recognise me and my brother, but at others lost in her own past to the point she didn't know me. Periodically, she seemed to think she was still ten years old, late for history class. Somehow, she could reconcile this idea of herself as a 1950s schoolgirl with her presence in the nursing home, with the uniformed staff, the blaring TVs, the old, wrinkled faces in the rooms she passed. It was chilling to see the stories that the mind could tell itself, the way she could return, against all evidence, to the notion that she needed to hurry to catch up with her childhood friend Jane, who would already be walking to the old brick schoolhouse at the top of the hill.

She had come to the cottage the summer before, in fact, and though it had been hard work to accommodate her, she had seemed happy. She didn't always know where she was, but she liked the light, the sea air. She was kind to her grandson Andrew. We'd set the living room up as a bedroom so that she wouldn't have to climb the stairs. The only problem was that Ruaraidh and I, on the floor above, couldn't hear her waking in the night. She got up, turned on lights, wandered around. She didn't go outside, but two mornings in a row I opened the fridge to find seashells.

Ruaraidh and I collected shells, which we stored on the windowsill of the kitchen extension. Mum seemed particularly drawn to a conch that Ruaraidh had brought back from a conference in Florida. On consecutive mornings, I opened the fridge to find it next to the yogurt. My mother was back in bed both times. When she got up after the second instance of this, I mentioned the shell and she looked at me like I was the one losing it. I don't know why I wanted her to acknowledge the strange act when that recollection was clearly beyond her. Her confusion was old news, but it disquieted me. Taking the conch shell from the fridge, I had run my fingers over it. It was a lovely yellowish white, shading in places to dark caramel. The outside was smooth, but the inside where the crustacean had clung into its home was lightly ridged, pinkish. I shifted it around in my hands, felt the natural mathematics of the thing. Cooled like this, held in the clean light of the kitchen, the object was blissful to grasp, and what alarmed me was not the illogic of my mother picking up the shell and putting it where she had, but a feeling that I almost understood why she had done so and a resultant fear that similar impulses could live latent within me.

But I was different from my mother, I told myself. I ate blueberries in the morning, I taxed my mind. I have a memory of her during my childhood speaking on the phone to her sister, my aunt, saying, "Of course, Hannah has all those brains . . ." I recall that she sat on the sofa in the living room, her back to me as I passed down the hallway, and there was an odd distaste to the way she said those words, as if she were describing "those brains" as a condition, like the eczema rashes which prompted her to rub lotion onto her forearms each morning.

In the house alone, I argued with Mum, continued conversations with the woman begun twenty years before.

This time, the weather was improbably good; too warm, by all rights, for the Western Isles. It was 2025, another summer of climate breakdown: fires on forested hillsides in Turkey and Greece, mudslides in Slovenia. It was the period in which the acceleration of these crises was still a shock. There had been reports the week before I arrived on the island of the lobster fishermen in Stornoway pulling up their creels to find octopuses, drawn north by warming seas. *What does a Scottish fisherman do with an octopus?* I asked myself. It sounded like the start of a dirty joke.

The urge to find humour in it was a defence, I suppose. Every summer was worse, but also better, Ruaraidh pointed out, than the summer that would come after. He was becoming bitter. It only took a newspaper article about green capitalism (and there were plenty) to set him off on a rant about greenwashing. I was bitter too, I suppose, but for different reasons. Fusion seemed to me such an easy solution, were it funded appropriately, were the gatekeepers of projects not so inflexible. Ruaraidh, I know, struggled to believe in the purpose of what I was doing (or had been doing). "We're not where we are because of a need for *solutions*," he had said. "They could solve the climate crisis tomorrow with the tools we have at hand." (Who *they* were I didn't ask him to specify. Governments, I guess. CEOs. Investment bankers. The category seemed to get broader as Ruaraidh ranted, until eventually it became *us*.)

This particular day—the one I am trying to explain—was hot, right into the late evening, after dinner, when I realised that I had lost my watch.

I walked around the house lifting cushions, scanning over surfaces, cutting through the stuffy inside air. I looked in the bathroom, I looked on the bench outside the back door of the cottage. I tried to push aside thoughts of my mother moving trance-like through the same rooms. Then I remembered the swim I had taken in the afternoon. *Of course*, I thought. I was being too slow. I'd drunk too much wine with dinner. I had forgotten that I'd taken off my watch before I headed into the water. It would be down on the beach, on the rock on which I had left my clothes.

Jasper had been padding next to me as a I searched the house, wagging his tail, sniffing the things I moved as if it were all a game. I put on my shoes. I opened the back door and Jasper bounded out past me, thrilled by the unexpected expedition. He was a vizsla: ginger, skinny, all bones and muscles. He dashed out into the long grass in front of the house, which was tall in the middle of the summer, swaying and rippling in the warm wind.

I have explained my doubts about premonitions, but that night did already seem special. Everything was vivid. I remember, for instance, the bank beside the path to the cove. The slope was covered with small yellow flowers. These quivered as they were struck by the wind that came off the sea and channelled up the gulley down which the beach path descended. This night, these little heads all shook with a strangely even frequency, which made me think of the way that old VHS tapes would shiver in place when you paused them. I remember being a child in the early nineties and pausing a recording of *Star Trek: The Next Generation* in order to take in a tracking shot of the *Enterprise*, to examine the spaceship thrumming there, in dark space, on the old cathode-ray TV. This was all connected, somehow. Held in the moment.

Jasper barked from lower down the path, already halfway to the sand. I followed him, taking care stepping down the dry, muddy footholds kicked into the grassy bank.

There was a brackish, salty, vegetal odour to the air. Jasper was crouched on the beach chewing on a washed-up stick of kelp. The tide had come in some way since I had swum and the sound of the waves breaking echoed off the high cliffs of gneiss.

The beach was small, invisible from the road, unmarked on Google Maps, and so seldom visited by tourists, even in high summer. The prints of my own bare feet from earlier, leading to and from the water, were the only ones I could make out.

I walked to the rock from which those footsteps originated. My watch was there, glinting. I felt a suffusing relief. It was a man's watch, actually; my dad's. Gold, with a leather strap. I picked it up and put it on. It had been warmed by the sun, and this warmth meant that, fastening it, I felt that someone else—my father, I imagined, gladly, then—had been wearing it.

I sat on the sand, my back to the rock, and looked out at the water.

The sun was descending to the sea. Already the water had darkened. It had been clear blue when I had swum earlier, the clumps of weed puckering underneath me, the riffles and ridges of the sandy bottom visible below. Now the waves were like pewter, holding their light, glinting only where burrs of curling surf caught the slanting rays of sunlight.

I dug my hands down into the sand: the warm dry upper layer, the hard-packed cooler grains beneath. Jasper was sniffing around the rocks behind me. I shut my eyes. I could feel the slight warmth of the dusky light on my face. I listened to the sound of the waves, the noise of the water fizzing in and retreating whisperingly out. Gulls, riding updrafts from the cliffs behind, called. It started then, I suppose. I opened my eyes again, and there was what seemed to be a flash of light on the horizon. I couldn't quite understand that. I doubted what I'd witnessed, but I also knew that I had seen *something*. My pulse jumped.

Jasper had arrived beside me, wagging his tail, watching me enquiringly. I dusted sand from my hands, looked out at the water and the reddening sky. Was it the light from a ship that I'd seen? I could make out no boats on the horizon. Was it some strange manifestation of the northern lights? The waves curled and broke and I scanned all that water ahead of me. Jasper pressed to my side. I could feel his ribs against my ribs. I could feel his own small heart thumping away.

I don't know how much time passed before I saw the shape in the sea. Perhaps it had been there since the flash and I had been merely finding a way to see it, to parse what was in front of me. It was unmistakably a figure. That was the first thing I thought. I spent no time considering any other possibility—that it may be a rock or a seal, for instance. I just knew.

A dark figure stood in the surf.

The water rose and fell around its chest. I had the steady sense that it was looking at me. The waves slipped by it. I realised then that it was moving towards me.

It approached the beach. Each wave struck lower against it as it came towards the shore. It didn't swim. It advanced steadily, walking up the rising seabed. I could make out its torso then. It had a heavy head, thin arms. The water didn't disrupt its patient progress. It walked as if through air.

Then it was in the breakers, which curled and frothed and spluttered around the figure. I saw its knees rising, its careful stride.

It trod through the flat, foam-latticed water ahead of the waves and I could make out the entirety of its legs, which were thin and long in comparison to the thick body, vaguely amphibian to my mind.

The figure was larger than a human. It had a giant slab-like body and a wide head, lumped, neckless on top of that. It was like a golem, I thought, like some kind of animate statue.

I didn't move, though. I was not capable of it in the moment, I found. To stand seemed as impossible to me as rising to a hover and flying off.

Instead, I just looked at the figure as it stepped onto the beach. I studied its feet, which were striking bird-like things, with three toes and a fourth toe behind the heel. I watched the prints made by these feet in the soft wet sand, saw waves advancing and spluttering into them, erasing them as the water drew out again. It made the creature more understandable, somehow, to see the marks it was making on the world.

It walked over the flat wet sand, and then the smooth crescent beyond that, and then the dry pitted sand on which I sat.

I was still.

It stopped just ahead of me.

Jasper stood. His tail came out from between his legs and rose behind him. A ridge of his short ginger fur stood along his back. He barked, and I felt a pang of love. What could he do, the skinny dog? But he was trying.

The being was a couple of metres away, its long shadow cast over me, laid out over the rock behind. Its skin was markless but matte, like silicone, I thought. Where water clung to the creature, it hung in round droplets.

I was still frozen against my rock. Jasper approached the creature, barking. The creature began to lower itself, bending its thin legs, moving its hands towards the dog.

I waited.

Its knees pressed into the sand. Its hands were large, with thin fingers. It moved one of these open hands right up to Jasper's barking head. I held my breath. The hand didn't move. I released the air from my lungs slowly, as I realised that the creature was holding a palm in front of Jasper for Jasper to sniff. Jasper realised this himself, sniffed, sat back on his haunches, and watched the large figure enquiringly.

Now maybe you see why I first spoke of my doubts, to gain the leeway to say this, to show that I didn't want to believe the sight before me. But I did. I knew too that, despite the great stature of the figure, it was human.

Perhaps I could have worked out that what I saw was a suit, could have calculated the way that a body fitted within. But at the time, I didn't. I merely felt with certainty that I was being faced by a human consciousness.

I looked up at the figure. Quite suddenly a portion of the suit—a dot on the headlike lump that topped the torso—became translucent, and there, hanging like a bug stuck in amber, was the glowing face of a young man: boyish, freckled. He blinked. He smiled down at me. He said, "Hello."

I said (I was shocked that I *could* say), "Hello?"

The boy's illuminated face said, "I imagine this is a surprise for you."

I said, "It's like a strange dream." But that was me being stumped for how to reply. It was nothing like a dream. I felt awake. The rest of my life was the dream, I felt then.

The boy nodded from within the suit. He had a gentle expression.

"Who are you?" I said.

"A human," he said. "A human like you."

"I do have some questions," I said.

Jasper was still sitting on his haunches, looking up.

"I can imagine," said the boy.

We both laughed then.

The sea came in and out. The sun was nearly down over the horizon and the sky behind the figure was still blazing.

"I'm from the future," said the boy. "I know that sounds hard to believe . . ."

In that moment, forgive me, I could believe it.

The boy said, "I know who you are too. I've come here to see you."

My heart fluttered. I wanted it, I realised. I wanted to believe it. He had come for *me*. Across time. It was mad, and yet I could feel in my bones that it made sense, or that it could make sense.

Maybe we are all, deep down, waiting for something like this to happen. Or perhaps it was just me, the entitlement that Ruaraidh had long lamented. I felt, I'm sorry, that what he said was true. *I have been waiting and haven't known I was waiting*, I thought. He had come for me, and though I knew—yes—that I should doubt, I didn't.

2

ANDREW

2057

T*he clear summer light flickers through the train carriage, and yet Kenzie* still sits hunched forward, staring at her screen, her strawberry hair tumbled down, moppish, shielding my view of her face. These screens are different from the ones we had when I was a kid: anti-glare, dynamic contrast, hyper-focal. I know these marketing concepts, though I never consented to learn them. I want to believe in them for the moment, however, to delude myself that it doesn't take wilful effort on her part to keep looking at the device in her lap, as the light dances all over her, dappling as we move through a forest of young aspen.

She is eleven and already prodigious in her ability to be embarrassed. She senses my pride to be on this train that I spent so long campaigning for. I've mentioned nothing of my party business, not the hours I spent collecting signatures and lobbying for this new line, nor the hearings I picketed, nor the citizens committee I sat on. She sniffs it out like a dog, though, knows by instinct that if she looks up, she will have to face my ill-concealed pride, my stubborn parental failure to understand my irrelevance. Which is fair. I must allow her that. A child's prerogative. I did give her the forward-facing seat so that she could see the heather and the hills, but I resolve that I won't make a thing of it.

She'll grow away from you anyway, I remind myself when I wake in the night and toss and turn, trying not to wake my wife Lina and falling into argument with my own jabbering primate brain, doubting the plan to stand for Parliament and lamenting all the time with Kenzie that I will give up. It's not a bad thing to let her have her space, but still, I can't help myself. The forest is behind us now. The train whispers up past the dam at the head of Loch Glascarnoch, which is lower than ever. It's another dry summer. The old road is revealed as a slantwise line across the rawish, lichen-speckled rockscape where the water has drawn back. I can make out Beinn Dearg in the distance, sunlit, behind other clumped rounded peaks. We will tip over into the descent towards Ullapool soon. I lean forwards in my chair and touch Kenzie's knee. She tosses back her hair, glares. "Look at those hills," I say, gesturing, realising as I have begun speaking that I don't really know what I am directing her towards. "The light . . ." I add, lamely.

She is biting her bottom lip, spits it forward to speak. "Right," she says. "The hills, and yeah . . . the light. Sure. Nice." The polite way she brushes me off, and the pity manifest in this courtesy, would hurt were I to linger on it.

"And the waterfalls," I say. "Look. Up there."

Her gaze follows my finger, and she says, "Yes."

"I just love the landscape here."

"Metamorphised sandstones. Schist and gneiss. I did a school project on it." She is back to her screen again.

"Yes, but . . ."

"Scotland has a varied geology, it's true."

"It's magnificent," I say.

"I could recommend some texts if you want to study the subject." She is playing now, impish, still looking down.

"You know the structure," I say, "so you don't need to look?"

"Pretty much," she says.

"Don't you feel any romance in the land?" I say. "In your ancestors' land? Doesn't it stir your Celtic blood?"

She looks up at me again then, baited, unable to resist me setting her up like this. "Mum's family is from Germany," she says, "and your family are lowlanders at best."

"At best?"

"If not displaced English."

"Shush," I say, pretending to be offended. "Your grandad's parents were from Mull."

"His dad was a sailor from Liverpool, moved to the island after he left the merchant navy . . ."

"Another school project?"

She shakes her head. "I read some of the family genealogy."

"You're very clever," I say.

She sighs in feigned exasperation. "I'm not," she says. She looks up again, fixes a smile I haven't seen for a while. "I just seem clever in comparison sometimes."

"To me?"

"Of course." She lets out a giggle that carries through the carriage and wakes her to herself, causing her, as soon as she has heard it refracted back, to shrink in her seat again, to return her blushing face to staring fixedly at the screen.

I let her be now. I sit and watch the view as we descend towards the sea, which reaches inland as the long finger that is Loch Broom. The early afternoon sun is high over the water. The train slips through woodland along the shoreline. The brakes come on a couple of miles outside Ullapool and the flickering of light between trees starts to slow in line with the motion of the train itself, as if we are all at a show where the band has decided to play something mellow.

The world is still beautiful, of course, but I missed that beauty for so long. When I look back, I realise that I was depressed for a long time. Not that I knew it then. It was just the way it was. My state was a filter that coloured my days, inseparable from the way that I perceived the world. I wasn't down all the time, and maybe I was even good company on occasion, but I was always on the edge, a man who spoke back to you from the edge. The thing that changed it all was the birth of this girl, Kenzie. I wanted to serve her, wanted to give her everything I had. But what really saved me was the sheer *reality* of her. I had a descendant and I realised that for a great deal of time my despair had been about the future, about the world I was leaving to the hypothetical people of the future. And yet, to have one of those people in my care suddenly, one of those *real* people, changed everything. I had no choice, I suppose, but to reject that despair. It was cognitively essential. That is how we think, isn't it? Post facto. I had to hope where I had never hoped before. I went to political meetings, and then I spoke at those meetings, and I found rising within me something that my little girl had given me. I noticed all the people like me, recognised the longings in them that I had felt myself. I had previously thought most people apathetic, but I came to believe that they were instead *hesitant*. They needed a route by which to exert their energies, by which to address their fears together. I felt that I could play a part in that great drawing together. I really thought for the first time, *We can do this. We can save this world for her. Part of this world, at least. Enough.* I ran around animated by that hope, by that sense that suddenly I had to do it for her. But now that resolve is leading me away from her.

Because the day is so nice, we sit on the rear deck of the ferry as it leaves the dock. The boat makes a long arcing turn into the channel that leads out between the Summer Isles towards the open sea. We face back up the loch and Kenzie still studies her screen and I look at the hills of the mainland, the cottages that dot the shore, the group of kayakers, insectile at a distance, paddling around the rocky headland beneath Rhue Lighthouse.

When we reach the open sea the water is dark, rougher. The wake of the ferry is wide and flat, like a thumbprint dragged across butter. The air is cold, and Kenzie and I go inside and sit at a high bar table beneath an old poster—outdated even when the ferry was launched—that lists the whales and dolphins that could once be seen when making this crossing. I buy myself a coffee from the cafeteria and Kenzie a cup of water because that is all that she drinks. She is not unlike my mother, her grandmother, in her preference for regularity in sustenance and routine. Food is only fuel for both of them, and I wonder what they will eat for the month they are together. Though of course Mum does, unfortunately, drink more than just water.

I sip my coffee and I tell myself once more that things will be fine. I am on Mum's side for now, her advocate in the decision to put Kenzie into her care over the holidays while I kick my campaign into gear before next summer's election. "Don't you spend most of your therapy sessions talking about how she neglected you?" Lina asked me in bed a few weeks ago.

"Maybe," I said, "but Kenzie is the age where she wants to be neglected."

"Is that so?"

"Mum only drinks in the evening," I said. "She's got genteel pretentions about her decline."

"She's a bit mad, you must admit."

"Duly admitted," I said. "I just don't think it's contagious."

I was lying back, ready for sleep, or ready to fail to sleep. Lina was staring sightless at the book she'd been reading for months, in the minutes snatched between her late return from work and turning in. The conversation was largely symbolic. Lina raised her points to have them knocked back. Lina's hospital caseload left her no time to be home. We'd agreed that I should be allowed my political career. We spoke of the subject only for our own reassurance.

At the port, Mum is waiting next to the battered ancient Land Rover, which she runs on biofuel.

We cut out from the flow of foot passengers exiting the ferry terminal. We walk across the car park towards her, over the vacant parking spaces.

She looks at the two of us with eyes narrowed against the wind. She wears a yellow fisherman's coat and wellies. A scarf flutters, peeling from her neck like a flag. Her high cheeks are red, marked with burst capillaries: the complexion of a drinker, I think, though maybe the weather of the island has caused such an effect. I'm trying to be generous, to let her be only a person and not the parent forever falling short of an ideal I must abandon.

She pulls us both into a hug. Her breath smells not of wine, I'm glad to find, but of that strange fruity chewing gum she loves. She steps back and looks at my daughter. She says, "Good to see you, Kenz." She is not the kind of grandma to squeeze a cheek or remark how much her granddaughter has grown. That is an asset when facing someone like Kenzie. Mum treats everyone as an adult. When I was small, that felt like a wall between us, yet it is just what a girl like my daughter, phobic of being patronised, needs.

The Land Rover croaks as it starts up, and Kenzie, sitting in the back, on one of the bench seats that run over the wheel arches, shakes her head in wonder. "A combustion engine?" she says. Mum nods. Kenzie's been in the vehicle before, but years ago when she was a tiny giggling girl in a denim smock, impervious to the fuel this strange vehicle ran on. We lurch out of town getting looks from the tourists, though locals calmly acknowledge Mum, who must be a well-known local eccentric: the scientist lady in her dilapidated cottage, fired from every university and institute now, persisting, against all reason, with a design for a particular type of fusion reactor that she is still so sure can be miniaturised.

Beyond town, Mum speeds up. She takes the turn onto the smaller road across the island without slowing, and the old tires screech. "Jesus!" I say. "You'll put us in a ditch." She only laughs, though, glad to have scared me. This is her vibe: exceptionalism. The rules of the road are for others, just as she thinks the laws of physics are. I see her looking up at the rearview mirror to catch Kenzie's eye and wink.

The house is grubbier than before, but still as I remember it, liable to make me a boy again. I carry Kenzie's bag up the narrow staircase to her room. I have the feeling that I am visiting a half-sized replica of the place I knew as a child. The stairs still creak in the way that used to scare me. The model of the ship still stands on the window, casting a spiky shadow into the room. I came here every summer until the divorce. When Mum moved out here properly, I was allowed to see her less often. Dad was resentful, and Mum didn't need me out here where she was so patiently unravelling her life on her own.

Kenzie drags up the wetsuit that Lina bought her for Christmas, the legs of it slapping up the stairs behind her. "It'll be nice to use that," I say, as she hangs it on the back of the door.

"Sure," she says.

"You'll be okay here?"

"Dad . . ."

The windowsills are dusty and there are moats of dog hair in the corner of the room, but the bedding smells clean. I fuss around until Kenzie stares me down with a steadiness that sends me out of the room.

Downstairs, Mum says, "All good?"

"Yes," I say. "I think she'll like it here."

"I'm sure."

"She has some work, some summer projects . . ."

"So do I," says Mum. "All the better."

I sit at the kitchen table and Mum makes tea. She brings the cups over, tinkling on a tray in her shaky grip. She sits with her back to the light, the cooling evening sun. "So you're becoming a politician?" she says.

"Well, I've been working in politics for a while. I'm running for Parliament now."

"Yes."

"I have my doubts, if I'm honest." I gesture upwards, at the first floor, at Kenzie, who is clumping around loudly, likely wearing her headphones.

"She'll be fine," says Mum. "Don't give it up on account of her."

I feel an opportunity for a rebuke, a chance to say, *Of course you would say that*, but I don't take it. "I wanted to be there for her. She was the main concern. The politics was secondary, but now . . ."

"We're serious people," says Mum. "We start a thing and we take it seriously. We don't know how to give up."

Again, I repress a reaction: the urge to reject the assertion that we are similar.

Mum puts two spoons of sugar into her tea, stirs it slowly. Maybe she wants me to ask her about her research, to indulge her view of herself as a working scientist on the edge of a breakthrough. I can't though. We look at each other silently, and she gives me a wan smile. There are gulls in the sky behind the house, riding updrafts above the cliffs. We sit for a long time, finishing our cups of tea. Mum clears her throat. She looks at me for a moment, then turns away and stares towards the sea. It is like she is preparing, but then when she turns back she doesn't speak. The resolve in her expression is gone. Her hands on the table are the wrinkled hands of an old lady. I look at them. I watch them coming to life, whitening in places as they press against the wood. Mum rises from her seat until she is silhouetted against the bright window. She says, "Will you join me in some wine?"

We eat dinner—a surprisingly tasty pasta dish made by Mum—as the light turns scarlet at the horizon. I am shocked to find Kenzie a useful partner in cleaning up after dinner. She dries plates with a tea towel, dances around the kitchen putting them into cupboards. She leans over the thick wooden table to wipe it clean, leaving behind rainbow-shaped arcs of suds. Mum sits outside, on a bench underneath the kitchen window, drinking another glass of pinot grigio. I go out. She looks up as I crunch along the gravel path towards her. "A nice night," I say.

"Every night here is nice in its own way," she says.

"I suppose so."

"This is what it's about, isn't it?"

"What?"

"What we're up to," she says. "trying to save this."

"I suppose," I say.

She appears to note my scepticism. She says, "Each of us in our own way."

I take a seat next to her. The sound of the sea is lovely: coming softly in, dragging hissing out.

"I'm glad you're doing your politics."

"Don't say *your politics*. You make it sound like a silly personal obsession."

"Maybe it is," she says. She laughs. "I speak as someone with a silly personal obsession."

"Do you think your work is silly? Really?"

She turns and fixes my gaze. "Of course fucking not," she says. She looks away again. The long grass in front of us is shuddering in the evening wind. "It had its costs, my work. I know that."

"Okay."

She raises the wineglass to sip. I hear the faint ting of the rim striking her teeth. She swallows, exhales unsteadily. "You're not me, anyway. You have a connection with Kenzie. You understand each other. You can talk."

"Yes."

"Believe me, I wanted that with you."

I don't need this now. Is it better to think that she was regretful in her neglect? Is this preferable to the feeling that she didn't see me, didn't recall the life she once had back in Edinburgh? On impulse, I take my device from my pocket, check my messages. The signal is usually spotty here, but the connection is strong for the moment. I browse to clear myself. To reset. I come to the video that I have shared so often amongst my bubble in disgust and fascination. It starts to play again, silently, subtitled. I hold the screen towards Mum. "You've seen this?" I say.

She frowns. "I need my glasses to see something so close."

"Axel Faulk. Tevat."

"What's Tevat?"

"It means *ark* in Hebrew, apparently. They've used up the Greek and Latin names. They're getting biblical now."

"Like the weather," says Mum.

"Yeah."

"He's the Mars fella?" she says. "I know him."

I draw the screen back. The man is speaking at a conference somewhere in California. Behind him looms a projection of the planet Mars, bubble-like structures adhered to its surface like boils. The subtitles say, "The time to depart is coming ever closer."

"We had a call," says Mum.

"Wait. What?"

"They were interested in my designs."

"Really?"

"Nothing came of it, though." She shrugs. She presses her empty glass down into the gravel under the bench until it stands straight. "I don't think they really understood them. They were more interested in the *idea* of liking my designs than the actual work. They relished the idea that I was a *maverick*. That was their word."

"You never told me this."

"I didn't know you were interested."

"This man is why I'm going into politics. He's moving here, escaping the new regulations in the U.S. He's made a deal with our government to coordinate his Mars mission from Glasgow. These people who just want to give up on the planet . . ."

"I was just after some funding . . ."

"We've gone from a denial of how bad it will be to total surrender. They're retreating to space, for fuck's sake."

Mum looks at me wearily, and I think that she is bored of me as Kenzie is bored of me. They are not ideology people. They are logic people, uninterested in changing minds, concerned with solving problems in a technical sense. Mum thinks still that her magical power plant will save us, yet we already have the means to save ourselves. Our diminished world is still enough if we work together, if we share. There is enough food, enough land to support us all, if we manage it to our mutual benefit. I could say this, but then I know what she would ask me back: *Why aren't we saving ourselves, then?*

I stand from the bench and walk down the lawn, past the odd pile of rocks that Mum built beside the house in memorial to her old dog, Jasper. The sun has set now. The sea still reflects the maroon glow that lingers at the horizon. I walk towards the bay along the lumpy path. I stop at the top of the cliffs and look down at the small crescent of beach for a while. When I turn back to the cottage, I see that Mum has gone in. The cottage is a silhouette against the purplish eastern sky, the lit, uncurtained windows standing out lanternlike. I see her move through the rooms, getting ready for bed. I can smell the gorse, the seaweed on the beach. It is bliss to be out here. Mum turns from the kitchen, moves upstairs. It feels somehow easier to know my affection for her from this distance. Close, I am too short with her, liable to apportion her blame out of scale. I must try harder, credit her efforts to connect. The temperature of the day is delicious now, the air cool and soft. The wind gusts, and the grass in front of the house comes alive. I look back towards the wash of the sea. For some of the older ones in my party it is treachery to think that nature can still be sublime, as droughts spread like bruises over continents and monsoons flood whole nations. Yet isn't it the point, that there are still things worth saving here, worth sharing? We must cultivate love, I tell myself again.

3

ROBAN

2098

My teachers at school have said that my phrasal dictionary is a fitting tribute to life in the Colony, while my mother, who is laconic, said that the dictionary is yet more proof that I am worryingly precocious. "I was just playing with dinosaur toys when I was your age," she told me. Though later, when she was being sincere, she said that she understands my dictionary, my need to gain a solid grasp of this strange world.

Really, I prefer it when she is being laconic because the sincerity makes me think of her worries for me, of whispered conversations spoken beyond my earshot in institutional settings. She frets for me, for difficulties of mine that she thinks extend beyond those problems that other children of my generation have. Mostly, I think, she is *projecting*. That is psychological terminology that describes the way that she imagines her own problems to be mine. My Other Mum died in a mine collapse when I was three, and Mum still misses her and expresses loneliness by talking to the child therapist about how I do not have a "rounded home life."

Maybe there is also projection in the way that Mum sees my dictionary. She thinks of it as an attempt to resolve *my* problems with language, rather than—as it really is—a remedy for the unacknowledged irrationalities of her own generation. What is strangest to me is to be in this place and still be talking as if there is inside and outside, as if there are trees and fields, blue skies, seas, a single moon dragging the tides around the planet. What is odd is not to want to change this way of speaking, but to carry on with it as if it is normal.

When she means to say that she is confused, Mum says that she is *all at sea*. But what could that mean on a planet on which water is only mined from deep in the rock, pumped through pipes in the Colony, and held in fountains, sinks, baths? She intends to say, as far as I understand it, that she is lost, adrift. But even the word *adrift* is one that relates to boats, to vessels floating on a large body of water, and there are no boats here in the Colony, no bodies of water for them to float upon. In my phrasal translation, I have decided, she should say *I'm all in space*. As in, she is free-floating, not subject to the gravity of a planet. She means really that she is *lost*. But even to be lost is an old concept, because what succession of systems failures would one have to experience to not be able to locate oneself?

"You are dogged," Mum says, when I talk through my latest definitions to her, and I wonder whether I should allow that, because I look up *dogged* and find that it comes from the stubborn characteristics of the dog, and there are no dogs here in the Colony. I am browsing on the screen in the kitchen, and Mum is heating the noodles that she brought back to the unit on her way home from the lab. I speak my thoughts aloud, and she says that all such comparisons are somewhat mythic anyway, and I ask what she means, and she says, "Even when there were dogs, many dogs weren't dogged."

There were, in fact, once dogs here. Mums bought a dog with them on the Long Voyage. I say, "Was Larry dogged?"

Mum thinks and says, "Yes, actually. Larry undermines my point because Larry was very stubborn."

On the screen I open Pictures, and flick back through the years until I reach the point that I was one year old, and there is Other Mum holding me and Mum sitting next to her with Larry the dog sprawled across her lap. Larry is beige and brown and has a small, wrinkled face. His mouth is turned down in what seems to be an expression of anxiety, his long floppy ears framing his head. His eyes are like shiny brown buttons.

That was all in the Early Iterative Stage, when things needed to be done quickly, and mistakes were made. No one had realised the problems that animals would cause to the first generation of children like me who had no exposure to many bacteria and suchlike. A lot of children had acute allergies to the pets in the Colony, and so it was decided that the animals must be *euthanised*, which is a word derived from ancient Greek meaning easy or happy death. Mum doesn't really like to talk about Larry, because, like talking about Other Mum, it makes her sad. Euthanasia is a *euphemism*, which is an indirect way of saying something that might otherwise be too blunt. Larry's death was probably not actually a happy death (though I'm sure the Colony authorities took all the steps they could to make it as painless as possible), and so doubtless it is an unpleasant thing for Mum to recall. But today she must be feeling a little better than usual in this respect, because she says. "You would have liked Larry. I'm sorry you don't remember him."

Mum knows that I like to hear about Larry, because when I was a small child I used to ask about him often, as well as about Granddad, who needed to be left behind because of the unforeseen rapidity of the Terrestrial Collapse and the limited capacity of the transports. Mum brings the noodles to the table, and I push the screen away and take up my ortho-fork. "What did Larry like to do?" I say.

Mum thinks. "He liked to run and smell and lick, I suppose. And the Colony maybe wasn't the best place to do any of those things, so perhaps even before the end bringing him here was a mistake."

"He didn't like to just sit?"

She lifts noodles with her chopsticks, swallows a mouthful and thinks. "He did like to sleep," she says. "But dogs are physical creatures. They need to run."

"Yes."

She looks at me, and I have the familiar feeling that I often have with Mum that I know what she is thinking. She is worrying that her assertion that running is so important to a dog might be offensive to her son who cannot run naturally. I am not offended, though I am well aware that the problems of my generation discomfort our parents, however much they might deny this. I would prefer, actually, that they spoke of it all more clearly, rather than avoiding the subject. I like to be direct, as is probably obvious.

Because there is a silence, I ask our OS to play music.

"Not this," says Mum. I've been listening to experimental Terrestrial music recently, and Mum dislikes it, says it sounds like a factory.

"Change, please," I say in my OS voice. Then I say, "This is better?"

She says, "Thanks." Then she says, "Sorry, R, it's just . . ."

"You don't like it as much as I do?" I say.

"I suppose so."

I twist my noodles with my ortho-fork. "Like Rute noodles . . ." I say.

She laughs. "I don't know whether to pity you for never having tasted food from Home, or whether to envy the fact you have nothing to compare this against." It's a joke, of course, based on the well-known fact that Homers like Mum would prefer the food from Earth, but it's also a little disrespectful to all those people who worked so hard to find a way to grow Rute efficiently in the Martian regolith, and all the folk who developed processes to turn this Rute into noodles, and breads, and chewy buns. I look at the OS receiver, wonder what the ArtInt is making of this. I suspect that her flat sarcasm slips by the system, and anyway her work is Category One, meaning that she is highly unlikely to be flagged for Attitude Assessment and potential Downrating. Still, to compensate, I say that Rute is crucial to our survival on the planet, and that I like it, and that anyway it's certainly better than eating nothing at all, which is really the only other option when you think about it, given the Terrestrial Collapse, and the difficulty of growing Legacy Foodstuffs here. Mum listens to this and her expression is momentarily brittle, but then she softens her eyes and nods and says that of course I'm right, and she shouldn't have made her silly joke, and she reaches across the table and touches my hand.

Mum is Category One because of her work on the Stellar8Rs, without which life here would be impossible. She doesn't like to talk about this, but one of the teachers at my school explained it to me, amazed that I didn't know that it was Mum who designed the first mini-loop system. That was why her picture was on display on Pioneers' Day. Without her, our teacher Yao said, we'd be shivering on this rock with nothing. Life in the Colony is hard and requires good attitude and energy. Lots of energy. On Home, maybe, there was just water sitting in pools, waiting for people, and food just grew and there was air to breathe, and a temperate atmosphere. But here we need to use so much power to get our water and our food, and to make the very air we need, and to warm us in the long nights and to cool us in the blazing days. Without Mum's systems, we would have managed only subsistence, if anything. On Home, they never managed such power. It is Mum's designs that allow us to live fulfilling lives here, and to feel assured that with terraforming we will find a way back to an easy self-regulating biosphere like the one which existed on Home, and which so many people back in Terrestrial History were so complacent about. You would expect Mum to be proud, but she is often regretful. She can be sad (though it is a sadness that I do not think others notice so easily, a sadness she carries lightly, that lives around the corners of her eyes).

When I have finished my noodles and Mum has given up on her own, we clean up together. I lean against the counter rinsing things, and she stacks the washer. She says, "You can have your sawmill music on," and I must query *sawmill*, because it isn't a word that's familiar to me. I realise that it has to do with the preparation of wood, which they used to use at scale in the production of buildings back on Home. Mum comes over to me as I sit at my screen and together we watch an ancient video, similarly mesmerised, in which a tree trunk comes down a line of whirring circular blades, being shorn of its brown outer skin (its *bark*) and sliced and turned and cut until the huge tree has become a series of uniformly shaped beams that trundle off the end of the conveyor belt, clacking together gloriously as they fall into a stack.

I am always early to school, because I wake at the same time as Mum, who likes to be at work in her lab before her colleagues.

I go to school at school number three. I am in the fourth school intake of the Colony. I was born at the end of the second M-year, after the Great Generation Gap. The GGG is another thing that preoccupies Mum. Often, she says, "You don't know how to be children."

No kids travelled on the transports after the Terrestrial Collapse, so the youngest person here, before anyone started having kids, was twenty-five Earth years old. There is a gulf between us and our parents.

For Mum, this is a problem. "We've lost the culture of childhood," she says. "The games, the sayings, the funny voices . . ." I don't agree, because, thanks to the digital archives, we have better access to Terrestrial Culture than any generation before. I can watch all the movies that Mum watched when she was my age, read all the books that she loved. She insists we miss simpler things—little phrases and gestures passed in emulation—and maybe she is right. Yet is it bad that we are growing up quickly? We are not just any children, but those living in the middle of the hourglass, some of the few thousands alive after the loss of so much humanity, amongst the few custodians of our species preparing the way for the Great Repopulation when this place is terraformed and when other habitable planets have been located. I want to be doing something real already, not playing, not mimicking.

On weekdays, as it is today, I wake at six, and Mum is already in the kitchen area of the unit making coffee. I sit at the table and drink my juice. Because Mum's work is Category One, we have a nice unit, a view of the Outer Plain from the large window in our living area. On winter mornings like these, the plain is still dark at this time, the uneven frigid ground illuminated by the light spilling out of all the units overlooking it, striped by the long shadows thrown by the scattered rocks.

Mum doesn't eat breakfast but insists that I eat quinoa porridge. Like all parents, she still hopes that just the right food, or just the right exercise, might somehow cure us, even now. Though she would never say this.

After I have finished my breakfast, Mum needs to go to work, so I return to my room, and begin to climb into my Interior Exo Suit, which I can do alone, but which I still like to put on while Mum is home in case I encounter any problems sliding into the piloting seat. Today, I get it on without great difficulty. I flex the knees of the suit in a quick squat, spread and draw in the arms. I took one pill today, because my pain was not terrible. Mum comes in, to check on me before I leave, and as always there is that momentary flinch when she enters and sees me standing suited. I smile at her via my Avi face on the suit display. She smiles back.

Then Mum has to go. The hour before her colleagues arrive, she says, is her sacred working time. She dashes around the unit collecting her scattered belongings—her glasses, her thermos, her screens—and dumping them into her big bag, before running out the door in time to catch the shuttle. I can never understand why Mum and the other Homers like *things* so much, why they must carry so many little items. They are still unused to this place, in which the necessities of life are designed to be close at hand.

I depart myself after Mum has gone. It is still too early to leave for school, but I am in my suit already, so I set out. Outside, the transitways are busy with Homers on their way towards the West Central Node. I am the only one in an Exo. Most of my classmates will still be in bed. To the left, the rail of the shuttle track whispers and tings as cars approach and pass. I have time, so I don't stop at the station, but walk amongst the flow of people heading to their destinations on foot. I pass a man in Corporation-blue overalls, who is conferencing over a head mike, gesturing as he talks. On the outside of me, next to the long windows which look out to portion B7 of the Inner Plain, a couple of women jog past. Their strides are exaggerated, the way they pump their arms cartoonish. Despite the years they have been living here, M-gravity is still strange for Homers. In my suit I am 2.5 metres tall, and above the heads of those passing I catch only snatches of conversation. The women are talking about preparations for the coming Solstice Holiday. "Raspberry and white chocolate," says one of them.

Her partner says, "Divine."

I wonder for a moment whether *Divine* should be replaced in my dictionary. A brief Systems Query confirms that the word comes from the Latin for God, means Godlike, which is not necessarily disqualifying, but which feels too tied to the old religions of Home. I mark it in my reminders as a *maybe*.

At the next interchange, I stop to think. I worry that I look purposeless, but Homers don't notice me. They stream past me as if they are simply negotiating another of the pillars that hold up the arching domed ceiling. It is still only seven a.m., and so I decide to walk via the West Crop Hangars: enough of a detour to occupy at least half the time I have to wait for school to open.

The transitway that leads to the hangars is crowded with Homers in khaki shorts and shirts, clocking off from the early morning shift tending the crops. Compared to other workers, they are broader, strengthened by the physicality of their labour. Their clear complexions benefit from the lights they work under. The next Mini-Node echoes with their happy voices, laughing at jokes, shouting out their goodbyes. I turn from the workers and ascend the ramp that winds around the outer wall of the node, rising to a public walkway that crosses over the crop hangars.

The Colony Administration put this in to let people see the greenery, which is apparently calming. Mum is always telling me to come here, as plants are in the category of things that she thinks might benefit me in ways she cannot explain. I do come before school sometimes. I've never seen another First Gen up here. Mostly the walkway is deserted but for old, retired Homers who sit dozing on the benches spaced along the span.

Halfway along the walkway, I stop and lean over the rail. Beneath me, my Data Feed informs me, are tomato plants. They grow from hydroponic tubes, raised from walkways along which the workers pass when tending to them. From above however, these walkways are obscured by the spread of leaves, so I look down as if seeing a forest canopy from a film of Home. I can smell the odour of tomatoes: a dusty, sweet smell. I could pop my visor and take this in more fully. But I hesitate. What if someone were to arrive suddenly and encounter my real face? They wouldn't want that, and neither would I. I stay visored. The air in here is warmer than the air in the rest of the Colony, and even in my suit I can feel the humidity. Then there is a hiss. The sprinklers above the plants are turning on. These plants get water through the tubes running around their roots, but the leaves are sprayed sometimes too. The sprinklers sprout from thin pipes that arc over the canopy, raining down fine jets onto the foliage beneath. I have only once before witnessed the sprinklers in action, and, as at that time, I am amazed by the thick smell that suddenly rises off the plants, the damp lushness that floats up to me. It smells like metal and chocolate and something slightly foul I cannot place. I think of my dictionary, because rain is a major problem. The Homers still talk about it as if it should be natural for us to imagine a world in which at any moment you can suddenly find water pouring over you. When Mum last got a raise, she said she was putting some coin aside "for a rainy day," and I had to ask was a *rainy day* a good or a bad thing, and she looked at me in a tender, sad way.

I watch the sprinklers for a long time, and I realise that small clouds are forming amongst the leaves of the plants beneath me, coiling white wisps of smoky condensation that reminds me of footage I have seen of Home a hundred years ago: rain forests, giant orange monkeys roaming through the foliage. I watch as these clouds thicken, until there is a plain of white beneath me, pierced only by the larger of the plants. I have never seen clouds before. I crack my visor and warm wet air rushes in, bringing the odour of growth and dirt more fully into my nostrils.

As always, at moments like these—when faced with a phenomenon that takes my breath—I realise that I want to see Miz. The time is 7:23. Suddenly, with a high-pitched squeal, the sprinklers turn off. The clouds start to dissipate. Farther along the walkway, an old man in a light blue suit walks steadily on, uninterested in the view beneath him. I click my visor properly closed and think that—yes—I will see if Miz is well today.

Miz's unit is big, because Miz's dad is also Category One like Mum, and her family is larger than ours. The unit is off a dead end which offers views of the mountains to the west. I ring the staff bell because it is early. Mehan, Miz's primary carer, comes and opens the door.

She frowns at me. She is okay, Mehan, but she is so protective of Miz as to be hostile at times. I try to be a little childish. I am not beyond acting when I need to. I say, "Is Miz well enough to have a visitor, because I miss her, and I would very much like to see her?"

"Roban," she says. "It's early."

"Yes," I say. "Sorry." I do not say that I know Miz's family well enough to suspect that her father will already have left for his job supervising the First-Generation Paediatric Unit. Her mum will already be running her classes from the screening room. And Miz, who sleeps hardly at all, will be awake. I say, and I must admit that this is sneaky, "I can see that it's not a good time. I'll message Miz to say that I came by."

Mehan wrinkles her nose in the way that Homers can do. She knows that Miz will not be happy to hear that I came and went. Despite all her issues, Miz does not hold back if she thinks she is being babied. She is dogged (if we're still allowing that). Mehan sighs. "A quick *hello* probably won't hurt."

"Thank you," I say. I stay kiddish. I draw on some of the Terrestrial movies I have seen, hoping I hit the right note to charm a Homer. "I very much miss Miz. She's my best friend, you know."

Mehan does smile then, suggesting a certain amount of success on my part. "She's a special girl, isn't she?"

Miz's room is next to the food quarters: a space that in most units would be a dining area, but which the family use to accommodate the large machines that Miz needs. The blinds are still down, but Miz is awake in bed, her face uplit by a screen that sits on the covers.

"You have a visitor, dear," says Mehan from the corridor, behind me, and Miz looks up to see me ducking through the door. She smiles then: an expression on her face that I know to be a smile, because Miz and I are like brother and sister, comfortable seeing each other Real, outside of our Exo suits. I pop my visor, and kneel down beside Miz's bed. I smell the sweet scent of the lotion that Miz uses on her blistered skin. "Roban!" she says. I understand the words, even though they are borne very lightly on thin breath. None of us First Gens speak strongly, but Miz speaks like the whispering of breeze through conditioning ducts. She shifts, and I realise that she is trying to loosen her right arm from where it is tucked under the covers, and I think of telling her not to, but then I think that my pleading will not discourage her. Her white hand rises and we both look at it, as if it is connected to neither of us: a third thing, a plant from the crop hangars seeking light. I move my suited hand and clasp it. I can feel the beating of Miz's pulse through my dermal sensors. "I'm glad you came," Miz says.

It is true what I said to Mehan. Miz is my best friend. We were born weeks apart, took our First-Gen Rehabilitative Classes together. Miz is older by nineteen days, and for a long time I followed her. She was the first of our class into a bipedal Exo, when she was only three M-years old, because her father was a big advocate of the technology and because Miz never met a challenge she didn't want to try. I emulated her in adopting the suit. Though I wasn't ready, and the suits, recently adapted from outside space walkers for Homers, were fiendishly difficult to manoeuvre in those days. They were unwieldy to pilot within the walls of the colony, where they had never intended to be used. The saddles and controls were made for large Homer bodies, not our own smaller, fragile frames. Mum helped me pad out my own suit with cushions so that I didn't tumble around inside. Still, I struggled to grasp the joystick. My movements in the suit were blundering. Mum said it was like living in a bungalow with a horse. A bungalow is a small dwelling from back Home and a horse, of course, is something we know about from Terrestrial History, in which the creatures served an important role in Transport, Warfare, Economics, and even Culture. Horses did not go inside living units in the past, I believe. Mum meant that I was very awkward and borderline dangerous. I broke many things in the kitchen and living room, and once I got myself wedged in the doorway of the bathroom cubicle. Miz, in the same period, was so graceful. I visited her house and she cooked pancakes as if she were a Homer using their own hands, pouring and whisking and frying in the suit. When we began to use Exterior Exos, Miz was the fastest, clambering so fluidly through rock fields, always the first home in the long race on sports day.

It was in the fourth M-year of school that she started having setbacks. She had always been small and it was growth that undid her. The rest of us grew with great pain. The interventions of Miz's father and his colleagues were excruciating but effective. We had surgeries to help our joints bond properly, took bone supplements and courses of hormone therapies to promote growth. Yet, though Miz was more determined than any of us, her body rebelled from the programs. Her bones didn't knit. Her muscles wasted. The hormones caused her skin to flake off. Surgeries gave her infections. She needed pills to cope, and the pills made her nauseous and tired all day. It all compounded. She had fevers. She stopped being able to eat certain foods. She bruised so easily. She became so delicate as to be unable, most days, to sit in an Exo.

I've won the last three big races on sports day. Some kids, who have forgotten the ways things used to be, would find it unbelievable that Miz—the girl who makes it into only a quarter of classes at school—was once so much better than me.

Now, at her bedside, I say, "Will you be at school today?"

She moves her mouth in a way that suggests *No*.

"That's a shame," I say, quickly, wanting to spare her the effort of speaking.

She smiles. She says, "No algebra for me, at least."

I laugh. Her eyes look very tired already. I say, "You should save your breath," thinking as I say the words that I sound like Mum.

Miz's eyes widen for a moment. "For what?" she says. "Tell me something new."

I think, and then I remember the cloud in the crop hangars. I say, "I saw rain clouds, sort of . . ."

Miz grins fully then. She says, "No shit."

One thing she has done with time at home is learn to override the parental settings on Digiarchive. *No shit* is an expression that young Terrestrial people used to use, that perhaps even our parents used to use, before they came here, became so proper and careful due to their sacred duty in the centre of the hourglass, between the great loss and before terraforming. As I understand it, it is merely a crude expression of incredulity, though *shit* in other contexts refers to excrement. I laugh. I start to describe the crop hangars. I speak of being up on that bridge, smelling the tomatoes, and then hearing the sprinkler systems clicking on and seeing the fine spray coming down, the cloud forming like froth around the plants.

"We'll go," I say. "We'll go and see very soon."

4

KENZIE

2071

Some of our colleagues listen to spoken audio as they do the checks: stories of other jobs—detectives or celebrities or sportspeople—as if our own work is not enough. I don't. Maybe I'm being too much of a prig, a stickler, but Justine, my partner, is even more of a hard-ass.

We move around the reactor room without speaking. Our plimpsoles squeak against the concrete floor, our boiler suits crackle as we crouch to examine the prototype. We sigh or grunt or exhale, as, say, one of us pulls back a panel to check a connection.

It's eerie in the reactor room with just one person, the machine gleaming in the middle of the white space like some strange altar in a chapel. Inside this thick shining stump is a small donut-shaped passage, ringed with electromagnets around which our fusion reaction will be sustained. We don't open the machine, because the gasses that will form the plasma are already in there, sealed away. Instead, we check the many connections of the wires that sprout in bunches, spaced around the reactor at intervals. We check the attachment of the outer panelling. I attend to the little screws that hold these plates in place and see my own anxious face reflected back to me in the gleaming aluminium. Justine works on coolly, a couple of meters to my right.

The checks were the idea of our boss, Sani. The big test is in less than a month. We're all counting down, stressed. He has gifted us this long list of things to examine, this thought-obliterating drudgery. We have done our calculations and the ArtInt has checked them. The simulations have gone to plan. The partial run-throughs have been satisfactory. The likelihood of finding a single wire or screw misplaced is infinitesimal, but we must do *something*, so the team has been paired up, each of us assigned a day on which to work. Justine and I will spend each Tuesday here for the next four weeks, double-checking parts.

Still, I find that this busywork leaves me time to worry. The government is already counting on the technology. Their Reversal and Resilience Plan relies on us getting reactors linked into the grid within the next five years. They need the electricity for the vertical farm projects designed to counter the supply shocks. They need the power to heat new homes and fuel the construction of those homes. They are counting on raising revenue by building plants in other countries to power desalination and CO_2 drawdown. Dad, of course, has questioned all of this in Parliament. They're fine ideas, he said to the house, but what is the backup? My focus is on making our plan work, but he is right that if it doesn't the country's strategy has a great hole in it.

I study the checklist on my screen. I grasp my multi-tool. I tell myself to be like Justine, who works so steadily. Yet my train of thought squirms away and I worry about her as well, fretting that I am irritating her with the clicks of my tongue that I cannot help but make as I move through the numbered points.

Justine is Sani's lieutenant. She's been on this project from the start. She moved from Glasgow University to Edinburgh five years ago, poached when Sani first got funding for the project. Her speciality is magnetic reconnection in plasmas. She coauthored important papers on the subject during her Ph.D. Now, in helping manage the project, her purview takes in broader aspects of the design. Working on the numerical model of containment, I report to her, yet we have only interacted occasionally. I'm a little awed by her research, which I have studied, and which is beautiful. She's only a couple of years older than me, yet she holds so much more authority. Even in the room now, in the funny outfits we wear—boiler suits and hairnets and thin purple latex gloves—she seems assured. The hairnet makes me look like a grandmother, while the legs of the suit ride up my shins, accentuating my tallness into comic gangliness. Justine's suit just fits her, and she has done something magic to stop the hairnet mushrooming out. They have a knack for everything, people like Justine.

I'd hoped to be paired with someone easier, to be honest. Justine is formidably driven. I come in early to work each morning, but however early I arrive I still encounter her sitting at her desk, headphones on, clicking determinedly through the plans and calculations of those working beneath her. In these recent dark February mornings, she has been illuminated only by the blue glow of her screen, the city still dark behind her. She's young-looking in this low light. She has good skin, strong cheekbones. Her hair is short and spiked. She has a tattoo, a phrase in Bengali in tribute to her mother as our colleague Ruslan has explained to me, that worms up her neck over her carotid. On these mornings, she looks fixedly at the figures and graphs on the screen in front of her. I wonder whether she had even noticed my existence before being paired with me.

We are in the third hour of our checks when I drop my multi-tool. It is a heart-stopping moment. The tool is a heavy little block from which fan out screwdrivers and wire snips and hex keys. It slips from my grasp with the Phillips head folded out as I tap off a checklist point on my screen. I see that it is tumbling towards the reactor itself. I drop awkwardly to the floor, trying to get my hands underneath it. (I was never very good at ball sports as a child.) I manage to half catch the tool, but then I too am tumbling towards the machine, and in a panicked instant I somehow calculate the need to scoop it away, high up into the air, like I am a volleyball player desperately rescuing the ball. I do so, and I get a hand down to arrest my fall into those billions of pounds of magnets and wiring. I twist and come down to the side of the reactor, onto the cool concrete floor. Then I look up to see the tool arcing up over the machine, out of sight. I wait for what seems like an eternity, and then there is a hollow crack.

My stomach lurches and I stand. I start to run around the reactor. The top of the thing is domed like a huge button. I rush around, looking up. I am expecting to see the tool or a mark made by the tool, but there is nothing. I get to the other side of the reactor. Has it gone into the machine? I wonder. For a moment I consider a scenario in which the whole prototype must be disassembled to retrieve my tool from its centre. I think of our boss Sani's expressive face. He always smiles broadly, because he is a kind man, yet his eyes, set above his freckled brown cheeks, have recently seemed to express such exhaustion. I imagine a weary look of disappointment levelled my way and my feeling of sickness intensifies. Yet, as I turn, I see a mark on the glass window that looks into the adjacent room which holds the banks of monitors and computer systems used to control the reactor. It is a chip as might be made by a bit of gravel thrown up onto a vehicle's windscreen. I look down at the floor, and there is the tool. I look again at the mark in the glass. The noise was just that! My heart is beating up my neck, seeming to sound in my ears, and I experience a relief so exquisite that it almost hurts. There is another sound, though, that it takes me a moment to understand. I think at first it is my own breath, but I then realise, turning, that it is not coming from me at all. Standing next to the reactor is Justine, panting with laughter. She has her hands clasped and her eyes are streaming. She crouches, she breathes, she rises again, and masters herself just enough to say, "Fucking hell, Kenzie. What the fuck was that?"

We talk then, and I am thankful for my own idiocy, because things are easier. It makes me shudder to recall the falling tool. Yet the minutes in this room now pass more comfortably. I didn't think I was someone who needed to chat, but as we go back to our tasks we make small talk—about the weather, about articles recently published in our field—and it is welcome, calming. Then, when she is working right next to me, Justine sighs and asks, "Do you think it's going to work?"

I say, "Of course."

She nods slowly. "I don't believe in it, for some reason. I have a bad feeling. Isn't that stupid?"

I say, "You're probably just nervous." But I regret the sentiment as soon as I have vocalised it, deserve the look of slight disappointment she gives back to me. I too have felt the apprehension she speaks of. I have known researchers who truly believe in their ideas, their projects, and I do not think myself gripped by the kind of faith that I observed in them. I have experienced my own doubts, yet I can't bear to share them; hadn't really, even until this moment, admitted them to myself. Justine has always seemed so assured, and it hurts to see her disavow this apparent certainty. "What will you do if the test doesn't work?" I say, hoping vainly, I suppose, that she can see some alternative, some other solution in case of catastrophe.

But she sighs. "Despair? We needed this design to work twenty years ago."

"Yes." The project proposal calls this design "the Model T of reactors." We're supposed to deliver easily reproducible fusion plants after all those giant temperamental designs that could barely produce more energy than they took to run. I look at the wiring that I am supposed to be examining. The connection is solid.

Justine says, "Maybe I'll go on the Mars mission."

"Really?"

"When I was a kid I always wanted to be a space explorer, but I didn't have good enough eyesight, even with correction."

"Right. And now you don't have a spare billion for civilian shares in Tevat?"

She laughs. "I haven't checked my account recently, but *no*. I don't think so."

"Oh well." I sigh, mock-disappointed.

"Don't you think it would be amazing to stand on a new planet, though?"

"I suppose," I say. "I'm just not sure I love the idea of the project. All the resources going that way . . ."

"But leaving the politics out of it . . ."

I channel Dad. "Can you do that? It just feels infantile, wanting to run away to space."

Justine laughs again. "Don't you ever feel infantile, though?"

We are both ghosts in the city, I suppose. I grew up here in Edinburgh, but to look at my activity map on my health profile is to see only the thick furrowed line of my route to the university and back and the circle that I jog around Holyrood Park on Saturday afternoons. I do see Dad occasionally, but he's busy with his own work, so we tend to just call each other. I get dinner from the Szechuanese restaurant beneath my flat most nights. Chinese takeaway is my comfort food. It's all that Dad and I ate after Mum died. The restaurant beneath my flat—Tian Tian—is not authentic. The supply shocks mean that they must make substitutions: cooking noodles with kale rather than bok choi, bulking out everything with too much onion. But I can tolerate the improvisation. I appreciate their resolve to push on.

I guess that elsewhere in the city Justine is living in a similar limited way, even nursing her own losses. I heard a rumour that she was married once, to another woman, back when she was doing her Ph.D. Did this woman—another scientist, I think—know some hidden side of Justine? They chose to be together, but then they chose to be apart.

I ponder Justine as I walk back to my flat in the cold rainy darkness after the first day of checking the machine. Buses tear along the damp roadway. Cloud is low over the city. Beneath the streetlights, the slanting raindrops appear from the grimy darkness, so that it looks like the lamps themselves are showerheads washing down a steady stream onto the pavements. I buy dan dan noodles from Tian Tian. In the flat, I change out of my wet clothes and into my pyjamas. I eat in bed, splattering oily red drops onto the bedclothes.

In the morning I wake to the smell of the takeaway, half-finished on the side table. It's five a.m. I dress and clean up and set off for the university. The rain has stopped, but the streets are still wet. The cloud has sunk, threatening to become a haar. At the campus, I can only make out our tower as I reach the parking lot, at which point it looms suddenly from the murk.

I realise that I am climbing the stairs quickly, short of breath. I am excited to see her, I guess. Or intrigued. Maybe I am just intrigued. I remember her laughing at me the day before, and I feel glad.

Our floor, the fourth, is dark still. I step into the open plan and there at her screen is Justine. She looks up and nods, and I nod back: firmly enough to be noticed, I hope, though not so firm a gesture as to suggest I am overthinking the flash of her attention towards me.

I go to my own desk and flick on my light and get out my thermos of hot water. I put my face to the log-in scanner and the tracker rakes down over my pupils. I tell myself that I am a fool to be thrilling at a simple greeting. It is nothing, but then I think again of her laugh: gasping, then rising into a playful sound that filled the reactor room.

The others come in and the silence is overtaken by their chatter. They talk of ordinary things—series that they watched, their children, what they'll do on the weekend—as if this is just a normal job, as if the failure or success of our project can be put away at the end of the day. Do they not worry, as I do, that every moment of thought directed elsewhere might be one they regret if the project doesn't work out? I put my headphones on and try to work.

Dad often tells me that I'm too serious, and I say to him, half-joking, "I didn't ask to be born into the apocalypse."

And he too has his typical response: "Lucky that we're fixing that, then."

He is an optimist, Dad, and sometimes I think that I made myself dour in contrast to him, made myself too practical in the face of his vague insistence that people are good, that people will *come around* (as he repeats so often). He even asked me on a recent call whether I've thought of starting my own family, and I told him to shut up.

He just laughed and said, "Don't make yourself lonely."

I sit at my desk until noon, and then I go down to the canteen, which is subterranean (one floor above the reactor, in fact). It serves a reliably terrible menu in a space with a reassuringly purgatorial vibe. I sit and eat in the harsh timeless light, and then I get a cup of tea and nurse that.

I come back to my desk and recheck old data until most of my colleagues have gone home and the cleaners have clocked on.

I get the dan dan noodles again. I send Dad a call request, because it's been a while. He reads it and messages back, "2 mins?" I sit in my chair and adjust the light so that I won't look dark and miserable. Seconds later, his face flashes up on my screen.

He says, "Kenz, how are you?"

I say, "I'm fine, Dad."

"Yes," he says. "Have you saved the world yet?"

The hubris—the exaggeration of our aims—is one of our shared jokes. I say, "Not yet."

He nods. "Don't leave it down to me," he says. "I'd rather take a holiday." He is in the living room of the flat to which we moved after Mum died. The bookshelf is behind him, that ugly clock on the sideboard. The strange alpine painting that Mum's brother did hangs squint on the wall. "I haven't either," says Dad. "But I did give a good speech on housing resilience, if I say so myself."

"I haven't seen it, I'm afraid."

"You'd recognise it. The classic riffs."

We are a team, became one on the other side of Mum's thing: the strange illness, and then all the tests at the hospital, and then the recovery, and then her turn to the worse again, and that brief panic when the specialists thought it might be contagious and we were quarantined and people in hazmat suits came to spray disinfectant through our flat. Eventually, the hospital decided that Mum was not infectious and she was allowed back home. But the treatments were not effective and, frustrated, she gave up. We had to watch her simply waste away then, unable to convince her to try gene therapy. It was all so tiring even to explain to friends, a burden that I didn't want to pass to others. So I held myself away and never reentered the world on the same terms that I'd lived before. I was thirteen and I stuck close to Dad, who was coping in his blinkered way. While other teens were rebelling, I was patiently waiting for him to get back from work. We moved to another flat. I got a bigger room, though the place was less nice. Dad did his best always. There are times I resent, sure. Like every child, I'd guess. He and I lived for one summer outside the Parliament in a tent, when he was a backbencher and seeking to protest the government's house-building policies. I didn't relish being rolled into his publicity stunt. It's not great to be fifteen without privacy or running water. (Which was his point, I suppose.

Though why *I* had to demonstrate that point, I still don't know.) The protest got quite a lot of news coverage, and even now in adulthood it's not unusual for me to be stopped by strangers and asked whether I'm the "Tent Girl."

Mostly, though, I stuck happily with Dad. I dressed like a little version of a middle-aged man, in many-pocketed technical trousers and sturdy shoes, because Dad did all the clothes shopping and knew only to dress me as he dressed himself. (Now, in fact, as his career has progressed, his aide, Miles, has got him in well-cut suits. It's only me still looking like a hiker at work each day.) He says now, "You sound different, Kenz."

"Different?"

"Uh-huh."

"I'm nervous about our upcoming test, I guess."

"The big one?"

"We're going to run our prototype all the way, try to reach one hundred megawatts."

"How exciting!"

"Yes," I say. I think of Justine, of her concerns. "I'm just nervous. It needs to work."

"I think it will."

"I thought you didn't believe in our project."

"You know that's not the case. I argued there needs to be a plan B. I still support plan A."

"Is that so?" I say.

Dad says, "It'll work."

"How do you know that?"

"I don't. But I haven't seen you fail at much."

"This isn't an exam. This is the fundamental behaviour of matter."

He says, "You sound happy, though. I think it will work."

"Well, I suppose I can let you believe that."

He looks away, and I guess that he is getting a message on his other screen. I make the excuse that I have things to do myself. I end the call. I go to the kitchen and make myself a cup of tea. I sit in the soft chair. From upstairs, I can hear the hum of my neighbour's feedback treadmill as they traverse their way through some meta-scape. The rain is still falling outside, lightly. It's a warm, calming sound against the windows, like cereal shaken in the box. Am I happy? I wonder.

When Tuesday, and our next turn to check the machine, arrives, Justine and I talk for the whole time we are together. I don't think I'm a natural conversationalist like Dad. Yet I find it easy to speak with Justine. I ask her about growing up in Glasgow, about her parents, her first degree. She doesn't tell me about her marriage, but I sense it between the things she does discuss; a hole in her history. That space feels like it speaks of some method to the conversation, work on her part to present a certain side to me.

And what do I try to protect in turn? Granny, I suppose, though Justine knows her work well. "You must get asked about her a lot," she says.

"More the Tent Girl thing," I say. But Justine is unaware of that, or uninterested. She wants to know more about Granny. I hint that it's a sad story, but she pushes me to explain what I mean. I say that Granny alienated a lot of people with the way she worked in the end: her rejection of collaborators, her insistence that her stellarator designs were the only kind that could work. "People think she was a zealot," I say. "She scared people. I suppose I try to play the connection down at work, because she didn't have the best reputation later on."

"I can understand that," says Justine. "What did you think of her?"

I stop seeking the wire I am trying to check. I sit on the concrete floor for a moment, because I realise that I have not truly worked out how to vocalise what I think. Granny's story has always seemed so set, like a heavy moral tale for children. Dad and I were the only people at her funeral in a low grey crematorium on the outskirts of Falkirk. The manager had asked what music she would have liked played at the event and Dad had thought for a long time and said, "I never really heard her listen to music."

Afterwards, we'd stood outside the building, and I'd tried to avoid looking at the tall chimney, and Dad had sighed and just said, "Well . . ." a resignation to those words (though not necessarily a hostile one). His tone seemed to imply that it was all so lamentably expected. A slushy kind of snow began to fall, and we hurried to a covered bus stop against which this snow struck damply. We were both sad, but I realised Dad thought Granny's life a great waste, and my sadness was different because though I saw her failures plain enough, I had believed her, believed all the while that what she obsessed over was possible.

I try to explain this to Justine, who stops working herself, who sits cross-legged on the floor next to me, her knee millimetres from my own.

"She was unlucky?" tries Justine.

"Perhaps," I say. "The wrong circumstances. The wrong time."

I think then of the time that Granny first spoke to me of fusion. I was interested in dinosaurs and fossils when I was young, and she once saw me studying an image of a trilobite on my device at her kitchen table. She took a place next to me and said that the fossil proved her work, because if our sun burned on any other fuel, our solar system and planet could not have lasted the millions of years since that little creature swam the seas. She rubbed her hands. "The sun would have just . . . extinguished." She was thrilled by the little proof. "But it didn't, right?"

"And so you're trying to make a sort of sun?" I had asked.

And she had laughed and said, "Yes. I suppose you could say that."

A week later, on our last checks, I feel sad that all this must end. In the reactor room, Justine and I have reached a complementary way of working. Where we have to move past each other, we do so easily. The first time Justine tapped me on the shoulder, it was a shock, but now it feels natural that one of us should place a hand on the back of the other. I feel graceful in her presence in a way that I am not usually graceful. When her checkpoints are high up on the machine, she will ask me to look at them on her behalf, because I have the extra head of height on her.

The night before the big test, I go to the pool. I swim three times weekly and run on Sundays. Yet this evening I am swimming on what would normally be a rest day. I need to move.

The pool is on the fourth basement level, two floors beneath the reactor. It is an incongruous space, gifted to the university by a Saudi prince whose son studied biosciences here. The prince used his favourite architect to build the pool, and the result feels jarringly out of place on the otherwise shabby campus. Perhaps because of this dissonance, people don't think to come here. This evening, as usual, I am alone.

The basement is lined in beautiful dark blue Italian tile. I walk towards the empty rectangle of water from the changing room. In the day, light wells tunnelled from the surface far above drag more light than it should be possible to capture from the Edinburgh sky down to illuminate the pool. Now, at night, the place is lit by a giant rectangle of LEDs hanging above the water like a white-hot brand.

The water is warmer than a proper Olympic-sized pool should be, a temperature for splashing around, not for exercising. I stand and crouch and dive with decent form, staying down, taking a couple of strokes, rising, pushing on.

This is not a proper way to train, of course: going straight at it, exhausting oneself. But I am not training. I'm merely burning something off. I am here to lose myself in the process of taking a stroke and then a breath, and then reaching the end of the pool and tucking and turning, repeating and repeating.

I'm good at this, but I used to be exceptional: a Scottish Schools Champion in three different age groups, a British Schools Champion twice. I was barely beaten, until one day a couple of the other girls caught up with me and I began to lose, and soon after stopped racing altogether. It was always an activity justified only by proficiency. Without unqualified success it felt ludicrous: all those hours in the water, those long journeys to compete, the strange foods and supplements and recovery routines.

I learned to really swim in my first long summer on the island, benignly neglected as Granny worked in her shed. Dad and Mum had spoken of her work as folly, but I had been surprised by the steady resolve which saw her at her desk, piled with old computers, hard drives, and ink-stained notebooks, at seven every morning. When I found her out in the shed after waking on the first morning of my stay, she had been welcoming, but her manner had been strained too. She was wanting to be kind to me but was itching to return to her work. So I swam that summer, watching her seriousness only from a distance, trying to cultivate a determination of my own.

When I got back to Edinburgh in the autumn, I went to the old Commonwealth Pool. It was different: no waves, no seaweed, no seals popping above the surface to observe me with their quizzical whiskered faces. But I still found a pleasure in the swimming, in the rhythm and then in the attention that my proficiency won me. It mildly vexed Dad, who couldn't understand my need of money for club fees. He said, "Why don't you go down to Portobello and swim in the sea for real?"

"In that water?" I said. "With the sewage overflow, and the road runoff, and all the plastics and bacteria?" As usual, he was thinking of the environment of his youth, when it was cleaner, recoverable. I didn't want a similar argument to the one we had about the foraged meals he had been trying to make a few months previously.

"People do it," he insisted. "People survive. There's a club that does it together twice a week. That's real swimming."

Maybe it is, I thought, but then I considered being in the pool, and the races I had started doing, and the feeling of swimming as hard as

I could, conscious only of the blood pounding in my skull, and of my limbs shaping for the next stroke, and the searing satisfaction of raising my head to gasp a breath and glimpsing how far behind the other girls were. I felt that that too was *real*, but in a way that a man like Dad could never understand.

It is late when I start home, the roads nearly deserted. I walk with my head down. An AutoBug comes past from the casino out of town, the occupants all well-dressed, laughing at something. In the flat, I make a quinoa porridge and stir chili sauce and peanut butter into it. Sometimes I find it satisfying to make a dinner that others would think truly foul. It is evidence of my own self-knowledge, I guess. Mum, home late from work, used to eat raw broccoli dipped into mayonnaise.

I look at my watch and see that it is ten hours now until the test will be run. I won't be able to sleep tonight.

Dad texts to wish me good luck. He calls it *my* test. It's a kind gesture, though it also makes something go taut behind my breastbone.

I set the light settings on *cosy*. I sit in my chair. An ambulance passes, splashing its siren light up against the windowpanes.

A few hours later, I shower. I heat my hot water and fill my flask. I walk back to work. I ascend to our floor, pad down the corridor. But when I reach the open plan she isn't there. It's only me. I sit and drink my water and the others slowly fill the big room and Justine arrives at eight for the meeting, which is less of a meeting and more of a halting nervous speech from Sani. "We've done all we can," he says. "Remember that."

In the observation area, there are lines of chairs set out. Sani and Ruslan sit at the screens in front of the window which my little tool chipped. I have watched documentaries about the old fusion experiments when Granny worked, and back in those times proceedings were monitored by dozens of people at computers. Yet now we have ceded those responsibilities to the ArtInt. We aim for reproducibility, automation. Sani and Ruslan at their screens are merely observers themselves, and the rest of us, pressed together on the small plastic chairs, are merely observers of the observers. I smell soap, toothpaste. Despite the early hour there is an odour of perspiration amongst the group. Terror sweat, I think. We have all got here by concentrating on theory, fundamentals. It should work. It *must* work to allow us to move to the next stage. The First Minister called Sani personally, apparently, told him that the government are ready to expedite production once the prototype has proven itself. The university chancellor stands at the back of the room, accompanied by Masha, the head of the College of Science and Engineering. The chancellor looks on, impassive. He reaches up and fiddles with the knot of his tie. Masha whispers something to him and he nods. Two days ago, I saw eight crates of champagne being unpacked into the refrigerators in the canteen. For us, no doubt. I try to hold to that fact. It will be fine. It should be a triumph. But then, that is what those running the many failed projects in Oxford and Padua and Innsbruck must have thought. Justine sits a couple of rows ahead of me. I can see the tattoo on her neck. She sits straight-backed. She doesn't fidget as others around us do. In the main space, technicians are moving around the reactor. Then they withdraw.

The test goes like this: On the screens Ruslan and Sani initiate the start-up procedures. The systems should be beginning, the flows of tasks we have planned and refined over the years set rolling. The reactor stands static within the white room. The drama of the run-through plays in the data fed back to the computer monitors. In another room, giant flywheels are already running, holding the massive amounts of power necessary to set going the fusion reaction.

First the gasses will be heating, readying to form the plasma. Sani turns and says, "Soon the centre of that machine will be the hottest part of our solar system." We know this, of course, it is a sound bite we give to visitors, to half-interested friends and family members, but still, as we hear it now, reasserted, defamilarised, there is a murmur among us, an involuntary response to the strangeness of all that we seek to achieve.

At the screens, Sani and Ruslan fidget as the rest of us wait behind them. The reactor room is well miked, feeding speakers in this observation space, and from those speakers comes a fine, high humming.

Eventually Sani turns and says, "Let's get this thing moving, then." On the screen he begins initiating the next stage. The magnetic coils will power up, the plasma will be pushed in, suspended. Hopefully the containment will hold and the reaction will continue steadily.

We all wait, hardly breathing. I look through the window at the shining machine. Another tone comes through the speakers, so high as to be almost inaudible, a sort of sonic shimmer.

It's all running as the models predict, as previous, smaller tests have indicated it would. But then quite suddenly there is a rattling sound from the speakers—a noise from a different sphere of life, like a faulty washing machine. We are in the world of physical things, of course. That is the issue. Is the noise so loud, or do I merely hear it as such because of what it portends? Everyone around me is twitching. At the front, Ruslan is clicking furiously at his trackpad. Sani turns, "Um," he says. "We're just pausing things."

The noise ceases, and there is some relief in just that. They are stopping the reactor. My heart is going like I'm running. What strikes me now is the silence of all of us who watch: a different quality to this silence than the one we held before. We are all making private calculations, I suppose. The issue, I am guessing, will be the breeding blanket. The reaction is not being properly contained. Something is being shaken. That could be a problem with the materials, or it could be an issue with the coils or the fact that the plasma's behaviour differs from our model. The last is partly my domain, and I wonder whether I want to know that defect is within my purview, something I might understand or even help to solve. Or would I rather it were others' problem; a thing that has just happened to me?

What I cannot really face is another, bigger thought, sunk so deep in me as to resist examination. Surely a problem so large as to make the machine rattle will not be solved by a simple reboot? Still, the others are quiet, I tell myself. Perhaps I am wrong, not thinking clearly. Perhaps things are just fine.

Sani stands and goes out of the room. In response to some subtle signal, Justine rises from her chair and follows him. Ruslan is typing at the computer. Justine comes back in, takes her seat. Sani reenters the room a little later, whispers something to Ruslan, then turns to all of us. "We're just making an adjustment," he says. "We're going to run it again."

There is no great risk with a fusion reactor. The reaction just stops if it fails. Yet I still wonder at the wisdom of this decision. I turn to the back of the room and see that Masha and the chancellor have departed. Others seem not to have noticed. Sani initiates things on the screen.

And it goes longer. I have no sense of time, no understanding of what time of day it is now, no notion of how long the test has been running. The reaction *is* happening, we have gone past break-even. "Climbing to fifty megawatts," Ruslan announces. The aim of this micro-reactor is a steady hundred, and we are almost there, I think. Yet then I hear a wheezy kind of noise above everything else, which might be a phantom, I think, until I understand it is being heard by others, until it increases in volume and once more Sani and Ruslan are frantic at the controls.

Sani stands and says that they will not run the reactor again today, that they will make some investigations, run the test later in the week. Suddenly everyone in the chairs around me is rising, almost panicked in our desire to leave the room. We do not believe in his thin veneer of calm. We cannot take sitting here pretending to. Of course they will not be able to resolve the issue in days. It might take months to even identify the cause. "This is fucked!" shouts Tobi, who is a specialist in low-activation materials. Someone else kicks over a couple of chairs.

Out in the corridor everyone is raging, arguing, telling each other to calm down. There is a low-key scuffle at the bottom of the stairs. Elsewhere, people are in tears. By the fire extinguishers, Oksana, manager of the materials team, is vomiting onto the concrete floor.

Rather than ascending the stairs in the flow of my colleagues, I find myself walking down. What will they do upstairs in the office but lament the failure of the test together?

I go to the pool. My swimsuit is in a locker. I change. I wash my feet and walk out onto the tiles. It is quiet, as always. I stride to the edge and dive in. I swim two hundred meters as fast as I possibly can. It feels quick. I would have done well to swim like this in my days of training and competition. Maybe this isn't so surprising. At twenty-five, I'm in my prime, I suppose, in terms of muscle growth, lung capacity; even though I don't train.

I lie back and float in the middle of the pool. I can taste a little blood in my throat from breathing so hard. *My prime*, I think again. *What have I done with that?* I close my eyes. The sound of the water echoes off the low ceiling. The lapping makes me think of being out in the sea at the cottage. I recall the crack of strong waves coming down onto gneiss, the taste of the sea on my tongue.

Then I think that maybe I *can* hear something. I open my eyes. A person is swimming slowly in my direction. It is Justine. She has a swimming cap on. She has a rueful smile on her face.

She begins to paddle in place. "You swim?" I say.

"Sometimes," she says. "I know that you do. I thought I might find you here."

"Oh," I say, surprised. My heart is going quickly.

She says, "So . . ."

I say, "So . . ."

Our words are hard in the echoing space, with the supressed effort of staying above-water.

"Do you know what the issue is?" I ask.

"No," she says.

"What did you and Sani talk about?"

"Why not try again, we said, basically. He was worried about damaging the reactor. But I felt like the risk was worth taking. There's no slack in the plan."

"Right. It needed to work."

"Yeah."

"And now?" I ask.

"Months to even diagnose . . . And I suspect it's a more fundamental issue. The containment was failing." Justine begins to swim a length now, with a leisurely breaststroke. I notice that she twists her left leg, making her stroke uneven. There is no reason that she should be a perfect swimmer, and yet it feels wrong to do anything more easily than she does. I swim beside her. I have so dreaded a failure like this, and now I am here living it, surprised somehow that the sky has not fallen, surprised that I can still feel gladness at having Justine next to me. I say, "When do you start saving for your Tevat shares, then?"

She laughs, says, "Fuck." The word echos and reverberates around us.

I go to work to swim now. It becomes clear in the first week after the test that, as Justine suspected, the cause of the fault is not simple. The system record does not yield a ready answer. The ArtInt comes to no firm conclusions. We are redeployed to rake through the data from the start-up process. Sani talks of running the machine again in the first days, but then, tellingly, that resolution drops away. One morning, I encounter a canteen worker in the car park wheeling away boxes of champagne.

I spend the workday waiting to descend to the pool. At five each day

I meet Justine down there. She swims slowly and I swim fast, and then we paddle around together and talk.

It takes me a long time to believe that she seeks my company as I seek hers, but it is true. Sometimes in the changing rooms we get lost in a discussion that sees us sitting on the hard benches in our towels until we're both shivering.

What do we talk about? The loss of the project, the sense of being unmoored suddenly.

She has her theories, little ways to tweak the ideas we've been working with. "We could do things differently," she says.

"Who?"

"Me and you."

I feel flattered. I feel foolish that I feel flattered. I say, "Where? Here?"

"They won't give us funding to start again here. Not after this."

"At another university?"

Justine sighs. "I don't think any university would take me on right now."

I wait. I'm sitting wrapped in a towel, cold but still unmoving. I don't have the stomach to joke as I usually might. I think of Grandmother, actually, of Dad saying, "Well . . ." in that cold crematorium car park, the long grey chimney and the grey sky behind that chimney.

Justine says, "Have you seen that funding application online?"

"Of course. But it's Axel Faulk. Basically Tevat. Is this your Mars thing? Are you actually serious about it?"

"This has nothing to do with Mars. It's just funding. This is about carrying on."

Justine has a crescent-shaped scar on her shoulder, and one day in the changing room she catches me staring at it. "I fell off a bike when I was a kid," she says. "I lost control going down a hill."

I move forward and look at it, because she seems to want me to do so, and I say that it looks painful, and she nods, and says that it was. She rubs her finger over the raised white flesh. I say that I can't imagine her ever losing control in any situation, and she smiles very widely.

I didn't mean it in such a significant way, I guess. It's too much, like a movie line. Yet she still steps forward and puts a hand on my arm, moving to clasp my elbow and pull me towards her. "On the contrary," she says. "Sometimes I can't control myself." But then she laughs, and I laugh too. It is too much, too cheesy. But she still has hold of my arm.

She is bolder than I am, and that is probably a good thing, a thing that lets us fit together.

The kissing is nice, but maybe I'm not good at it, because our teeth clash. She pulls back and looks at me, and I say, "I'm sorry."

Justine smiles and says, "You apologise too often."

We do work on a plan, then. We use data from our tests at the university, we use insights from other labs, other studies. The problem with a large project like the one we have previously been working on is that it's slow to turn. "Like a tanker," Justine says. Working alone we can make little changes, refine our concepts in ways that we wouldn't have been able to do in a larger organisation. And I find that, crazy as it might be, I do believe in it all. I am glad to hurry back from work together, to my flat or to Justine's, where we will eat very quickly and then work until it's nearly morning. Or perhaps I just believe in her. Or I hunger for a certain look she gives me when she is impressed. I am a Labrador with her, I suppose. I am eager to please in a way I have never been before.

"You look so well, Kenze," says Dad when I meet him for the first time with Justine. We have found a table in a café in Bruntsfield. It is one of those March afternoons in which the approach of summer is finally plausible. Outside, the streets are busy with people, red-faced because, though the day seems to promise heat, it is still bitter in the wind. Dad shakes Justine's hand, grins widely.

One thing I hope is that this new relationship might soften my admission to Dad that I'm making a proposal to Axel Faulk, the man he spends half his time in Parliament railing against. Perhaps his relief that I have found someone will compensate for what he will see as a betrayal.

I feel proud of the three of us, doing these normal things. We eat and he and Justine seem to get along. He asks Justine about her research, about working with me. She has watched quite a few of his speeches, listened more carefully to the specifics than I ever have. She quizzes him about his energy policy in exacting detail, and he loves this. He eats his chips with his fingers. He says, "You're better than my opponents on this stuff. You should go into politics."

"That's not for me," says Justine.

"On second thoughts," says Dad, "that's good. I don't want competition."

"I couldn't smile enough," says Justine.

"The smiling is hard. Yes."

A woman comes in with two greyhounds, one of which creeps over and sniffs at Dad's leg. He feeds it a chip. "Don't do that," I say.

Dad ignores me. He looks at Justine. "What will you do now your project is kaput?"

"I heard you talking in Parliament about it," I say. Trying to waylay him.

He shrugs. "I warned them, didn't I?"

"We're designing our own project," says Justine. She reaches out and touches my shoulder. "We're going to try and make our own prototype."

"At Edinburgh Uni?" Dad says.

"They won't have us," I say. "We're done there."

"We're trying for private funding, actually." Justine pushes on. I give her a look. She returns the glance sternly. I know she won't let me swerve this.

"Private?" Dad says.

"Yeah," Justine says.

"Not all this money Faulk is throwing around?"

"Yep," Justine says.

"Oh," says Dad. He is quiet for a long time. The dog comes back, sniffs at his leg again. He shoves it away. He clears his throat. "Do you trust them?"

"If they give us money," says Justine, "we'll take the money."

"Is this for their Mars project?"

"This isn't Tevat. We'd get some lab space in an innovation campus. And some money. A lot of money, actually. We'd pursue our own plan."

Dad tuts. "But they'd maintain some rights to your plan."

"If it works, it works. It's in the world. Then we can argue about who uses it."

"They'll patent it to fuck."

"At the moment we have nothing," Justine says. "So that'd still be an improvement."

"We just want to do our project," I say. "We're not endorsing the Mars project. We're not part of that."

Dad levels a long stare at me, parental in a way he isn't usually. "These people aren't looking out for the likes of us."

I say, "We'll take our chances."

Justine says, "We hear you."

"Okay," Dad says. He is looking at me, trying to catch my eye and make me complicit in his doubt, but though I feel his glance I don't turn to it. I hold my gaze on Justine.

5

HANNAH

There is an argument against time travel that's so neat as to seem stupid. It goes like this: If time travellers exist, then where are they?

The question has a comfortable logic. Because they would come back, would they not? Years ago, some MIT students organised a time travellers' convention to which no time travellers came. A gimmick, of course, but a clever one. It's not as if these invitees could be allowed the excuse that they missed the conference.

But what becomes, I wondered, of this nice little proof in the face of someone who actually claims to have arrived from the future?

Where are they? you say, and then they answer, *Right here*.

What on Earth do you say next?

It was a midsummer, Hebridean dawn. The grid of the dormer windowpanes shadowed a cross on the linen curtain that hung in front. I sat up in bed. I'd slept a bit, I think. Maybe I hadn't. It was hard to tell my dreams from the strange thoughts that turned over in my mind.

Einstein once wrote that the difference between past, present, and future is only a "stubbornly persistent illusion." (Whatever the subject, there's always a pretty Einstein quotation to reckon with.) This was in a letter to the sister of a close friend who had recently died, so it has been assumed that the words are just the physicist's version of the platitude that the recently departed is "smiling down on us." Sitting in bed, I found myself annoyed to consider the dismissal of the idea due to its context. Just because it was written in a state of emotion, does that mean it wasn't what he believed? Did his grief preclude sincerity?

I had walked off the beach with the figure, the boyish man. We had climbed the steep bank, and I had followed behind him.

I had tried on the idea: There was a human curled inside the body of that large figure, riding within it. It seemed possible. The figure squatted in its walk, like those Boston Dynamics robots that I had watched in YouTube videos. Even in the future, I thought, their machines walk like a child who has filled a nappy. I looked at the hands, held by the side of the torso, and thought that no one on Earth could right now craft such hands. But then maybe, one day . . . ? The funny bird-like feet curled and grasped the dirt on the incline, leaving crescent-shaped scratches.

He wanted to be taken out of view, so I showed him into the low stone shed next to the cottage. (In the large suit, he could not have navigated the interior of the cottage itself, with all the furniture, the tight doorways, and low ceilings.) The shed had once been a home that shielded its occupants from the wind off the Atlantic with thick low walls and a heavy thatched roof. Now the thatch was gone and the structure was covered with corrugated iron, rusted orange. One felt the breezes coming between the cracks in the stonework like small grasping hands. On bright days, the sun cut through the holes in the roof, forming illuminated pillars where the dirt from the packed earth floor eddied up to be caught in the shafts of light, but in the moment, after dusk, the creaky wooden door opened to a bluish gloom. The figure had to crawl under the lintel, but inside could move forwards kneeling. He was still taller than me on his knees, but now his shadowed shape seemed merely the height of a big man. I said, "There's no light, I'm afraid."

The boy's face shone from within his suit. He smiled. He said, "No problem." As he did so, a warm glow rose from his chest, illuminating the space around us. There was wood piled near the back wall, two old sun-bleached kayaks, a wheelbarrow with a deflated tire listing in the corner.

I sought a better sense of what was happening then. I had put on an act, I suppose. I'd believed him. I'd walked behind him, studying. But now I wanted to fathom him. I said, "What do I call you?"

He seemed to consider this. He said, "Red. Please call me Red."

I said, "You're from the future?"

"A hundred years from now," he said.

"A hundred years?"

"From 2110."

"That's eighty-five years."

His face smiled. He said, "I knew you'd be a stickler."

"You know me?"

"I read your research," he said.

"On what?"

"Fusion, of course."

"I've published little of note."

"The work you will publish. The work you will publish soon."

He kneeled still, just ahead of me. His face, lit within his suit, grinned. I didn't know what to do with my hands. Jasper was next to me, pressing his side against my shin. I smiled up at the boy's face, nodded. He told me that he had come back to talk about fusion. "In my reality," he said, "we managed it. But it was too late for all this."

"This?"

He moved the thin arms of the suit, the large articulated hands. "For this planet."

He left me silence. The wind hummed around the shed. Jasper watched Red intently. "Where did you come from?" I asked.

"Mars."

"You live on Mars?"

"With considerable problems," he said. The face was wincing a little now, almost unsure. "That's why the suit, actually. I'm not used to this planet."

"Earth?"

"No."

"You've never been here?"

"No." He said the word sadly.

"I'm sorry to hear," I said.

He said, "I've come back to try and save the planet."

"And fusion will do that?"

"I don't know."

"Oh."

"The reactors are our most important technology in the future."

"I see."

"And you said yourself—"

"Myself?"

"You *will* say yourself, I should say, in a paper. You will say fusion could solve the climate crisis, as you call it, allow societies to supply the needs of their people."

"I've always liked to be bold in my claims," I said, trying to be a little self-deprecating. Though perhaps that was lost on Red. I considered what he was saying. What if I could deliver practical fusion now, decades before the most optimistic timelines? We could electrify everything. Suddenly energy would be basically free. And what would it mean as a symbol, a milestone? To have leapt so much into the future? To have harnessed the power of the sun? A little sun, hotter than the sun itself, in fact. I thought of the funding that might be unlocked, the sudden faith in research, the optimism.

Red said, "I must be honest. This is not all planned out."

"The journey through time?"

"I don't understand it fully. I submitted to it. I came here."

"Submitted to it?"

"I was exploring space. It was a kind of accident."

"I see." I didn't see. But I felt that I needed to carry the conversation forwards.

"But I want to be here. I think I'm supposed to be here."

"Right."

"That's not an explanation," he said. "That's just a feeling. Something else."

"And you're sure that you can change time?" I asked.

The boy's face within the suit fixed eyes on me and nodded. "I'm sure of that, at least," he said. "My life was saved by someone who had come back."

Stephen Hawking, amongst others, thought that were time travel possible the alteration of the past by the future could not happen. The time traveller sent back to kill Hitler would necessarily find their rifle broken at the crucial moment. The person saving Lincoln from assassination would trip in the wings of Ford's Theatre. Et cetera. Et cetera. A force would not permit these things. The question turns on whether there is some solid state to the interaction of events across time, or whether things may alter and shift, or if, in fact, time splits into strands. I quizzed Red doggedly on this. He listened and said, "I was saved by a traveller changing his past, whether that was in one strand of time or in a totality I don't know. Maybe *my* future won't change. I'm not sure. But I believe that I can at least save you, *your* reality, *your* future."

It hurt my head. I felt the wine again, felt a sourness in my stomach. It was too much. It seemed impossible. My limbs ached. I thought of the story I had once read of Yuri Gagarin landing back on Earth after making the first manned spaceflight. He had been blown off course, coming down in the middle of the Russian steppe, miles from where he had been expected. He emerged from his craft to meet only a confused farmer, who looked with terror at this strange creature in a spacesuit, clambering from a sphere which had just tumbled from the sky. Gagarin told the man not to worry, said, "I am a Soviet citizen like yourself, and I need a telephone in order to call Moscow."

I am just that farmer, I told myself, confused by the limited nature of what I have seen before, needing to find my spaceman a telephone.

The morning after, I rose from the bed and walked down the creaking stairs into the sunlit kitchen. Outside, the air was very still. I could hear birdsong. Jasper dashed past me. The dog sniffed at a tuft of grass, his tail wagging. He cogitated on the smell, cocked a leg, and peed. I wondered whether he could smell the boy in the suit, whether the boy in the suit had an odour at all. I walked away from the house, still in bare feet. The short grass on the pathway towards the shed was very damp with dew.

I pushed the door open very slowly, feeling every second of the reveal—doubting, believing, doubting again—until I saw the dark outline of the prone figure. I realised that I was glad to see it. It lay back, like a sleeping giant, but there was something strange about it. The torso was big now, stretched upwards into a dome, as if the figure had a giant beer gut. As I watched, there was a clicking from within the thing, like a kindling fire, and this dome began to sink, until the body was once again as it had been. It sat up. It kneeled. Red's face appeared again on the front of the figure's head. "Good morning," he said.

"Good morning," I said. "You were sleeping?"

"The body becomes a sort of capsule," he said. "I lie down in it and sleep."

"I'm sorry to have woken you."

"It's not a problem," Red said. "We should start anyway."

"Start?"

"Your lessons," he said. "Of course."

He told me to be ready to take notes, looked down with curiosity when I brought in a notebook and pen. He seemed to notice me studying the front of his suit, the lit face held there. He gestured with the arm, said, "It's not my real face, by the way."

"Okay?" I said.

"I just wanted to level with you. It mirrors my reactions. It's not exactly me."

I wondered why it mattered to him to say this. I said, "It feels very natural to talk to you."

"I'm glad."

I tried a joke: "Do you want me to pour a mug of coffee into your suit?"

He paused and then laughed, the illuminated face grinning. "I think I'm fine."

There was an old table stacked at the back of the shed, and I retrieved that. I brought a chair from the kitchen, a blanket for Jasper to lie down on. Like this, I made a little working area. I saw on my phone that my husband had texted with a screen grab of a long email from his university about a new prohibition on single-use coffee cups. "I guess that will fix everything," he wrote. I thought, *Should I text him back and explain that I'm having lessons in nuclear fusion with a freckled robot man from the future?* I decided not. Instead, I sent the crying laughing emoji, then the crying emoji, then the crying laughing emoji again.

Outside, the sun was rising. The shadow of the house, thrown across the lawn in front of the doorway, drew shorter. The metallic cool in the air diminished.

Red kneeled and spoke of the failure of current fusion reactor designs. At times, an image would appear on the chest of his suit: a diagram, a dynamic sketch in which lines knitted themselves into a picture. He wanted me to understand the deficiencies in current thinking. Then, he said, he would explain where my work should go in the future. He spoke haltingly, rushing through details, stopping, working back to clarify. "This isn't my natural area," he said.

I assured him that he spoke well. He talked of how a tokamak reactor could not be sufficiently refined. He explained the difficulty of containment in this configuration. He told me that many of the assumptions that researchers were making about the behaviour of plasmas were still a little off. "Of course, you must suspect most of this already."

I wasn't sure that I did, but what he was saying made sense to me. I was on the cusp of these thoughts, perhaps. I told myself not to doubt. I told myself that it was not impossible that I would have managed these insights alone.

It was all fascinating. I wrote and wrote and worried that I wouldn't be able to reread these frantic jottings. He looked at me. "You're okay?" he said.

"Why are you telling me this?" I asked. "Why not just tell the government?"

The projected face frowned. "The world needs this. But a government wouldn't share it. They'll use the technology for themselves only. Governments are selfish and shortsighted. This is what history will show. This is what I learnt at school."

"I see," I said. It was possible. I could believe it.

"And how would I explain it to them anyway? I'm here to impart this information as subtly as I can. You research this stuff already. You can take it, pass it on as if it's yours, naturally. No strangeness. No mystery. You can publish."

"But I'm just one person."

"It will be messy if I make my appearance known generally. Who knows what I would change if suddenly everyone was aware of me? Here"—the arms of the suit gestured a line between us—"it's just you and me."

"Our secret," I said.

"I think of it like surgery. Minimal intervention."

"I think I understand."

"Apart from the big thing." He laughed then. "Apart from an invention that solves everything."

It felt special, yes. Perhaps it was vanity to accept it so easily. There was a limit to all that I could take in, but I tried to be worthy of his choice. His ship, the craft that he had arrived in, was out at sea, beyond the bay, he told me, resting like a rock on the seabed. It was like a fairy story. Though the ship had a reactor within it, he said. It ran on science, not on fairy dust.

The postman came at ten and, hearing tires on the gravel, I walked around the shed and watched the man—middle-aged, wearing shorts, the cheeks above his peppery beard blushed red by wind—jump out of the red van and push some unimportant bits of junk mail through the letter box. I waved at him, and he waved back and drove on. Seeing the vehicle move towards the farm at the end of the track felt thrilling. The world continued oblivious.

I asked Red if he wanted to eat something. He smiled shyly. He said that he had food supplies for himself. "I don't know how I would react to food from here," he said.

I pitied him, of course, his alienation.

"You should eat," he said. "I'm asking a lot of your concentration."

I made more notes in the afternoon. I could write a whole book, I thought, on just the insights that I had gained so far. As far as I could follow his ideas, they seemed compatible with what I knew. I was inclined to trust those claims he made that stretched my understanding.

He talked into the evening. He was worried that I was tired, but he was tired himself, I sensed. There were times when I had to ask him to repeat what he was saying. I imagined what it would be like to describe, say, a computer to a Victorian scientist. "Tomorrow," he said, "I'm going to start explaining how to construct a usable reactor. I just wanted to frame the context, the limits of the current approaches. You need to be able to present the design as your own."

"I understand," I said.

He said that he needed to return to his craft to recharge his suit, and so when the dark came in fully he and I walked down to the beach and he waded out into the water. It was a clear night, but the moon was a thin crescent. The waves were small. I watched him walk beyond them and sink down through the water. Now that I was not shocked by his arrival, I could really look, could study his steady step through the waves, the even way he sank away. There must have been some system in the suit for buoyancy, for equalizing pressure. His head disappeared, and there was just the shifting skin of the sea. I saw this. It's still strange to say that I did.

I walked back up from the beach alone.

I looked at the hills behind the house, their eerie presence in the low light. But for the wind, and low sound of the waves coming in and out, it was silent. The dogs at the farm down the road were quiet. Jasper padded next to me. I thought of all the people who had lived on the island in the past. Once, a century and a half before, the land had been thickly populated, peppered with small village communities of men and women farming narrow strips of land—runrigs—the outlines of which could still be made out, scraped across the landscape, as if a giant had run a comb against the rolling hills. Even in the low light, I could see some of these furrows on the shadowed land. The people must have put so much work into that soil, I thought, to make it yield enough to survive in their limited way. They burned peat in their stoves, lit their houses with oil and candles, arrived in the twentieth century in this way.

For some reason, I felt galvanised by the thought of these people of the past. Their lives were unimaginable now, the crudeness obscene. I pictured an old lady burning a single candle to sew by a hearth. What those people lacked was energy. They could work their land only as much as their tired arms would allow. They had limited light. Coal and then oil—powering cars and machines, and lighting homes, running the factories to which they moved for work—brought these people into the modern age. Was I, I wondered, in Red's eyes, closer to such people than I was to him? I had always believed in the usefulness of fusion, of course, but, walking in the dark, placing my feet on the uneven ground, I felt a sense that history could click, lurch forward. I had a feeling that in due course what would seem odd would not be the invention Red explained to me, but the lack of it, all the time we had lived without.

I slept properly. When I woke, still early, I went to the shed and I pushed the door and felt again the giddying relief that he was there, returned, sleeping in his suit.

He didn't wake. The suit didn't shift this time. I walked with Jasper. The dog bounded out ahead, sniffing at fence posts and rocks and tufts of grass and bracken. In the rising sun, these features threw long shadows, tiger-striping the green land.

Jasper and I walked down to the water, which was clear and blue, a different sea from the sea of the night before. Red's footprints led from the tide line. I stood on a rock and watched seaweed, below the surface, billow with the motion of the water. I wanted to swim, but I wanted to work even more urgently. I had been thrilled by nothing as much as I was thrilled by this. I recalled the strange thing that Red had said about feeling that his journey back was fated. It seemed wishful, but in a less rational part of myself I believed it too. I was ready for him to come.

I made coffee in the bright kitchen. I went out to the shed with my notebook. Red sat up in his suit, leaning against the wall of the shed. "You're charged up?" I said.

His false face smiled at me, and he said, "My *suit* is charged up, even if I'm still tired."

We began to talk about making a working reactor. I sat at my desk. He knelt ahead of me, speaking earnestly, flashing images across his chest when necessary.

He spoke of a stellarator, an elegant incarnation that I could only half grasp the idea of. "It won't work," he said, "until one day it will."

He spoke of the ways in which this model accounted for the deficiencies he had identified in a tokamak design. He said of the stellarator, "It's like the plasma has a way it wants to move around, a path we need to *accommodate*."

"It sounds almost mystic," I said.

He laughed a sweet laugh at that.

He tried to link the lessons of yesterday to today, synthesising problem with solution. I thought, oddly, of things my husband had explained about political thought, Hegel and the idea that history should lead somewhere, should narrow to a point. I tried to imagine this reactor he spoke of: the rings of magnets, the plasma twisted and flowing like blood through a vein.

Some questions of mine vexed Red. I felt his indecision when he tried to answer them. He was working to project assurance, I could see, even if I only saw him refracted, through his simulated face. "This is not my field of expertise," he said, "so you must forgive my slowness."

I asked him who had tutored him in the subject, and he said that his mother had, and that he would have loved her to be speaking to me. I felt his sadness again then. Could he get home? I wondered. Did he have a plan to return? Forgive me, I hadn't even considered that. Perhaps it was a necessary oversight. There was work to do, I suppose. He was resolved on our lessons, and so I had to be. I tried harder to frame my questions, to narrow down and clarify. We moved more slowly than Red wanted, but we moved. I told myself, *I can do this.*

We paused and carried on and suddenly the dark was coming in. "We should stop for the day," Red said to me, and I staggered out into the blue dusk towards the cottage. I climbed the stairs. I slipped into bed and opened my notebook. I felt inspired, not yet sure of everything I needed to be sure of, but certain that I was gaining a sense of the route I needed to take. Jasper burrowed under the duvet and slept. I wrote in a panicked way, fearful of missing a single glowing insight. I wrote until the room lightened again. *Keep a grip on yourself,* I thought, but I continued scribbling. Jasper got up and circled around in the middle of the bed and then burrowed back down. I rose unsteadily because one of my legs had gone numb. I walked over the creaking bedroom boards, trying to gain back sensation. I hadn't drawn down the blind when I climbed into bed the night before, and now passing the window an impulse drew me to stop and look out.

The window faced west, towards the lawn and the sea. I looked at the blue sky and at the winding path to the beach. Movement drew my gaze back to the shadow near the shed. There was someone down there, I realised. My sleep-deprived mind took longer than it should have to understand. It seemed that there was an old man—the farmer from down the road, perhaps—creeping around the barn, stooped, one hand against the stonework. Had he realised that Red was there? I wondered. Was he investigating? I was about to rush downstairs and confront him, when the person straightened and I saw from the face that it wasn't an old man, but a skinny ginger boy.

He needed the wall for support. He was moving away from the door, walking his hands over the stone as he shuffled his feet in the same direction. He wore loose black trousers and a black sweatshirt. His feet were bare. His head bobbed, as if it were an effort to hold it up. As I watched, he stopped and pressed himself to the wall, then began very slowly to turn, leaning against the stone. It was then that I saw his face, and I am sorry to say that I was shocked. Even from the distance, even as he stood in shadow, I could see that his face was long and uneven. His brow was crooked, and his chin was tiny. I regretted my reaction as I had it, but I couldn't control the revulsion, the impulse that saw me split between the desire to turn away and the wish to stare. If he looked like anything, I thought, he looked like one of those sickly princes of history, those pale frail boys whose health failed them too early. He seemed to be gulping air. I could see his long pale neck moving. His eyes were closed for a long time, and then he opened them and stared ahead of him. He shook and took a step, and then he took another. He was like a man walking into the strongest storm, though from the way that the long grass moved down there, I could see that the day was quite calm.

I watched his progress across the grass with fascination. I knew deeply that I shouldn't go down, that he intended to do whatever he was doing alone. He shuffled forwards, seeming always to be on the verge of falling.

I had trimmed the lawn around the house when I arrived a week before, and he seemed to be heading for the place where I stopped mowing, where my property gave way to meadowland. The shadow of the shed was stretched by the low sun, and as he moved out of this shadow I glimpsed him fully, vividly, so that I could see the pain and concentration on his strange face. He stopped. He let his head droop. His arms were ahead of him. He began to fall. He tumbled onto his front, lay there curled on his side for a moment. I almost went to him. Then he thrashed around until he was lying on his back. He cast out his arms and legs. I understood what he was up to then: he lay starfished in new light, feeling, I realised, the sun on his bare face for the first time in his life.

6

ROBAN

2103

There is a whole universe beyond the base. That is what I want to communicate to Miz. I knew this before, sure. Of course, there is so much that is not the transitways and hangars and nodes. Yet I didn't understand the true difference between life in the Colony and life beyond. For my whole life I have lived in spaces made for human occupation. Often this is annoying, because a particular place will be designed for Homers, not for First Gens in Exos. Yet there is an appreciable reason behind each little choice: the way a doorway is shaped, a button placed, how a window lets outside light through a room. Yet, in training, on the far side of the planet, we are away from all that. Yes, we have our base—a spoked wheel of transitways and hangars—but on most days we are out in the beyond, learning to fly the expedition craft or moving across the rocky terrain in our Exterior Exos.

I traverse a boulder field in my Exo and the thrill and difficulty of the task is that this landscape was not laid out to facilitate my travel across it. It just *is*, and I must reckon with it. I bend the knees of my suit to land on the upslope of a large boulder. I take a stutter stride to reach the top and prepare for a long leap off the rock onto a flat slab about six meters beyond. I hit this slab and stride and then tuck my legs to leap onto another rock. I crest that and roll forwards, springing back to my feet as I come off the end and carrying on, through the rubble.

When I fly the craft, there are updrafts and dust storms that I have not encountered when training on the simulators. On flights, the controls become slippery with the perspiration that pours off my palms. But I love it. This world, this real world, is not a test set with an answer already in mind. It is itself.

The days of training are so hard. As I will tell Miz, they are days of three or even four pain pills. But they are revelatory days. The twelve of us new recruits—all First Gens—share a dormitory block. We wake early and take our supplements. We do our exercises. Then we suit up and run for hours through the uneven landscape. Then we are back to eat. We fly in a craft after that, paired up. We rise away from the surface and practice manoeuvres. We eat again. Finally, we rehearse taking samples from the rocks around the base. For the first month of training, my hands were in agony from grasping the controls of the suit and gripping the flight stick. My palms bled, but then they scabbed, and beneath those scabs formed callouses. At some point in the bewildering run of days I found that I could walk more easily from my Interior Exo to my bed. I looked at myself in the mirror and my posture was different. I held myself up.

Now my first leave is imminent and I'm unsure whether to relish or dread its approach. These relentless days have given me so much. I want to stay here, tempering like metal, yet I understand that this intensity cannot go on forever.

The week before leave is due to begin, the recruits of a previous intake check into the dormitory block down the corridor. They're an M-year older than us, these cadets, just back from their own leave, granted after their missions prospecting the planet and the asteroid belt. They were the first intake of First Gens to be trained, the oldest of us in the Colony. They are doing the job already, the real work, and we newbies are shy when we pass them in the transitways. We encounter their group on Exterior Exo maneuvers. When we do so, there is always one of them out ahead. Though I know that I should be concentrating on my own progress, I always find my gaze drawn towards this figure, moving in their suit like a virtuoso: a balance of stillness and speed. The figure leaps and lunges and yet carries their own core so steadily. Their foot speed is amazing. I learn from rumours that the figure is Vishay Simms, the top recruit from that intake. I see him in the canteen sometimes, with the older group. He is smaller than the others. He eats with his head down. His cohort have a bravado that my intake, new to all this, have not yet gained. They joke loudly. But Vishay doesn't join in with the antics of his comrades. He holds himself back, seems to be granted licence by those around him to do so.

When our leave begins, the twelve of us who have trained together file up the gangway of a transport bound for the Colony. We are in our interior suits, and we strap ourselves into the bench seating that runs down the length of the hold. The air smells of the last cargo: the algae stock used in the base kitchens. The craft shakes as it takes off, rising up through the air lock and out into the swirling dust. When the thrusters really engage, the resonance changes and the shaking dies away. We are up above the local storms, just the thin atmosphere and then the darkness of space over us.

Others around me watch entertainment on their suit displays, yet I just sit in the dim holdspace. I feel that I need to reflect on how I have changed, to prepare to feel new in an old place. Thoughts of recounting my training to Miz have kept me going, yet I am unsure about how much to bring back to her. Miz was so good in her suit when we were young. At school, as I kept gaining confidence in suit manoeuvres, I waited to be passed by Miz. I expected her to recover and return, impatient as she had once been. It took too long for me to realise that we wouldn't graduate together, and when this realisation did come, I felt embarrassed by it, unable to vocalise my disappointment at a fact she had come to terms with long ago. I won the Exterior Exo race in the final year, still feeling, as I paced back to the Colony in first place, that Miz should have been ahead of me. I got top grades in most of my classes too, and at graduation I received the Faulk Medal from Virginia Faulk, Axel F's daughter. I tried to give the medal to Miz. I went straight from graduation to see her in her room. I dropped the thing onto her bed, where it made a crater in the crisp white duvet. We looked at it together, and she said that she was proud of me. She would have loved to meet Virginia Faulk, because she idolises Axel F for all the work that the man did to bring us to this place. Yet she wouldn't accept it as a gift. "It's yours, Roban," she said. "You earned it." The most she would consent to was to look after the medal while I was away.

And still, coming back, I cannot cure myself of the thought that she should be here with me, first amongst us recruits. I still have in mind an alternate timeline where she is healthy and we are doing these things together. I sit in the rattling transport craft and wonder what I should say to her. She will be glad of my success, but I don't want to give her too much cause to consider what she is missing. I think of a run that I and my fellow recruits did three weeks before, where we came out of a thick sandstorm to encounter the sun rising over a craggy ridgeline. The colour in the sky was unlike anything I've ever seen. It all felt like another world, truly, and I resolve that if I can find the right moment to do so, I will tell her about this.

We touch down. I disembark and say goodbye to the other recruits. I stroll along the transitways feeling distant from this home I know so well. Everything is smaller than I remember. I open the little unit door, to be met, to my surprise, by Mum. She stands halfway to the door. She must have been at the round table waiting. I say, "You're here?" I'm not displeased. It's just a shock to find her missing work. I suppose that I had anticipated coming into an empty unit, counted on time and space to acclimatise to being back. I squat in my suit and embrace her. "It's great to see you. I just didn't expect—"

"I'm sorry. I've surprised you."

It is all wrong, I think. I want to begin this again.

Mum points to the table, to a pot steaming there. "You want tea?" she says. "You should get out of your suit."

"I'm going out again."

"Really?" she says. "Stay. Have tea. Take off your suit."

"I'm going out. I'm sorry."

"Roban. Please. You're just in." This isn't like her, I think. She is talking, but her eyes are saying a different thing. I feel panicked. I look at the table, at the pot. Something else catches my eye, resting on a folded cloth: the Faulk Medal.

I stumble to my old room, sloppy in my suit, knocking against the doorframe as I pass through. My system tells me that my pulse rate is high, begins to play me soothing music. I release myself from the suit, and the work of that gives me something to concentrate on. I slide the visor up, push away the controls. The chest opens and the saddle lowers. I free my legs and step onto the padded floor of the bedroom. I take care to shut the suit away neatly, as I don't always. As long as I'm here, going through these steps, I realise, it is not confirmed, there is a tiny possibility that nothing has happened.

"We return her to the earth," the celebrant says. Through the glass of the memorial wing we mourners watch two Homer women in Exos lowering the small coffin down into a grave dug into the dusty ground. Behind are the winking markers of those who have been buried before.

Once, when I was a baby, this was an empty space, and now it is half full. They will have to demark a new graveyard soon. Somewhere out there is Other Mum. The celebrant stands at a lectern in front of the window. He casts his eyes up only briefly, as if he faces into blinding light. His words irk me, in the same way that words used to irritate me when I was obsessed with my dictionary, before the teachers explained that the plans of the Corporation rendered the dictionary unnecessary because the old terms will strike true again when terraforming begins.

You don't return *her to this earth*, I think. *She did not grow from this soil, was not nourished by it.* The symbolism is wrong up here, but the man persists with the story.

Her heart gave out one night. Painlessly, her father reassured me when he called to invite me to this memorial service. "Sometimes that just happens," he said. "The body's resilience reaches a limit."

I don't want something just happening, though. Her death is not merely a thing that occurred, I think. *It happened* here*, in this world that you made, in this world that you all purport to control.*

The Homers wear dark clothes, clasp their hands in front of them. Those of us in Exos stand farther back, mimicking the gestures of the unsuited.

When the celebrant has finished speaking, the women outside begin to shift the dirt manually, using shovels. This is not the most efficient way to move dirt in an Exo, but it is all theatre, bearing us away from the terrible reality of what we watch: Miz down in the ground, and regolith beginning to rain onto her, rising now as it is disturbed. Above the hole a cumulus of dust builds to a tower, like steam coming from a boiling pot.

Afterwards, Miz's father comes over to me. "Roban," he says. He is a handsome man of Korean heritage. Everyone in the Colony knows his face from the informational videoshorts in which he appears, explaining treatments available to First Gens and speaking hopefully of developments the Corporation are making in medical science. He was so often at work in the first years that I knew Miz that I didn't meet him for a long time, and when I did I was surprised, not because he was not like the man in the videos, but because he *was*. There is no alteration in his manner from his public appearances. He speaks clearly. He fixes his green eyes on one. Even now, there is an undertone of optimism—doubtless habitual—to what he says. "She liked you, Roban. You were very special to her."

"Yes."

"I'm very sorry."

It's her bereaved father comforting *me*. I am aware of the wrongness of this, guilty that I am not the one doing the work.

He fixes his gaze on my Avi face. "We all tried so hard," he says.

I feel something turn in me, hard and sour. Maybe I am doing enough to just be silent. Miz's mother arrives and puts an arm around him. She says, "Roban." We are two people with nothing in common, now that her daughter is gone.

I nod in the suit. I turn away. My mum is at the window, looking out at the graveyard.

I leave the memorial wing. I pass the doors to the eternity vaults. When I was younger, I used to love coming to look at the high, uplit entranceway with the Latin inscription above, the sentries standing by. Here are the gene banks and seed banks and cultural data banks, though, of course, in the Early Iterative Stage when there were power and resource issues, we lost a lot of recorded biomass and a few centuries of Eurasian culture. Mum's second Stellar8 design was crucial in recovering the facility after that. She and her team made refinements to their reactors, increased redundancy so that the demands of mining wouldn't, as they had before, cause outages in the colony grid. In fact, I have a memory of being here as a child, before my Exo, at a ceremony at which she was awarded a medal.

She was allowed on a tour inside. It was just white corridors, she said, and the faint humming of the refrigeration. That's what the future looks like, I guess: nothing much, unless you really believe in it.

I cross the elevated path over the crop hangars. Beneath me are potatoes. Miz and I never came here together in the end.

At the funeral her youngest brother was in his Exo, moving jerkily through the mourners. Now there are better interventions to relieve conditions that First Gens suffer. It has even been suggested that our genes might start to adapt naturally, that those generations that come after us might be better suited to the planet. Nature, I suppose, finds its way, even up here.

A quotation of Axel F's that we all know: *Everything is iterative*. We lurch towards perfection.

Yet I think then of the way adaption actually happens, of school lessons in biology. The holders of certain traits prosper. Others die away.

I wander for a long time along transitways, through nodes. The working day is done, and people are back in their units. The shuttle dings by sometimes. Outside the windows the dust and rock are dark. After much aimless walking I go to OldTownSquare, which since my return has seemed so small. I used to love the trickling fountain in the middle, the façade of EatTown market, rendered to look like old stone buildings back on Home. I can hear the vendors closing up there, yet the square is empty. I sit on one of the benches facing the fountain, awkward because it is set too low for someone in a suit. When I was a kid, before I wore the suit, I clambered to the edge of this fountain and dipped my fingers in this water. Now, of course, I'd never let myself be seen unsuited in so public a place. The fountain is a round basin with a little island in the centre, on which stands a man, a Homer, holding the flag of the Corporation. Little jets spray out from the base of this island. I've seen it so often that I can hardly really see it, but today I sit so long that I notice the motif punched at intervals into the outer edge of the basin: little hourglasses. This was a way they measured time back on Home, apparently. I researched that once. Sand fell from the top chamber to the bottom, and when there was no more sand to fall, one knew a certain time had elapsed. None of this is the reason that sign is used. The symbolism merely relates to the shape of the graph: all the people before, all the people to come, and us, now, in the pinch. I always felt so privileged to be here when so many others were *not*. Yet now, in this moment, I feel the constriction. I believed, as I was told as a child, that all of this was a triumph. I used to detest Mum's ambivalence, in fact. She was never as enthusiastic as other children's parents. She wore only the most basic decorative sash on Corporation Day. Her work powered the place, yet it seemed she used the leeway that gave her to mope, left it to others to keep alive the hope so necessary for our community. Sometimes her sadness felt like a warm little secret between us, but mostly I wanted an affirmative parent, like Miz's dad, with his wide smile and his steady gaze.

I stand and walk back to the unit. When I arrive, I must squat my suit as I always do to tap in the entrance code. I duck through the doorway, the shoulder of my suit knocking the lintel.

Mum is waiting for me, out of her funeral clothes. She sits on the sofa. I go to my room. I climb out of my suit and get changed into my lounge outfit. I walk slowly back into the main room. I go to her. I embrace her. She smiles and I do not explain what I am thinking. (Could I even do so?) But I hope that she understands.

7

KENZIE

2071

O*ur application to Tevat fails. The notification arrives early on a Saturday* morning. It is only in this disappointment that I come bumping against the realisation of all that my infatuation with Justine has made seemingly possible. Of course, a hasty plan from two refugees of the field's most notorious recent failure was unlikely to come off, and yet I sit up in bed and read the message on my device and feel a thudding surprise. Justine returns from the bathroom of my little flat and she looks at me and seems to know before I even speak. I make us coffee and Justine makes calls. She hears that an old colleague of hers, a man called Jack, formerly of Glasgow University, has received funding for a fusion project. "He's no better than us," she says, and shakes her head. I wonder what we will be after this, devoid of our old shared purpose, our obsession.

"What do we do now?" I say.

I am thinking of Granny then, of the cottage, the sea, the shed, cool in the mornings. The thought of retreat to a place like that is understandable now, appealing. I say, "We could take a holiday?"

Justine sips her coffee. "Like ordinary people?" she says. "Why not?"

We set off five days later. En route, we stay at Justine's parents' house on a quiet cul-de-sac in the outskirts of Glasgow. Pictures of Justine and her brother receiving awards line the route along the hallway and up the carpeted stairs, the siblings' ages and levels of achievement increasing, through school, then university, then postgraduate degrees. "What happens at the top?" I say to Justine, on entering the hall, studying the first of these.

She makes a pretend grimace. "You sound like Mum," she says. "I suppose it better be good."

Her dad is a broad man who moves slowly around the neat garden. Her mother is bright, watchful, drawn to her daughter but wary, then, not to crowd. I sense Justine's irritation, and I, motherless for years now, want to tell her to relish the attention, the misguided care. Though I don't.

We leave after breakfast the next day, with a lunch packed by Justine's mother.

We depart the city's northern suburbs, ride past Loch Long, past the old naval base where the submarines used to dock. The hillsides are blistered. I stare up at yellowed grass; at dark clumps of heather, burnt the summer before. The sun is out, though, and the loch is bright, marred only by algae blooms at its head.

We change trains and ride the smaller line up through Skye, the craggy peaks glowering down at us, cloud-crowned and reassuringly indifferent.

This is one of the routes that Dad campaigned for, and I am surprised at the shabbiness of the train. Dad and I used to take the other route to the cottage in a similar kind of train, and I remember it pristine. The seats of this train are stained, and we look out of the window through the curled lines of a graffiti tag that runs the length of our carriage. There is no conductor, and from Broadford there is a man in an adjacent seat playing a loud military role player on his screen without headphones, looking at us occasionally, daring us to object.

When we come to the house, I am ready to be disappointed. Yet we summit the final crest of the road in a Bug and the cottage stands pretty above the clifftop, cast in afternoon light. The Bug won't drive the last yards where the track is unsurfaced. We get out and shoulder our bags as the little vehicle sets off whirring back to the port.

I last came to the house five years ago with Dad, arriving in a van to haul away Granny's stuff. It was a horror show. She hadn't been coping for those final years. She'd died in care, in exile from this place. The floor was discoloured from the time prior, when she'd had a fall and lain for two days before a postal delivery person found her.

I remember all the boxes of wine beside the back door: a cheap brand decorated with an antique picture of a sunlit Italian vineyard, which seemed mocking in its quaint unreality. I stood examining that image, repeated and repeated in a jumbled pile, collapsing, sodden with the winter drizzle.

Yet now the house is pleasant. It's not as characterful as it was with Granny here, but it's clean.

I watch Justine unpacking our provisions in the kitchen. Her presence is a way that I can see it all afresh. She runs her fingers over the heavy table. She touches the shells on the sill, raising up clouds of dust.

Then I worry that it is *too* nice, that she will think that I am spoiled by all this in contrast to the modest camping holidays that she took with her mum and dad and brother (and, of course, I am).

We stroll down to the small beach, which is striated by the clumps of weed left behind by the tide.

The air smells bad, because two gulls lie dead amongst the rocks at the far end of the beach. But even the foulness is bracing: a different kind of stink from that of the city.

Justine comes to me, and we nuzzle together, against the wind and the pounding of the surf.

Over the course of the week, Justine admonishes me that I don't know how to relax. I'm too set on filling our days. I plan walks along the coast.

I prepare complicated lunches. I should just spend time with her, as she is telling me to do, but I cannot.

I get up before her and stalk the beach looking for shells. I call a Bug out to ride to the local shops for fresh scallops for a pasta dish. I study the nature guides piled in the living room—outdated now by extinctions and die-offs—so that I can identify plants on our walks together.

I ache with gladness still. It is a pleasure that feels at times like pain. I even wonder whether I want this joy to break. I half fantasise about a terminal argument. I almost want to see the other side of this love, to experience an end to my anxiety that it can't endure.

By the final couple of days at the house, we have walked every trail around the cottage. Justine looks at me exasperated as I pace around the kitchen. She takes her cup of coffee back up to bed with the old novel that she's been reading, and I know that I should follow her, but I can't.

I still need to gather, and this urge takes me to the one place here that I haven't yet had the courage to explore: Granny's workshop.

It was supposed to be my job to clear the workshop. I was finishing my undergraduate degree when Granny died, taking the first tentative steps towards a career in fusion. Dad thought that I would understand the mess, but the few books I looked at mystified me. It is odd to say, but I learnt little from Granny about fusion in person. I sensed the holiness of her work when I was a child (a holiness that, incidentally, Dad could never see). Her work, at least as she approached it in the years I knew her, seemed to take the energy and attitude of a punishing religious practice. She withdrew from the world, and I only watched from afar, learnt to trust her own belief. Later, at university, I walked into a second-year class in nuclear physics and listened to the lecturer speak apologetically of the many failures to implement fusion. I thought simply, *It doesn't have to be this way.* That was what Granny had given me, I suppose. Later, as I specialised, I did read her published papers. Long before my birth, she'd made her reputation with perceptive critiques of current fusion technologies. She'd also outlined some promising concepts for a reactor design: a stellarator, compact and ingenious. She'd found a way in which tritium production may be accomplished through low-energy reactions. This could have been her great achievement, enough for a single career, yet she wanted to put that tritium fuel to use, to truly realise her design. The stellarator plan won her funding and a lab of her own. Yet Granny couldn't create the finely tuned design that she had theorised. She was recruited to an Oxford-based lab then, where she'd worked before and fallen out of favour, and now she failed a second time. She went back to Edinburgh. She wrote more papers, some of which were well received. But every time someone wanted to develop a concept with her, the project fell apart. She couldn't compromise, couldn't tolerate others tinkering with her designs.

Later, when I joined the lab in Edinburgh, I heard stories from Sani that his supervisor had told him of working with Granny. She was brilliant but impossible. She could demolish others' ideas but could never fully explain her own. She took over projects. Colleagues lost patience with her. Every little aspect of a design was a thing to be fought tooth and nail. Two projects failed and then the university didn't renew her contract. Peers spoke of her as someone who had lost her way. She couldn't get another position. She wrote hundreds of letters seeking funding, first to institutions, then to private labs, then to philanthropists interested in scientific work. She was on the island by this time, divorced, alone. This was the long middle of her life when I knew her. Periodically, there was someone curious about her ideas. I remember the phone ringing in the night when I was a child and the way that Dad spoke. His speech was falsely animated, not far from the voice he'd use with my classmates on playdates. She'd be telling him about someone who might be ready to fund her work, but it never went anywhere. These funders were stranger as the years went on.

They'd seldom have the money that they promised. Once she came close to a windfall from the heir of a supermarket dynasty, but the guy was sued by his own children and his plans to finance Granny's project was used as evidence of his mental instability. Had she gained funding, I suspect that she would have quarrelled and dragged other researchers down with her.

And perhaps after her death I was still too young to be faced with her unfathomable notebooks. She had worked for so long alone. She'd developed her own unique references, a shorthand. It was a knot of thought, tying itself tighter and tighter as the years went on. And also, maybe, I didn't want to unravel it. Already then I had felt myself committed to a path because of her. I had gained my belief in my vocation from her example. I took a quick glance and I decided that I could not open myself to finding error or delusion in those books laboured over with such holy care.

The sea is shining as I approach the shed. The metal roof moans in the wind. I have to work to get the lock on the door loose, but it comes. The hinges wheeze and I remember why I couldn't tackle this before.

There is a pyramid of cardboard boxes in the middle of the room. There are parts of the old Land Rover against the back wall. There are odd bits of furniture: bookshelves, a child's desk, an old plastic chair faded from red to pink. A folded dog cage is leant against the wall by the door, spiderwebs matted between the metal latticework like loose skin on a skeleton. I move by it and the webbing shifts.

My focus is on the back of the room because there is a door in the floor there. I haul a ring and the hatch screams up. Dust rises like smoke. There are steps leading down to a basement area. Peering down, I can see that the bottom of those steps is obstructed by more boxes of notebooks.

Granny wrote by hand because it facilitated nonlinear thinking. I still remember her saying such words to a half-baffled eleven-year-old girl.

Could I do this? Make a place like this? Pages and pages every day, until those pages become books, become boxes, become close-packed rooms?

It is all time, I suppose: all these words written in heedless hope. This morning, at the end of the holiday, with a sense of dread rising up my throat, I ask myself, *Isn't that most lives?* All this waste? This building to nothing? I think of the proposal document that Justine and I have been working on for months. I stand on the steps, looking back into the shed, but then I ascend again. I fold down the door. I go to the pile of boxes in the middle of the floor, tug one open. The date written on the book is 2065, two years before Granny died.

I go out into the sun and sit with my back against the wall of the shed. It takes me a while to learn to read Granny's script, to fall into the way of it, but then I am fluent with it. I read. I skip. I read. There are pictures in the margins, sketches of plants. I read and skip. There is a diagram: part of a magnetic housing unit, carefully rendered. If she was deluded, it was a serious delusion. Like Newton's alchemy, I think. The text around the picture is small. I turn the book to track a line of words that runs spiralling around the drawing. It feels tantalisingly on the edge of something. I flick the page. Another picture. I read the clustered scribblings around that, I flick on, read more. Time gets sticky. I go back into the shed, rifle through more boxes. I grab another book. The sun is high in the sky, the shadow that the house casts over the grass diminishes. I read on.

I think, *Shit.*

• • •

We wait in a triple-height atrium. This is technically his home, but for a man like Axel Faulk the distinction between his own concerns and those of his company are negligible.

The tall window looks out at a Zen garden: raked gravel, stones and moss-covered rock; a rustling thicket of bamboo. Behind this are the rooftops of the Tevat campus. Out of sight, beyond, is the Clyde, rolling slowly towards the sea.

The bamboo sways. Justine taps her own knee nervously. The receptionist who greeted us returns from a back room, carrying a tray on which sit tall glasses of carbonated water. The woman places the tray on the coffee table in front of us. I watch the rising bubbles streaming around the shattered cubes of ice in the glass, breaking with metallic pops at the surface. Everything feels so *crisp*, I think, though I haven't slept properly for weeks.

Two months ago, we extended our stay at the cottage. A van delivered a scanning machine from the mainland. We worked through every one of the stacked boxes in the shed and in the basement below. We took it in turns to flick a page, scan, flick a page and scan again. Our fingertips blackened with ancient ink. Whoever wasn't taking the scans worked at the screen trying to organise the material. It took eight days of ceaseless work to get everything recorded, and then another week to decide where to begin our study of the pages. We reassembled Granny's old computers, downloaded the plans and data and models that she had built. We slept and we worked, and one day we were surprised to find that we hadn't eaten for at least twenty-four hours and that there was no food left in the house. We called a Bug and rode to buy food. I looked at the rounded hills, bays and lochs and the blue cloud-streaked sky, and I felt the landscape pulsing around me then, as if my unacknowledged hunger had let me through to a place of saintly ecstasy. We ate cake in a café. We went into the village shop and grabbed items nearly randomly. We rushed back to the house, where our screens waited for us.

We knew even then that we would build what we were organising into a proposal. I'd called Sani, said that we had both caught a strange flu out on the island. He'd said flatly that he hoped we'd get better soon. The prototype investigation still dragged. There was no urgency for us to be back at work. Then I'd called him again three weeks later, when we were back in Edinburgh, said that we had something he might be interested in. He'd organised a little conference room for us, down in the basement next to the café, let us speak and show him our diagrams. He'd watched like a parent at a school play and then said, "That's nice. That's clever."

"And?" said Justine.

"You don't want me involved, believe me. The government are cutting funding, the university are taking the department apart. I'm still hoping I might get a better idea of what went wrong before they shut us down completely."

"I'm sorry," said Justine.

He'd shrugged. "I'll make sure you both get paid through to the autumn," he said. He laughed a little bitterly. "Call me if you get funded and find yourself on the lookout for lightly used reactor parts."

Now the receptionist rises from her stool again. She wears black athletic wear, tightly fitted, creaseless. She smiles. She points towards the high double doors in the middle of the marble-clad back wall. "Axel is ready for you."

We ride up to his penthouse room in an elevator lined with butter-coloured wood. The doors open to brightness. Axel's penthouse has floor-to-ceiling windows on all sides. The city is spread around beneath: the pretty Georgian crescents, the trees in Kelvingrove Park, in full leaf and shifting just a little. Sunlight breaks through cloud to come down on the spires and towers of the city centre. Windows shine amidst the piles of soot-stained ancient stone. He's older than I expected. I've watched footage of him in interviews. In the flesh he is handsome, strong-jawed, as he has appeared in those videos, but there is something in the way he sits—

hunched on the stool at the other end of the room—that gives away the fact that he is an elderly man. He gestures to the open floor in front of him. The place is sparsely furnished, museum-like: no seats but his own stool, low bookcases, pieces of pottery on plinths. We step towards him.

He says, “Interesting.” His accent is strange: bland and unplaceable, like an OS voice. He grew up in Rio de Janeiro, I know, the son of expat American bankers. He is formed by gated living, Dad has asserted many times, the man’s philosophy moulded in retreat from the masses.

We wait.

“Your proposal, I mean,” he says.

Justine nods. “Yes.”

Axel checks something on his wrist display. His hair is colourless, his skin very light. He gestures that she continue.

Justine begins to speak about our reactor design, moving through the pitch that we have been practicing for days, word by word, pause by pause. Axel Faulk closes his eyes and listens.

Justine’s voice is more brittle than usual. She speaks too quickly. She is uncharacteristically nervous. I notice that Axel is now watching me observing Justine.

As she starts to explain the unique design of the magnetic coils, Axel raises his palm. “Thank you,” he says.

“We—” says Justine.

“I like it,” says Axel. A smile comes late to his lips, an afterthought. “I had my fusion specialists look at your plan. They’re working now, actually, building the prototype space.”

“Your specialists?” I say.

“The team I’ve been funding.”

“Jack’s team?” says Justine.

“They *were* Jack’s team.” Faulk gives a flat smile.

“Oh. Right.”

He grins, enjoying our surprise. "They'll obviously need a new leader . . ."

"Well, we can do that together," I say, trying to sound ready, capable.

Faulk wrinkles his nose as if taking in an unpleasant smell. "That's not how things work in my teams, unfortunately."

I say, "This is a design made by both of us—"

"But now it needs to be implemented." Faulk speaks deliberately, as if explaining himself to someone slow. "My teams are vertical. Accountability is a key principle. Everything else is just . . ." He waves a hand.

I say, "But this is *our* idea. We need to work on it together."

Faulk fixes his eyes on me and then laughs. It is a strange sound, coming from him, filling the clean still room. It is not a joyful laugh, but something sharp. He says, "Well. If you want to share your *idea* together, by all means hold on to it. If you want to use your idea to make an actual *reactor*, then I have certain expectations."

I look at Justine, seeking support, and see that she has closed her eyes. She opens those eyes. She says, "Kenzie will do it. Kenzie can do it. I'll step away."

In the night, a month later, I stare at the ceiling and wonder why I didn't object. Our new flat is in the centre of Glasgow. I watch the light that leaks over the top of the blind. The glow shone by a passing bus makes a parabola that lurches towards the chandelier and then disappears.

Justine has explained that she nominated me as the lead because the plans were my inheritance. "She was your grandmother," she said. I nightly weigh those words, trying to detect if there was a single note of bitterness in them.

Justine works now for a telecommunications company. She manages the technical aspects of their infrastructure: the connections, the cables, the physical hardware. The work is beneath her, but she does it without complaint.

Where is her credit? Where is Granny's credit? I think of them when I am at the lab, and I can hear both their voices telling me that credit was never the thing they wanted. They wanted only a solution to the problem itself: a fusion reaction set in motion, held it in place. *So make that happen*, I tell myself.

Each day I stride through the pristine reception area of the main start-up building and make my way down hushed hallways to a beautiful lab, so neat as to seem more like a gallery than a place for scientific work.

I have new colleagues, who listen to my every word and who queue at my desk to show me the way that they are trying to realise my designs. (Or my grandmother's designs.) Sometimes I lose track of my guilt and there is a tumbling thrill to it all. The project is a cornerstone of the ten-year plan for the company, Axel F has told me.

Still, it is petrifying to run a whole project. I have no practice at this. At the university I was part of a team, implementing directives, checking others' modelling calculations, occasionally speaking up in meetings to make my own modest suggestions. Now, as my colleagues stand and await my approval or correction, I feel like an unconvincing actor. I come in very early so that I can be alone, get to grips with the progress of the project at my own pace before I am asked to make a call on the latest unresolved issues. In the evenings I lean on Justine, who listens to me list points needing attention, who helps me consider the workflow plans and respond to the many questions of those labouring under me.

I visit Axel Faulk in his high room over the city. He asks me about my progress in a clipped, impatient way. Before I knew him, I thought that he was a charlatan. But I have come to see he is a genius, although not in any of the ways in which his supporters say he is. He has no particular vision, no special insight, yet he knows how to urge others faster to their goals. He gets in your head like a sort of parasite. I struggle to explain delays, complications, though my reasoning is solid, justified. He sits folded in his chair and watches me with his beady eyes. He likes to say, "You could be doing a little better, no?"

I work, and that is everything. Summer gives out into an oddly parched autumn, and I only notice because I am slightly cold walking to work in my jersey. Leaves, curled and dry, are blown scratching over the cobbled road outside our flat. The weather gets colder still, and the clocks change, and suddenly I am walking to work in the dark and walking home in the dark. I am in a tunnel, I suppose. And perhaps I love that.

8

ANDREW

2073

In the church, the woman plays the fiddle beautifully. I have been meaning to leave in order to get home in time to greet Kenzie, but now I linger at the back a few minutes longer than intended as the woman slices her bow backwards and forwards and the music rises and reverberates in the chill air beneath the dark vaulted stone ceiling.

I spoke to her before, as the soup and bread was served out. She's from a west coast town, emptied by the insurance crisis. She was shy to meet my eye, bashful as so many are at these kind of events. "I used to cross the road if I saw a gathering like this," she said. "I always thought . . ." She sighed. "I suppose I thought that those people weren't like me, that I wouldn't get into their situation. But then"—she laughed mirthlessly, held up her hands in ragged fingerless gloves—"here I am . . ."

I had the feeling that she hadn't really renounced that old notion she described. She projected shame still. She hardly ate at all, and held herself away from the others, who mingled, standing, rustling in their thick padded winter coats, their breath rising above them. Maybe her feelings about her circumstances would soften in time. Her situation was beyond her, of course, but perhaps truly believing this insulted her sense of personal agency. The ArtInt had concluded that variability in storm patterns, weather, and market fluctuations were too great to allow firms to underwrite certain small businesses, and the government had chosen not to step in with subsidy. Without insurance these concerns couldn't take loans, couldn't get equipment and materials on credit. As simply as that, there went most of the fishing industry and a third of small farms in Scotland. The woman had owned a café, spoke of how she'd always been in before six in the morning making pastries by hand. "But it didn't matter," she said, speaking carefully, as if trying to convince herself. "There was no one to come in."

"Of course not," I said.

Yet now, at the front of the church, the woman stands tall, her back arched slightly, in fact, as she bears up the fiddle and dashes the bow over the strings. Her face is inclined upwards, and her wool hat drawn off her head a little so that one can see her auburn hair. She has her eyes closed, and, playing this way, so absorbed in what she does, she looks younger. Speaking to her, I had thought her close to my own age, but now I wonder whether she is nearer to a peer of Kenzie's. I'm older than I think myself, of course, and Kenzie is no longer so young, and recent years have worn so many people down.

When she saws out a final, plaintive note, I turn and walk through the doors of the church, out onto George Street, nodding at the bouncers by the entranceway, sadly necessary at the shelter events now. It is actually cold this Christmas Eve, and the pavement is flecked with frost, the whole stone city liable to glint in the right light from the right angle.

I walk south, thinking of the woman still. Her coat was thin for this time of year, but she'd declined a new one from the donation box. "I'm fine," she'd said. "I like to move. I stay warm that way." People are loath to understand their situation as a general one. They think the crisis merely the isolated misfortunes of other people, until it comes for them. But it is a pattern, a whole rolling change, around us now. The conclusions of ArtInt are not wrong in this respect, at least. The government, Tevat, my daughter, even, talk as if the apocalypse is still ahead, beyond the horizon, to be surmounted or succumbed to in due course. Yet on nights like these, I feel a ready rebuke: it is with us already, in lives shortened and made wretched, in jobs and homes lost. It is not a discrete problem to solve, but a reality to reckon with together. We need a story, I think as I walk, not our individual narratives, but a tale of our destiny as a nation, as a whole species.

I make my way past the station and then turn up Cockburn Street, because the shortcuts via the steps and the closes will be hectic with street drinkers tonight. The shops on the hill are shuttered and barred and none of the historical light projections—the carriage that clatters soundlessly over the cobbles, the capering pickpockets, or the lumbering grave robbers—are turned on. Instead, there is a more genuine atmosphere of unease. From Fleshmarket Close I hear the sound of smashing glass and raised voices. At the top of the street a cluster of private security men, maintained by the local shopkeepers and restaurateurs, wait, their hands hooked into the inner pockets of their tactical vests, watching the people passing with narrowed eyes.

I turn right and walk up the Royal Mile, past Adam Smith, guano-splattered and glowering, and St. Giles' Cathedral rearing out of the darkness. A stiff wind, bearing the smell of the sea, chases me over George IV Bridge and then past the university and across the Meadows. I push my hands into my pockets and trudge, and eventually I'm in Bruntsfield, where I stomp up the stone stairwell into the flat.

The door opens to light and music because Kenzie has arrived already. I should have been back, I chide myself. There's no hospitality in leaving her to let herself in. She comes to the hallway, smiling, to greet me. Her hair is slightly shorter, I note, cut in a trendy way, even. She looks well. I try to change my mood, to will myself towards easiness. I take off my big coat, whirl off my scarf. I hug Kenzie and say, "It ran on a bit. I'm sorry."

She laughs. "You think I'd expect you on time back from an event? I just got in anyway." She gestures to her small rucksack by the door.

I smile, glad to be off on the right note.

The air smells of spices and hot fruit. Kenzie says, "I'm making glühwein. Merry Christmas, by the way."

Despite the fact that it has been years since Lina's death, we still do Christmas the German way in honour of Kenzie's mother. The two of us will eat a big meal tonight, on Christmas Eve, and exchange presents afterwards. Tomorrow will be a quieter day and Kenzie will travel to Glasgow to spend time with Justine and her family. Now I follow my daughter into the kitchen to receive a mug of scalding wine. "O Tannenbaum" blares from the kitchen speaker. There is a nut roast in the fridge, and I put the oven on to heat that. I ask about Justine, and Kenzie pauses her rooting in the cupboard and her complaints about the dirty crockery to say that Justine is fine, careful as she always is on the subject of her partner because, as we both know but do not say, it leads us towards the changes of the last few years: the private proposal, the connection to Axel Faulk, and the move to Glasgow. I ask about work, trying to make the enquiry light, normal. Kenzie tells me things are going well. "We've had a lot of a good tests. We're working on a mass-producible model." She takes out knives and forks for dinner, polishes them with a tea towel.

"I'm glad to hear," I say. "I'm proud of you. I knew you could do it."

She looks at me with a certain caution, polishing more slowly.

"I don't like your employer," I say. "You know that. But I'm glad your project is good. That was always your objective."

"Yes," she says coolly.

We carry the table settings through to the living room. With my daughter here, I always see the flat with different eyes, fret that it's too dirty. I've been to Kenzie and Justine's Glasgow flat just once and found it to be like a show home in its cleanness. It was the flat, I supposed, of women who spent most of their time working: minimally decorated rooms, mark-less parquet floors, great expanses of pristine marble countertops. My own living room is shabby, overpacked with furniture because the previous flat (the *family flat*, as I think of it still), which the chairs and sofa and table were bought for, was larger. This afternoon, I got the old box of Christmas decorations out and strung things up. Some moulted silver tinsel is draped over the fireplace. The old Christmas stockings, now moth-holed but still bearing the letters *A* and *K*, are tacked beneath. Around the bay window a tangle of lights glow and then dim with a woozy rhythm.

I watch Kenzie setting out the plates, taking care to align the knives and forks and napkins just so. There is a little black triangular burn in the middle of the table, from where the iron tipped over while I was making a Halloween costume for Kenzie when she was fourteen. I run my finger over the mark. In the kitchen, the oven timer starts to bleat. I look up to see Kenzie watching me. "Shall I get that?" she says. I return to myself, nod. She walks quickly to attend to the oven.

"You're too scared of being abandoned," Lina told me once. It was in the aftermath of some argument. We were sat at the kitchen in the old flat, softened towards each other, but still talking our disagreement through. "You're still the boy whose mother ran away to her island. You're still seeking loyalty. In your work, too. All that talk of collaboration, working together . . ."

She was right, probably. Though I'm sure I wouldn't have thanked her for the insight. I recall that I asked her—smartly, I thought—why she was a doctor then, and she'd straight-batted it back, sounding more Germanic than usual: "Because my brother was so often ill when I was a child, of course." I miss her acuity still, miss her especially at Christmas.

Kenzie returns to the table with the nut loaf steaming on a chopping board. Though she has started to eat meat with Justine, apparently, she was happy enough, when I checked, to have a vegan Christmas dinner. I slice the loaf with care, serve us both.

After dinner we exchange presents: the same things we gift each other every year. I receive a bottle of Edradour whisky. I give Kenzie a couple of pairs of the thick socks she likes (or used to like, at least). We sit in front of the fireplace, me on the sofa, Kenzie on the armchair which I still think of as Lina's. Though I drink seldom these days, though I have, in fact, three unopened bottles of Edradour previously gifted by Kenzie, I open the new whisky, pour us each a couple of fingers. I say, "I have something I want to run by you."

"Yes?" Kenzie says.

"Moira is retiring in the spring. I'm thinking of running for party leader."

"That's great."

"Yes. Well . . . It's a big decision. But I've been thinking I should give it a go."

"You should."

"It will be more work. There might be a bit more attention on me. Some on you, even."

Kenzie lifts her glass, sniffs at the whisky. "Sure." She sips.

"You don't mind that?"

"You once made me live in a tent for a publicity stunt, remember."

I laugh. I choose to take that only as a joke. I say, "Well, I'm not asking you to do that again. I'm sorry about that, by the way. I'm just warning you."

"*Warning* me?"

"Well. You work for Faulk, don't you?"

She puts down her glass, looks at me with a grave expression. "I receive funding from him for a project I proposed myself."

"Well, people might chase that down . . ."

"And . . . ?"

"It's your life. That's what I'll say if they do. I'm just mentioning it now."

"Just warning me."

"*Warning* was too strong. I'm sorry. It's not a big thing."

"No."

"No."

In bed, later, I lie and wonder at my own dissatisfaction. What did I want her to say? *I'll quit the company, Dad? I'll join the party too?*

I think of Lina speaking of my need for loyalty. Fair enough, maybe, to seek such a thing from a parent, a partner even, but one's child?

No.

It is Kenzie's life.

I hate the man she works for and it is an unbecoming hate, I know; compulsive, dirtying. I must not let it stain my relationship with my child.

I turn in bed. Outside I can hear two men shouting happily, wishing each other merry Christmas, in fact. The pub on the corner will be kicking out.

Upstairs, a neighbour walks across the room. A door closes. The water main, somewhere deep in the trunk of the tenement, runs and murmurs.

She chose her path, follows it. And that is fine.

I think of her swimming. Her bedroom when she was young used to smell of chlorine. I'd go to her events, and it always distressed me to see her at the end of those races gasping and cramping, needing to be helped from the pool. *This is what she* likes *to do?* I always asked myself. But it *was*. She loved giving everything, feeling she had given everything, going so deep into herself she became only that depth.

Still, there is an ache there. We were closer once. I did this for her, strange to say: the politics. When she was a child it felt so necessary, so connected to the girl I jiggled in my arms. I want just to agree. Though it is doubtless a facile wish, I feel it. I turn over, sleep thinly, wake to the sound of her in the kitchen.

She's made coffee. There's a mug for me. Her own is half-gone already. Her rucksack, packed, is on the kitchen counter.

I say, "Happy Christmas!"

"Happy Christmas, Dad."

"What do you want for breakfast?"

"Oh."

"I have bagels. Those ones you said were good."

She looks at her watch. Her grandmother's watch, in fact. "Yes. They're nice. But. It's just that there are only so many trains . . ."

"Of course."

"I'm sorry. But we did our thing yesterday, I thought . . ."

"Yes. Yes. It's fine. The trains . . ." I need to pull myself together, to not be like this. I try a joke. "I should do some more campaigning on the trains. Get better service on Christmas."

"Yes." Kenzie smiles.

"It could be my first leadership promise."

But the mention of the leadership seems to sour things again. Kenzie drinks the last of her coffee, nods.

I walk around the Meadows. The wind is up and the air is cold and biting, yet there are still thick piles of leaves around because the year stayed mild and dry well into November. A child comes by on a bike, screaming joyfully, the mother running behind. A Christmas gift, of course.

I walk for a long time, making laps, saying "Merry Christmas" with the right smile, the right voice, trying not to seem the sad older man alone on Christmas. The sun is slowly lowering, beginning to set over the links, beyond the spires and chimneys. I will make calls, I think, in the off time between Christmas and New Year's, begin sounding colleagues out, seeking support. My feet are icy cold, but I walk and don't realise why I walk, really, until I find myself in front of the old flat.

I count up three floors. The window is lit, white blinds down. A family in there, hopefully, having Christmas.

We left, Kenzie and I, two months after Lina's funeral.

She complained about that departure later, saying that the light was so good (and, God, it was). In the new place, my current place, she had a bigger room. But that was never enough. It didn't face the Meadows as this place did. All that sky ahead of you at the start of the day. Still, she was gracious about it. "I understand," she said back then, a year after we'd left. "It was too sad to stay."

But it wasn't that, exactly.

I stomp my feet to stay warm. A shadow in the room moves behind the blinds. I hear voices.

It was not so much that to stay in the flat was sad. Rather, I had wanted to preserve the last days in the place as they were. Strange to say, I felt those rooms like a sort of stage set, a venue for the performance of Lina's final months, which would only have been made unbecomingly ordinary by the patterns of daily life lived there afterwards.

It had been hard for me to take when Lina had told me that she wanted to give up on treatment. Each new therapy proposed had a more tenuous chance of success and worse side effects, but still I had been so invested in the idea of overcoming, in the notion that we should do anything for even the slightest possibility that Lina could live a little longer. Yet she, at the apex of all this activity, had seen things more clearly. That time that we had before she sickened irrevocably was not just time to be *spent* in seeking a cure, not just a clock against which we competed, but *life itself*. Lina's specialist, an ex-colleague of hers called Jawed, estimated that another round of gene therapy would have had a ten percent possibility of extending her life, and following the consultation I'd fixated on that one Lina in ten—for she was a fighter, was she not?—and not the other nine Linas who sickened and died anyway, using up the last of their days in waiting rooms and surgeries and endless tests. Yet Lina herself understood that her choice was not just about *ends* but *means*. Means were what one had to live with, the one certainty of a predicament like hers. We needed to make a choice that we could stand by on any terms. She showed me that, and though I was angry at first, I came to love that insight, carried it forwards, even, into my work. Kenzie, however, couldn't understand. "You're letting her give up," she shouted at me at the time. "*You're* giving up."

But no. I wasn't giving up. I felt that I was truly seeing my wife, engaging with her situation sincerely. It was summer in those final months. The flat, which faced south over the Meadows, was so bright. We looked out as the trees exploded into blossom beside the pathways across the grass. We saw that blossom fall. As the summer holidays began, the students flooded out with barbeques and guitars. Chatter rose to the open windows. I read to Lina and then, when she lost the concentration for listening to me read, we played her favourite pieces of classical music. We looked at photographs. Sometimes we slept late, until nearly lunchtime, and sometimes we woke before dawn. We took the days as they came. Lina was weak and grew ever thinner. She looked strangely younger and then so frail and gaunt, but her eyes were always still her own.

And maybe somehow it worked. There is a silhouette now, behind the blind, moving through to the kitchen. I can almost believe, want to believe, that I could go to the bell and ring 1F2 and say only, "It's me." I can imagine that I'd hear the buzz and the click of the door unlocked and stomp the spiral stone stairs that smell of dust and stone and ancient iron. Waiting at the open door would be Lina, perhaps sick, but still notably herself, her gaze set on me, ready to say just what I need: that it is okay, that I am doing all I should, that everything is well.

9

ROBAN

2103

W*hen I return to base after my leave, I* work. *I was previously the third-*best-testing recruit, but now I practice until I am top of my intake. I do extra reps of every exercise. I read flight manuals. I study technical diagrams of craft. I massage my palms to keep my hands supple.

Every tenth day on the base is a rest day, but I never want to stop. I'm avoiding reflection, I know, but this knowledge doesn't staunch my restlessness. On days off, I still get changed into my Exterior Exo. I do longer runs than I do with other recruits. I am now so proficient at conserving charge that I can nurse the suit further than anyone in my intake.

It helps to be exhausted, because otherwise I am angry. Pointlessly so, I guess. Because what can I now change? The thing I focus on in my moments of rage is the Faulk Medal, which I brought with me when I returned from the Colony. It sits on a shelf in my dormitory cubicle in its fabric bag. It's a chunky object, embossed with a profile of Axel Faulk in the centre. Around the bottom of the disc runs an inscription: *Pertinet ad nos in posterum*. "The future," my school chancellor translated for me when I received it, "belongs to us."

The slogan gets to me now. I thought blithely when I received the medal that "us" referred to we First Gens who competed for this award.

Yet with the loss of Miz, I now wonder at that assumption. What future did she possess in the end? What if the Corporation's plans have no real space for the likes of us? When I study the heavy disc, I experience an anger so pervasive that I wonder whether I actually relish it. I hold the medal and feel the rage swirling within me. I think of Mum's reactors, the plasma circling inside. Is that "us" just Homers, those who made this place as their escape, their retirement? Or the Corporation board? The Faulks? Is their sense of ownership hubristic or malicious? These are thoughts I could never speak, but they arrive in my mind. Sometimes I fall asleep holding the medal. I have vivid, furious dreams in which I am losing a fight, or trapped in a small space, giddy and bewildered in a panicking crowd. I wake to find my hands abraded from grasping the roughly textured disc.

It is toxic, I know. I need to grieve, to let myself be sad, as Mum has urged me to. Yet I can't free myself of the medal until one day when I think of Miz. I call her up in my mind—imagine her calm in her quiet bedroom, tucked between her soft pillows—and let her tell me what to do.

On the third rest day after I return to base, I dress in my Exterior Exo and slip the medal into one of the compartments of the suit.

Outside, I ease through the badlands that surround the base, pacing up slopes, using my momentum to charge through depressions. I summit a ridge and dash down a scree and then follow a rounded canyon bottom for twenty clicks until this canyon gives out and the land flattens to a plain. Fine dust moves across this flatness, swirling around the feet of my suit and giving the impression that I stand amidst a shallow lake, as there must have been here when this planet had surface water. I have run for three hours. The charge of my suit has dipped to fifty-six percent. This should be enough to get back to base, yet it is poor practice to have left myself without a buffer. Yet I wait a little longer. I imagine this land flooded with water, the light reflecting off that surface, a lake around me as I have seen in films and pictures of Home.

I squat. I scrape at the dust. The regolith is fine and the hole refills itself as it is being dug. Yet I persist and make a little bowl-shaped depression. This is a ceremony for her. I take the medal from my suit and drop it into the little well in the dirt. I will bury it out on this plain, this nowhere. I imagine the dark sky shifting and blinking above this spot, an eternity passing through the changing sky. I realise that I have not imagined this medal ploughed up or found by a wanderer beneath terraformed grasses, though the Corporation's plan should have this land around me changed in due course. Surely it should be found eventually by the *us* to which the future belongs. But I suppose that I do not have all of the faith I had previously, because I cannot picture such a discovery. It is strange to find myself dispossessed of convictions that I have held for so long. I feel giddy, loose. As I consider this sensation, though, I see a movement in the distance, at the horizon. My eye catches a dark shape approaching. I disbelieve it at first. I focus on it and realise that it is a figure in an Exo running quickly. I know then that it's Vishay, farther from base than I could get.

He must have seen me, because now he approaches with long strides. His knees pump evenly. The contact of his feet is perfect: heel to toe, heel to toe.

He stops ten meters away.

I realise only then that I have done nothing about the medal. I have merely gawped as he has come towards me. This disc is in the hole at my feet, glinting. A slight incline of Vishay's head indicates that he is zooming in on it, reading the inscription. I find myself wondering what he makes of it.

The communication channel opens.

"You're a ways out from base," he says.

"Yeah," I say. "I'm testing my range."

"Right," he says. "Good job."

Then he steps forwards and drops to a squat next to the hole. His hand goes down, and I think that he is going to pick up the medal. (To take it back as evidence?) Yet he doesn't. He pushes dirt over it, looks up at me, pushes more dirt over it, packs it down.

He's said nothing of the medal on the communication link, I realise. What he has done and what he saw me doing will not be logged. It would be an issue, disposing of this award, made with such difficulty from rare metals. I'd be lucky if I was allowed to remain in the prospecting corps with that on my record. Yet Vishay seems to be making himself an accessory to my crime. I don't understand. He stands and we face each other. "You're good?" he says.

"Yes," I say. "Are you?"

"Oh," he says. "Never better. I love it out here." He steps back from me, turns, indicates all the flatness. "It's beautiful."

"Yes."

"Most recruits couldn't get here . . ." Vishay's voice is even, conversational. He seems to be willing me to join him in this act, this pretence of normality. "What charge are you on?"

"Fifty-four," I admit.

"Right," he says. He will keep this to himself, I am suddenly sure. What is happening binds us.

"You?"

"Sixty-four. Let's go back together. We're both cutting things close."

I am going to agree, but already he has assumed my assent and started running.

After that, we run together on rest days. I labour to stay close to Vishay. I learn little tricks from him. He toggles the suit heating system off to preserve charge. He has customised his stabilisation settings. He has a way of swinging from leg to leg in rough terrain that I mimic. He rolls the hips of the suit, getting a little extra distance with each leap.

Mostly our talk is technical. I ask how he does something, and he explains as best he can. Often he just clicks his tongue and sighs. He says, "Practice, Roban." I weigh his words for evidence of why he helped me when he met me out there on the plain. What motivated him to share the secret of that buried medal? We haven't spoken of that meeting since. Running together we are well matched. (Though he is always faster.) My little ceremony for Miz has introduced me to someone new to emulate, to chase behind. Sometimes superstition—the sense that from beyond the grave she guided me to Vishay to help me, to replace her—seems as logical as anything.

Three months before my graduation exams, Vishay tells me that he is going out on missions again. "I've done good training," he says. "I'm ready." He has never seemed anything but strong to me. I wonder what kept him grounded for this time, what mission he must have done to need such a period of rest.

I mark his departure date on my calendar. We have two more runs together before he goes. On the first, he leads us back out to that plain on which we first met. He stands a couple of meters from me, obscured periodically by the upswirl of regolith. The light, cutting through these particles, is turned a deep red. I feel like we are inside a living body.

"I'm going to show you something, and then you're going to do it," Vishay says.

"Okay?" I say.

The dust patters against my suit. I can hear my own breath, a high tone, above it."R3, XN, BB5, R2, 778," Vishay says.

I tap the code. My system says, *Delete record?*

Vishay says, "Say yes."

It is forbidden, of course. Operational Transparency is a key principle of our work as Prospecting Cadets. To delete a record intentionally is one of the most serious offences, because why would one do such a thing unless one were acting against the Colony? I should refuse. I could try to flee. (Though of course he could catch me.) He has seen me bury the medal, though. Now his silence on that front is understandable. He took that as proof of my propensity to break the rules.

I could take charges for my misdemeanour on the chin, I suppose, while implicating him in this greater offence.

But do I *want* to?

I think of the medal itself, the nagging sense I have gained that the slogan on it spoke not to my own destiny but to the vain plans of others.

"Yes," I say. There is a ping.

He explains the mechanics of erasing conversational logs then. We're too far from the base out here for it to upload in real time, so it's possible to erase the log before it's taken up to the OS and scanned by the ArtInt.

He shows me the code to patch the space. It's ingenious.

"Why do this?" I say.

"I don't know," he says. "So we can really talk, I suppose."

"Okay?" I say.

"For now, though, delete this conversation too. We need to head back."

For the next ten days, I alternate between terror and impatience. I expect a knock on my door from my superiors, but they apparently notice nothing wrong with my logs. I have vivid dreams of being out on the plain. Sometimes I am suitless, and I can feel cool air swirling around me. I crawl and claw the dust. Vishay speaks to me, and though I recognise his voice I do not understand his words.

"Why me?" I ask him. His answer is jumbled, lost.

Then, on the rest day, there is a knock at the door. Vishay stands at the threshold in his suit. I follow him through the air lock. I chase him, placing the feet of my own suit in the prints he leaves in the fine dust. Until we've reached the plain, we don't exchange a single word.

He stops there and turns to me. The dust eddies around our suit ankles. I imagine the lost lake again, surrounding us. I open the communication channel. I say, "So . . ."

He says, "You're angry. I know it."

I ready to speak, but I cannot vocalise the right response.

He says, "I saw you burying your medal, remember."

"I do remember. My friend died."

". . . And you're angry about that?"

"It's just . . ."

"Not what you were taught would happen?"

"It feels like that," I concede. "They always told us at school that they'd come here for us, that the Colony was our blessed inheritance."

"I know," says Vishay. He says the words flatly, waits. Then, in a new firm voice, he says, "I'm going to tell you about my last mission."

"Okay."

"I'll tell you and then we'll delete the record."

I pause. I wonder whether I want him to speak at all, whether I am really ready to face whatever he has prepared so carefully to tell me. I was once so happy in my certainty, in my faith that the Corporation would lead us so easily to a fuller future. But there is no way to go back to that, I suppose. I inhale. I say, "Okay."

"I went to Home," Vishay says.

"To Home?" I say.

"An *Overflight*, they call it. They've decided it's good for us First Gens to do it. They're worried about desertion, so they send someone unready to land on the planet. I travelled in a craft without an Exo."

"But I thought Home was a dead planet."

"Well, that was what I was supposed to be checking . . ."

"How?"

"The Overflights stay at altitude, looking for signs of civilisation: heat of the kind that would come from industry, concentrated emissions. I orbited the planet four times."

I can hear my own breathing in my suit. "Did you see signs?"

"Nothing on the scale that they worry about."

"Worry?" I say.

"The theory is that anyone who has survived is not likely to be nice. They're anxious about being followed here."

"Is that possible?"

"I don't know. They say they have a plan to intervene if necessary." He says *intervene* in a certain way: articulating it slowly, disowning the word as he vocalises it.

"Okay." The connection hisses. The joints creak within my suit.

"There are plants down there, forests, river deltas. I saw the sea."

"Did you see cities?"

"Certainly. They're overgrown now. Except in the dead zones."

"Dead zones?"

"There are great empty patches. Weapons? Droughts? I don't know. If Command know that part of the history, they haven't told me."

"Right," I say. We were taught at school that there are no records beyond the contact break that happened one M-year after my birth. "What did it feel like to see it?"

"It was strange. It was like I've seen in archive footage: the water and the greenery. But to know it was *there*, underneath me, was different. The clouds over the sea were beautiful, and the shadows on the land. I did the scans they wanted me to do, but I was wondering all the time about whether there were animals down there. Or if there was someone walking through the forests beneath me. I wanted to know what it would feel like to be down on the surface."

"You wanted to descend?"

"Not exactly. But I thought, *We had all this once . . .*"

I know that I am not listened to by the ArtInt, but something—habit? a residue of my old faith?—makes me want to vocalise the Corporation's logic. "What if we're successful in terraforming, though? What if we can make that kind of land up here?"

"For our great-great-grandchildren?"

I don't know what to say to that.

"The land on Home is there *now*," says Vishay. "Damaged, but still . . ." We are both silent for a long moment.

"You're going back to Home on the next mission?"

"Someone else. I don't know who. Command let you do that mission only once. I'm just prospecting now."

"Why did you tell me all this?"

"I needed to speak about it. I dream of the place every night."

"Why me?"

"Because I trust you. Because you have your own doubts."

Did the sight of me disposing of that disc provide him with the same strange comfort that I experience now on learning of his mission, his fears and desires? He has been lonely, I suspect. I have been lonely. The channel closes. He steps back. He is deleting now. I begin the process myself.

We turn towards the distant hills. We both start to jog.

A week later, Vishay is gone. My final exams happen. I'm top of the class. They give me another, smaller medal. I go back to the unit on leave. I walk the Colony in the day. It is nice to see Mum, who makes a point to be home early from work, who is careful around me, keen to sit together with me in the evenings. Still, I itch to be back on the base.

I dream now of Home: Secondhand dreams from Vishay. Glimpses.

I am so relieved ten days later to climb back into a transport, to set off around the globe to the training base.

Four days after I have landed at the base, after I have returned to my routines of training and running through the badlands, I am called to Command offices. The room into which I am led overlooks the main hangar through one-way glass. Down there a craft is being cleaned by a couple of AutoDrones. The Homer who led me to the space nods quickly and then goes out, closing the door behind her. Left alone, I feel apprehensive. I look out the window at the jets of cleaning fluid sprayed by the drones. The liquid mixes with the red dust coated onto the craft, forming an uneven crimson puddle on the landing pad. The ring of orange landing lights around the craft simmers. After some considerable time, after the craft is long clean and the drones redocked, a door opens and the commanding officer of the base, Haley C, stands in the doorway.

Haley has spoken to my cohort on review, addressed all of us as cadets, yet I have never interacted directly with her. She says, "Roban," and I am surprised to hear her saying my own name, identifying me from the many other cadets from whom I've imagined myself indistinguishable. She is about Mum's age. She has mid-length black hair streaked with a few lines of grey. She frowns as she appraises me. She is sharp, I sense. She steps into the room and the door closes behind her. My stomach plunges and the nagging thought I have held since being invited here blooms: Command have found out about the deletion of the system records. There must be an anomaly, some fissure I didn't account for or cover. Haley looks out the window—readying herself for confrontation, I suspect—and then turns her gaze back to take me in. For a Homer, there is something very deliberate in the way that she moves. I realise that I should admit my wrongdoing before the charge is levelled at me. I can own the choice to bury the medal, I can say that Vishay insisted on teaching me how to delete the record, used his seniority to influence me unduly. I knew, of course, that it was wrong, against regulation. But perhaps expressing remorse unprompted will cause Command to be lenient. I could testify to Vishay's sharing of his classified mission, his description of Home. But then I think seriously of Vishay's account of dropping into orbit over the glowing planet. I imagine the whisps of clouds, the delicate whorls of weather systems that he spoke of. It is all so perfect in my mind, and I do not want to give this up to anyone, I realise. I do not want to give Vishay up either. We needed to find each other, I think. My goodness, yes. I recall the barren days before I knew him.

What was I even thinking? I can tell Haley nothing. I will hold out. I must.

Yet when Haley steps closer to me she is smiling. She inclines her head to the side. "You're the best in our latest intake," she says. "I say that purely factually, according to your tests."

"Thank you," I say, surprised, wrong-footed by the warmth.

"You're here because we think you're ready to deploy. We're pairing you with the best First Gen we have." I am glad to be suited so that my reactions are cloaked. I exhale slowly. My palms are sweating as profusely as they do on any training flight. My jaw aches with tension. I feel a relief that is in itself like a kind of burning.

The door opens again and I turn to see an Exo walking in, Vishay's projected face on the interface.

"You've met, I believe," says Haley. "We have high hopes for you."

10

ANDREW

2076

The greenkeeper, Douglas, looks almost too much like a greenkeeper. A stout man in tweedy trousers, a wax jacket and Wellington boots, he has grey-blue eyes, which he squints against the drizzly wind that blusters off the sea. It is all part of the job, I suppose: the costume, the steady manner, the sense that both give that he is but one in a series of men and women who have held this role over centuries. "Lasers," he says. "All over the place." He clucks his tongue. He is telling me about how the Links Society moved this part of the golf course inland, away from the rising sea. "People know the dimensions of the courses here to the nearest centimetre, but the contractors shifted every bloody blade of grass." He points to the bridge, which my assistant Miles explained to me in the visit briefing is a famous landmark of the old course. "They moved the burn, and they moved the bridge over the burn stone by stone."

Douglas waits for my response and the wind screams. We are on the fairway of the first hole at St Andrews. The tide is in. Beyond the rough and the dunes, the sea breaks over the flat beach, the horizon lost to low, ruddy clouds beyond the waves. On the tall flagpole next to the clubhouse, the saltire flaps and furls and the rope to which it is connected chatters. The man's attention to me is a thing I find, with a sudden lurch, that I want to describe to Lina. I'm thinking of a time years before, when she was pregnant and her father came to visit from Germany and suggested—because I suppose he thought it was what men should do together in Scotland—that he and I play golf. It was a hot day, and we gave it up after four holes and three lost balls. We had to return home to Lina, then, who was the one who had actually played golf in the long idyllic summers of her Bavarian childhood. She was unable to hide her amusement as her father and I came back into the flat sunburned and grumbling. *I'm an honoured guest at the world's most famous course*, I want to tell her. Instead I meet Douglas's gaze and say, "That's very impressive."

They are not my people, golf people. This is what Lina would understand. My people are teachers, civil servants, students, and proprietors of vegan cafés. They are not men like Douglas. Yet Douglas nods as if I have said something very wise and says, "Shall we proceed to the green?"

He walks ahead; his thin hair, previously combed across his pate, now rises and dances in the wind like a flame. I am thinking of Lina because I am thinking of how far I have come. I feel it quite suddenly, and, though Miles has been telling me this for weeks as he hands over polling numbers, I haven't fully understood my success in the way that I do now, tramping along this fairway. Maybe golf people are my people now? Maybe all people are? This whole indignant nation? Everyone is so angry. It is all I can do to not scream, *Where the hell were you?* But my days of screaming ("your stunts," as Miles calls them dismissively) are over. My objections to the status quo are on record. I am a man of integrity, as Miles reminds me. I am just trying to preserve my polling advantages, to walk this home. My collar is dampened by the rain, though I don't raise the hood of my jacket because it would obscure my face from the videographer who is standing on the dunes, getting far-off contextualising shots. The dampness spreads down my shirt, between my shoulders, to the small of my back. I can bear it, though. I smile.

On the green, Douglas lowers to a squat, spryly for his age, and pats the turf. I come down with him, trying not to groan like an old man myself, and place a hand on grass that is as even as a carpet. "It's a tough thing, a green," Douglas says. "You want it even, and you want it dense, but you don't want to compact it so much as to kill the turf."

The two journalists who have been following me hunch over us to hear Douglas above the wind. The videographer, moving in now, gestures them back.

"I have a little secret, though," says Douglas. He gives a beady wink.

"Oh yes?"

"Aye. Icelandic volcanic ash."

"Ash?" I say.

"From a certain volcano. I can't rightly pronounce the name, but we get it by the truckload. Perfect density, ideal pH."

He pats the ground again. I pat it too, mirroring him. He grins. Once, I would have been horrified by the idea: ash arriving on a ship from a thousand miles away, as families struggle to eat, as infrastructure collapses and wars rage at the edges of Europe. This is the first golf course, after all: the template from which others are made, so that now simulacra of this link land outside this small Scottish city are peppered over the whole globe, in deserts, on mountainsides, in swampland and tundra. A strange, nostalgic, colonial impulse, I guess. Presumably one could hit a ball over any landscape, but this place has been re-created with such difficulty in so many places that one can only conclude that the making, the mastery of the land, is part of the point. And then, atop that, the mad idea that this very landscape on which it is all *based* must be made more like itself. I think of the word that the Tevat people love so much: *terraforming*. The impulse to make land pristine, new; the hubris to think that one can do nature better than nature can.

Yet I am trying not to be the man attached to a critique like this. I am not my father, not a dry academic. I say, "That's amazing. You could play pool on this green."

"Five hundred years people have been playing golf right here," says Douglas, "and still we're making the course better."

"I'll see to it that you get five hundred more," I say. Miles is in the clubhouse, working on my pre-election itinerary, but he will be glad of this little sound bite.

Douglas stands and dusts his hands. He looks down at me. "Is that a promise?" he says.

"It is," I say.

"You won't run off, like the other fuckers?"

The full exchange won't be useable on the news feeds because of that swearing, but still that response of Douglas's gladdens me. Douglas's anger is so much more important than any folly I might identify in the game of golf. I am drawing men like Douglas in my direction. Two weeks before, a whole trove of correspondence between Tevat and the government was leaked, revealing how many ministers have been allowed to become shareholders in Tevat's Mars Colonisation Corporation and been reserved places on the first civilian transport. The documents laid out the self-described "hard limits" of Tevat's extraterrestrial settlement proposals. They can't take everyone, as should have been so obvious, though the fact is still impactful news, so starkly is it conveyed in briefings which also speak of the "questionable viability of the current median life quality in Scotland." I have tried to raise alarm about these issues for so long, and yet for people like Douglas they are newly shocking, provoking them to anger, to a sudden nostalgia for the ordinary. Douglas looks around and the rain still billows in, pattering against our jackets. He looks resolved, I think, and this makes my heart jump higher in my chest. Beneath all that urge to perfection is still the land itself, the gladness at the earth. I rise and I say, "I won't. I promise."

He winks again. "I'll be after you with my gardening fork otherwise."

When Miles and I reach the station, the drizzle has turned to a full rainstorm. We stand on the platform as water sheets from the roof to the tracks in elastic panes, torn by the inconstant wind.

I tell Miles that I finally understand, really, viscerally, that I can win. He looks at me in his exasperated way that is a joke but is also not a joke. He says, "Only now? Christ!"

"I knew, but I just didn't feel it." I touch my chest. My sodden shirt sticks to my skin.

"Well, get used to it. We've got to be sprinting from day one. These people don't know how to lose. These people will be after us."

He is speaking of Tevat.

"We need to legislate," he says. "We need the perfect package. We need to be on the offensive from the first minute."

I nod. My hair is sodden, plastered to my scalp. I give my head a dog-like shake. Miles looks at me, his mouth open a little, as if to say, *What are you doing?* I say, "I'm ready." And it is true. My goodness, how I am ready . . . Years of telling people that technology won't save everyone, that people must save each other . . . Years of digging into the boring detail of policy documents, the minutiae of projections of sea-level rise and peatland die-back. In morning meetings now, Miles and I rehearse the various coalitions that might be thrown up by the election, calculating how these groups might be maneuvered into the triage that must begin on day one.

We are in shock as a nation. Embarrassingly late to this, since whole countries have already fought and lost battles for their own existence. Yet people compartmentalise, convince themselves that Bangladesh, say, was a different place, far off, subject to other forces than those that impact our own nation.

Yet these forces *are* acting upon us too. Quicker now than we expected. Maybe I've been too sincere, too worthy, in the past, but surely now *is* the point to test grand, abstract ideas of nationhood, to ask whether we have a destiny as a collective.

I have an industrial strategy based around green manufacturing and resilience. Daily, the assistants in my office brief me on the modifications suggested by academics, unions, and industry specialists. My colleague Jun has an army of largely indistinguishable twenty-year-olds devising an economic strategy for the treasury. We're going to launch a crisis investment interest rate. We have a plan for a full employment government works strategy. There is an insurance rescue plan. Every now and then someone in my office will message me a picture of a vertical farm, or a floating solar array, or a kind of infrared heating panel they suggest we begin manufacturing. I want to do it all, to rush in the door of the First Minister's residence and greenlight everything while the public are so zealous, so clear-eyed in response to the betrayal of the last government.

Above the sound of the storm, I can hear the hum of the rail as the train approaches. I look up the curve of the track and make out the engine coming around the long bend that leads into the station. I look at my device. It's seven p.m., and I haven't eaten since eight in the morning. My brain is done. We get onto the train, go through the newly familiar routine of entering the carriage and noticing people noticing me. This fame, if that is what one calls it, has crept up suddenly. I keep smiling. Miles and I take seats facing each other across a table.

Yes. It is all strange, and I want someone to notice the strangeness, to recall me writing petitions about bicycle storage at the kitchen table twenty years ago. It's been weeks since I've talked to Kenzie, and I want to tell her about all this weirdness: the focused attention, the sense of being watched and estimated differently now. Perhaps she knows it in her own successes with her prototype. As I understand it, her reactor is nearly fully tested, soon to be mass-produced and christened the Stellar8R (with all the crassness typical of Tevat).

But then, her work is different from mine, not nearly so public. She bypasses my urge to persuade and seeks perfect plenty instead, beyond which the politics—the mechanics of sharing—becomes irrelevant. Mum would have been so proud of her, and I am proud too. I must communicate that. It is just that it sticks in my throat, the thought that her design will first be made for the Tevat colony. You can solve the formula, but still there is the question of who controls that formula. Always.

The station lurches, shifts. I reach the belated realisation that it is the train that is moving. Rain flurries rattle against the windows. Droplets streak against the glass as we pick up speed. Miles stares at his device.

"Tevat are announcing a competition," says Miles, studying his device, "amongst their staff. Countering the claim that they're not taking any Scots with them."

"How many people?"

"Fifty." Miles looks up, smiles. "I don't see how that placates the other six million in this country. They're losing a grip on this."

"Let's hope," I say.

"Aye."

I take out my device, prompted by this conversation and my earlier thoughts to send Kenzie a message. I write, "Everything going well, Kenz? Talk this evening?" I watch the read receipt for a while, waiting for it to flick blue. It doesn't, though, so I put the device back in my bag. The countryside of Fife flickers past: bushes damp and heavy with the rain, fields with puddles in them, benighted cattle.

Miles jogs my arm, and asks me whether I want to eat, waves an oat bar in front of my face. "Not that," I say. I've plateaued in my hunger. I'll save my appetite for a takeaway when I make it back to the flat.

We reach the Firth of Forth. The bridge is ahead of us. The sound changes when we are out over the water. The wind strikes the train, diminishing in instants when we pass through the shade of the bridge's thick iron frame.

Across the firth, we pass the buildings of Queensferry, and then fields. The suburbs of the city begin. We stop at the new Kirkliston station. An old man with a spaniel stands on the other platform, waiting for a westbound train. As we pull off, the dog strains on its lead, spotting another dog, disembarked from our train.

I look at the message again, but Kenzie still hasn't read it. I have no reason to be annoyed. In my own busyness I often leave messages from her unanswered for days. I want only to speak to her of my day, of Douglas the greenkeeper and his funny flintiness. I flash across a country that I might soon govern. *Isn't that mad?* I want to say. *And aren't your successes astounding too?* (I must say that. Must find a way to say that.)

We are in the suburbs of the city now and we will be at Haymarket very soon. Another train comes past in the other direction, rattling, flickering faces through my peripheral vision. Ahead of me, Miles is engaged in his screen, his brow furrowed. I recall the filthy flat awaiting me. I should get a cleaner, though I'm never there. Then again, I might be moving to a new address. I imagine the grand Georgian house on Charlotte Square, the First Minister's residence.

I think, *No. I shouldn't consider that.* But then I think, *Why not?*

11

KENZIE

2076

T*he rain carries on for a month. For the first week, people in the city tell each* other that the weather is just typical. Then in the second week, as the downpour stretches beyond what even Glaswegians are used to, they tell each other that what is typical is not the rain itself, but the way it comes in *now*, this biblical turn just when they needed an ordinary spring, a normal summer. In the third week, I wake and look at my device and there is footage of Dad from all the news feeds: overdue a haircut by a couple of weeks, standing in front of a flooded street, shouting to make himself heard above the wind. He has the air of a prophet now. He was surging in the polls before this. But now he is the man of the time. He rants about the failure of the government to prepare for any of the chaos. In the evening, there are clips of him all over the country: next to a torrential river; on a bridge over a motorway that is now a lake; wearing a pair of waders as he stands in the centre of a submerged town square in Fife.

At work, we forge on. The Clyde in front of the start-up campus is swelling, brown with all the dirt washed from the hills. The lab is in the basement level of the main building, but my desk on the fourth floor offers a view of the broadening torrent of water. Branches and uprooted trees drift down the river; plastic dustbins, sheets of tarp, a large truck tyre, spinning as it floats by.

On the news feeds the next night Dad is interviewed from a flooded farm in the Central Belt, swallowing down his veganism to lament the farmer's ruined livelihood, gesturing behind him to a cluster of cows on a muddy island in the middle of a field become a lake. The morning after, I look up from my desk to see a cow—maybe even one from that farm—in the water, dead and bloated, tailed by a speedboat full of videographers.

In the prototype room, the technicians argue about when the space will be flooded. They lament the lack of waterproof doors on the level. They work more slowly than usual, whispering that it will all come to nothing when the waters pour in and ruin the reactor.

This isn't how Axel Faulk works, I tell them. If the doors aren't there, then there is a reason behind this choice. His whole organisation is a data-crunching machine, a living decision tree. Before constructing the start-up campus on this land, his people will have run all the calculations: hundred-year floods, thousand-year floods, the trends of climate breakdown. Dad has a whole rant about Tevat's relocation to Scotland, lamenting the cynical way that the company fled the U.S. to avoid taxes and oversight, griping about the board's choice of a pliable small state trying to win a reputation for technological development. I agree, actually. The difference between my and Dad's responses lies in our perspectives. He, a moralist at heart, is only appalled. I am an admirer of systems. I can't help but be thrilled by their cold foresight.

The river breaches its bank on the south side, spreads its fingers into Govan. Tower blocks stand like still ships amidst the flow.

Lifeboats make their way between the flats, rescuing people from first-floor windows.

In front of our building, water spills over the river wall and floods the riverbank path.

But still we carry on. We have a team meeting in my office, the floodwater, glinting where sun breaks through the spitting clouds, unmentioned all the while.

The next morning I have a missed-call request from Dad, sent the previous night. We have been missing the other's calls a lot recently. Previously, he could count on me to be able to talk in the late evening, but now I have Justine and my own never-ending work, and he has yet to adjust his assumption that I should be reachable at nine or ten. Now, at breakfast, I try to call Dad back but don't get him, probably because he is on the news.

I flick on the feeds to encounter a report of a flooded school. There is a ticker of the dead now in the corner of the news feeds: people washed away in vehicles, people drowned trying to salvage property (or loot), fatalities caused by the closure of hospitals and by medical emergencies in villages cut off from assistance.

I watch all this on the big screen in the kitchen. Justine comes in and makes coffee. She says, "Have you applied?"

"Not yet," I say.

She is asking about my application to join the first full-scale Mars transport, the competition to become a shareholder and the first of the unfunded travellers.

"Just over a week to go," she says.

"It's just that right now . . ." I gesture at the TV.

"That is exactly why we need to do this," she says sharply. She is right. She stepped back to let me take my role, and the least I can do is use that role to save us both. Still, I do want to warn Dad. I've always said to him that I'm taking Faulk's money to realise our reactor plans and nothing more. I've let him think that I'm still sceptical of the Mars enterprise.

The fact is, though, that I agree with Justine in her desire to join the project. For a long time I doubted her desire to slip away to space; resented her simple notion that experience of a new planet should make up for the loss of this world and our abandonment of our species. She'd chide me that I was self-aggrandising, that I followed Dad in speaking as if every decision of mine could save or doom the world. "What if you just *live* in the world?" she once asked. "What if you're just subject to events like everybody else?"

I should leave for work, but I linger for a little while with my coffee. I watch Dad's latest videos on the screen. He stands in a shopping mall, people mopping water away from the glass doors behind him. He cuts his interviewer off when she tries to ask him about looting. "Look at all the people helping each other, though," he says. "The majority. People sharing what little food and shelter they have. This is the only way forward. Taking this on together." His hoarse voice hits me somewhere deep in my chest, but these days I have my doubts. Maybe we can recover from this flood, I think, but what of the next one, and the worse one after that?

Justine's mum is in a hospice now, and on Sundays Justine and I travel out of the city to a sprawl of ugly century-old buildings at the end of a crescent.

Justine holds her mother's thin hand, and they talk in low tones about years before: the static caravan they used to go to, the old dog called Max, Justine's grandfather and the shop he used to run.

I cut up kiwi fruits, because the old woman likes them and Justine and I are able to afford them with our well-paid private jobs.

Justine's dad usually sits next to me. The two of us don't talk because he isn't really one for talking, especially now. We watch the two women leaning together, bound by our pleasure at that sight.

Yet on the weekend of the fifth week of rain, Justine and I check the trains and see that they are cancelled. We look up a Bug, but the routes out of the city are all red. So instead we stay at home in the flat, the windows fogged in the damp weather, the rain still coming down.

I call Dad, and he answers but says that he is rushing to another interview. I don't tell him about the application.

I draft the application at the kitchen counter that afternoon, aware of Justine moving past, stealing glances. The transports have room for only a small portion of Tevat staff this round, along with the paying subscribers and shareholders and strategic partners. My reactor might be important to Axel F's plans, but that doesn't mean that he would never pass me over should there be others with more to give his new colony.

On Monday morning, the river has risen even higher, washing over the small expanse of parkland that divides the river path from the campus. There are young birch trees planted on neat hillocks between the asphalt paths that bisect the park. The water floods around the rises so that the trees stand out on little humps of grass, like strange variations on cartoon desert islands.

In the prototype room, the technicians are drinking tea. "We're a few weeks off," I say. The prototype is almost workable; not the one in the adjacent room that proved our concept two years ago, but a version that will be readily reproducible. Sebastian from logistics is already contemplating the production cycle. The techs just sit holding their cups, though, and I know that they are thinking about the floodwater. I say, "Believe me, this place is not getting flooded." They go reluctantly back to work, and I return to my desk, though now I do pause intermittently to watch the rain prickling the surface of the bloated river.

I stalk home beneath an umbrella. The walk takes longer than usual, because the drains on Argyle Street are blocked, and so the road itself is a river and I must go up and around. Still, when I get to the top of the road where it isn't flooded, my shoes and trousers are sodden. I reassure myself that at least I have avoided wading through the drain water and all that has bubbled out from under the old city.

I get undressed in the hallway. I leave my clothes in a sopping pile on the parquet. I stride quietly through the flat in my underwear, and yet Justine is not in the living room or kitchen. I think that she might be out until I hear a ragged breath from the bedroom.

She is tucked under the covers, facing the wall.

I climb into bed next to her. I rub her shaking back. After minutes of this, she finally turns to me. "Have you submitted?" she says.

"I'll do it tomorrow," I say. "I need to warn Dad, at least. He might have to distance himself from me if I go. He'll need a strategy. People still remember me from some of his campaigns, after all. The tent, certainly . . ."

Justine turns away again. I expect her to say, as she has said before, that Dad using me in his campaigns was manipulative, but she doesn't. She stares silently at the wall. I sit on the mattress and look at her. It is a long time—the light changes behind the sheer curtain, falling to dusk—before she turns back.

In the half dark, she tells me that her father managed to get up to the hospice and took Justine's mother out in the drizzle in the wheelchair. The weather was bad, Justine explains, but the old woman hadn't left her room for weeks, and so her husband pushed her around the crescents that surround the hospice. When the couple were turning back, two young men came up to them and started shouting.

"Who?" I say, as Justine pauses.

"Mum was confused," Justine says. "But then she understood they were telling her to go home."

"Like . . ."

"They're shouting at this old dying woman. Mum. *Fuck off back to where you came from.*"

"I'm sorry," I say. "I'm so sorry."

"That's how it is, I suppose. That's how it's going to be even more."

"Yes."

"I think, *Fuck them. I am going to fuck off.*"

"Yes."

I cook dinner. I watch the news feeds as I do so. Experts talk through different scenarios which might play out on election day. It's most likely that Dad will win at present, but he might also fall short of a full majority. The other big news is that the SOIL Party are polling at seven percent. There is a video of the First Minister getting into a car, a hand over his mouth as he says something to an aide. Now comes footage of Dad coming out of Parliament and being asked to rule out the possibility of working with SOIL. Dad turns to the bobbing microphone and says, "We're not going into coalition with them, no."

"But would you take their votes on a parliamentary bill?" says the woman holding the mike.

Dad thinks, looks uncomfortable. He says, "I believe in my agenda. I can't promise we won't seek their votes on a bill if we need those votes."

I have to stop chopping the peppers. I pause the feed. I walk laps of the kitchen. It's dark outside now, rain clouds cloaking any moonlight.

I go into the bedroom with my device, the video of Dad ready to play. I hold it up to Justine, who sits up in bed now. I see from her expression that she has seen it. "Those people . . ." she says. "Those fucking eco-fascists."

"Dad . . ." I say on the phone, but he knows before I need to say it.

He says, "I didn't say I'd go into coalition with them. It was a hypothetical. I was being honest. If they win the votes, they're part of the parliamentary process. That's how it works."

"*Our own, first of all,*" I say. The slogan appeared on a billboard that I pass on my way to work. It was quickly graffitied, I was glad to see; a stumpy cock sketched over the SOIL logo.

"I know," says Dad.

"*Our own,*" I say.

"I know," he says.

"Who is that? What could they possibly mean?"

"I take your point."

"Justine's mum is scared to go outside."

A silence. "Right," he says. "I'm sorry to hear that."

I sigh, and the microphone of the device crackles.

Dad inhales. "We have a really ambitious agenda," he says.

I cut off the call.

I walk to work. The rain comes down in a maddening way: intermittent, but never quite at an end. We're a whole city, a whole nation, undergoing water torture.

The river is around the thin trunks of the birch trees now, lapping at the bottom steps of the main building, washing up the wheelchair ramp like a tide breaking against a beach.

I work as best as I can, trying to check through the protocols for the reactor test.

At noon, a police boat cuts flashing across the brown water. I wonder why it is speeding so quickly—rising and thumping over the swollen river—until I spot it: a water-tossed tangle of clothes and a flash of reddened skin. I know as soon as I see it that it is a body.

My device bleeps and there is Dad's face, and I answer though I have let previous calls ring through. Maybe it is the shock of watching those police officers, standing in the rocking boat to try to drag the sodden body aboard, that inclines me to accept.

"I'm sorry," Dad says. "It's just that this is my whole life."

"It's everyone's whole life," I say.

One policeman is holding on to the belt of another officer as this latter man leans down over the floating mass.

"You make compromises," he says. "You understand compromises."

"But my whole game hasn't been moral purity."

"Sorry?"

"The number of times that you've judged this job I do . . ."

"I haven't," he says, but the denial is half-hearted. He waits, but I can say nothing. He says, "I'm sorry. I really am."

"Okay."

"The SOIL thing was only theoretical. I was trying to be honest. We're unlikely to ever need them."

"You can't talk about drawing people together and then work with a party like that."

"I'm not endorsing them. I was answering the question. If they're part of the process . . ."

"Uh-huh."

"We're polling well. The crisis is motivating people."

"I can imagine."

"I have a proposal, actually."

"Okay . . . ?"

"What if I made a role for you in government?"

I don't know where to start with this. "I have a job," I say. "I don't need a job."

"I know you have a job." He speaks slowly. "I'm suggesting something. What about you defect? Take your blueprints. Take your best people. We'll make reactors for the nation. Let Faulk fight us in the courts."

"You haven't thought this through. It's not so simple. This isn't just a recipe for cake. It's about expertise, facilities, supply chains."

"I know it's not simple. But why not try? You needed to prove your design. As I understand it, you've now pretty much achieved this."

I sigh. I wait. Could I do what he is proposing? Could we make his idea work? Not as easily as he thinks, of course. But perhaps. I still feel so fearful that my own project will melt in my hands, though. It is mad, precarious. A little sun in a box. Could I take it to him? Do I dare? The men out in the boat are leaning over the side, struggling. The boat wobbles. They're going to tip into the river, I think, but they don't. The shaking stabilises and the men hang on. The police officer at the wheel guns the engine to keep the craft in place. All around, the water, sunstruck momentarily, glimmers and dapples.

"And Justine," Dad says. "She could work for us too. I wouldn't shut her out like Faulk did." My heart thuds, and I think, *No, of course. No.* She would not take that. I have not promised her that. I think of her weeping in the bed.

"I can't," I say. "It's not—"

"But Kenz . . . Faulk—"

He is pushing too much now, and I am tipped into an anger, which is easy. "You should come here," I say.

The dinghy has drifted closer.

"I'd love to see you," Dad says, "but I have campaign events."

"Not that," I say. "They're pulling a body out of the river. Wouldn't that be a good backdrop?"

I end the call. Out on the water, the policemen suddenly tumble backwards into the body of their dinghy, dragging with them the bloated corpse. A pair of bare legs momentarily hang over the edge of the boat, limp and pinkish, until they are jerked out of view.

I walk home through the drizzle. There are sirens everywhere. A news bulletin said that the army is being deployed. As I approach the flat, I look down the street to see an armoured vehicle rolling out of the park.

It is another thing to live through this as two young women, I think. I should tell Dad that. I run my fingertips over the Tevat-issued mini-Taser that I keep in my breast pocket. I hurry to our door.

Inside the flat there is a smell of frying ginger. Justine is at the hob, cooking. Music plays softly. Dusky sunlight is coming through the windows. I realise that I can't hear the rain.

We eat in silence.

Afterwards, Justine looks up from her bowl. "You talked to your dad?"

I nod.

"You told him about the application."

"No." I say. "But it doesn't matter."

The next morning the sun is out. Patches of dryness bloom in the middle of paving slabs.

I walk slower than I usually do, feeling the light on my face.

From my office I look down at the river. It rises just a little more with runoff from the hills: right up to the final step in front of the atrium. I go down and stand at the front doors and look at the water that goes on almost forever. I imagine slipping down into it, swimming and swimming.

Then, late in the afternoon, it begins to draw away, as if a giant has pulled a plug somewhere.

It descends the steps, and men come out with brushes to scrub away the sediment left behind.

The technicians in the prototype room blush when I come in. They're working earnestly now, trying to make up.

"What did I tell you?" I ask.

I go back to my desk. It's late afternoon now. The grass of the park is becoming visible, dragged flat by the retreating water.

I open the tab on my monitor. I read the form one last time. I press submit.

12

ANDREW

2076

S*omething about the schoolchildren's singing is strangely affecting.* *Not* that it's good. In fact, quite the opposite. Yet the laboured nature of it resonates with me. "And we'll all go together, to pull wild mountain thyme," they sing flatly, standing in their matching mustard polo shirts, stretching the words, torturing every vowel. "All around the blooming heather. Will you go, lassie, go?" The end of the chorus has no questioning intonation whatsoever, as if they are tired of asking, really, as if they've relinquished all expectation of a response. I relate, which is perhaps why I am breathing evenly, trying, to my great surprise, to hold back tears.

There is just over a week to go and I am so sick of waiting. Miles reads me the polling each morning, and the polling is good, but what use is good polling until the election is actually here?

The school is in Livingston, composed of dated buildings, with drafty windows that sing as wind blows down from the Pentlands. We're in the hall. Behind the children, through French doors, is a view of muddy playing fields beginning to dry now that the rain has stopped for a week.

Next to me stands the music teacher, conducting, though his twitching gestures seem to have no actual impact on the perfectly even nature of his pupils' dirge.

The singing stops, finally, and everyone—the children, journalists, and teachers—looks to me for a response. I beam and slap my hands together, trying to fill the space with my applause.

I answer questions to the cameras. In my head, Miles's voice resounds, telling me to *hit the message*. "Unless you're bored of saying it," he told me in the morning, "the public haven't yet heard it."

I say, "This election is about these children. Their future. This is their election. Yet they can't vote, so I'm asking those who can to think about these children when they enter the polling station."

The camera people and journalists look out the window—at the gulls standing in the playground, at the sun breaking on the grass beyond, the denuded hills in the distance. They have heard this patter before.

Afterwards, I drink tea in an empty classroom with the head teacher. "You want something stronger?" she asks, winking.

"It's not a bad idea," I say. I wink back. "I should keep it together for a few more weeks, though."

I'm sat on a tiny chair, as is she. A child-sized table, on which our mugs of tea rest, is between us. This feels right for these days, I think. Everything the wrong scale, confounding.

The head teacher sighs. "It's true what you said."

"Sorry."

"This is *their* election. I do worry for them."

She's my age, I calculate. She wears a navy suit, square-framed glasses. She has short grey hair, hippyish jade earrings. She looks almost familiar. In another life, maybe, we'd be friends. She glances down at her hands, sun-spotted, laid on the low table. "I can imagine," I say.

"Some days I wake up and think, *We should be teaching them survival techniques, not singing.*"

"It doesn't seem like you've spent that long teaching them singing," I say.

She weighs that for a moment, and then laughs.

"I'm sorry," I say. "You were being sincere. I can empathise."

"It's okay," she says.

"I can barely think about the worst-case scenarios, if I'm honest."

"You have kids?"

"One. But she's grown up now. Married. An adult. You?"

She thinks. "Yes. The camping girl. Of course. Me? No. I chose not to."

A babble of voices arises outside the windows. Shapes move on the other side of the vertical blinds, flitting. The children must have been let out for their morning break. The headteacher still hunches in her chair. She says, "I don't regret it, but I suppose that I wonder sometimes. What if I'd been one of those people who could just believe everything would work out? What if I could have convinced myself that we'd all fly off safely to a utopia on Mars?"

"Yeah?"

"Do you ever feel angry that you notice? That you're compelled to care?"

I laugh. "Only a hundred times a day."

"I want to be wrong in all my alarm, but then I've made my choices on those terms. So it also hurts if I am. I was angry in the past, I suppose. I felt like I was serious and others weren't."

I say, "I understand that. I felt like that once."

"And now?"

"And now I have more hope, I suppose."

"That sounds nice."

"It's not always nice." I smile. "Sometimes it feels like staying on a tightrope."

The wall of the room that adjoins the corridor has frosted glass inset along its length. A dark shape moves down this corridor, bristling behind the glass, and something about its motion convinces me that it is Miles. The door opens and he comes into the room, frowning. He says, "Do you have a moment?"

The head teacher stands from her tiny seat, holding her mug to her chest.

Miles moves in and takes another chair next to me.

"I'm sorry to throw you out of one of your own classrooms," I say.

"It's fine," says the head teacher. "No bother. It was nice talking to you." She has read something on Miles's face. "I hope you keep your footing."

"Sorry?"

"Stay on your rope." She smiles as she closes the door.

Miles sighs. The teacher's footsteps recede. "It's about Kenzie . . ." Miles says. A great space opens up at my centre. *What has happened to her?* Though I cannot even speak those words, so I just wait, gaping, for Miles to speak.

"They've picked her."

"What?"

"To go to Mars."

A rush of relief, first, that she is okay. I even smile. I know I smile, because I see the reaction to that—the angry incomprehension—on Miles's face. He waits.

"Fuck," I say dryly, forcing it.

I thought it was even worse for a moment, but Miles is staring at me, urging me to truly connect with what he is saying.

"She has one of the fifty winning places on the next transport."

"Shit," I say. My words are flat, like those of the singing children. I really think for a moment. She is *going*. She is okay, yes, but she is going. I never thought she'd do it. I feel still numb to the fact.

Yet Miles has no time for my confoundment. He says, "It looks hypocritical."

I try to catch up. "It's not me, though. I'm not going. I'm not the one chosen. She's an adult . . ."

"You know it doesn't work like that."

"But I can't tell her not to go . . ."

"These fifty, they can apply to take family members. There's rumours already that you're going with Kenzie."

"But that's crazy. Why would I go? When I'm doing all this?"

Miles tuts. "Half the current government are going."

"But we're different . . ."

"Exactly. I think you understand our counter-strategy, at least."

There is another knock at the door. A woman comes in carrying a camera and tripod. She was in the hall earlier, filmed the children singing, me speaking afterwards.

"Neera will record your message to voters," says Miles. He stands and looks around, nods at the children's pictures on the wall. "We could have a worse backdrop," he says.

"I'm sorry," I say. "You need to take this slower. What's the plan?"

Miles kicks away a small chair, which briefly screeches across the wooden floor. He says, "We have to be quick and you have to be unequivocal."

"Unequivocal."

"You need to condemn her."

"Kenzie?"

"*Renounce* her, I mean. That's the word."

"I'm sorry?" I say again.

Miles paddles his hand in the air. "You're hugely disappointed. You fully condemn the Mars mission and your daughter's decision to join. Maybe imply that this is a personal break . . ."

"But . . ." I say.

"Seriously," he says.

Neera has set her camera up facing a well-lit wall, a couple of bright children's paintings. A dog climbs a triangular mountain. A stick family stand in front of a white house with a steeply pitched roof. I say, "I can't say those things right now."

"In my professional opinion you need to, though." Miles scowls. "Perhaps if you explain it now the public will understand. You leave it any longer, they'll feel like you're hiding something. There's been enough betrayal. You can't betray them too."

"I'm not betraying them."

He ushers me to the wall, points to where I should stand. "You have to prove it, though. You've got to give them something."

I stand for a moment and look at the lens of the camera. I think of a time long ago, when Kenzie was young and I left her to stay with Mum for the first time. We drove the rattling Land Rover to the dock and then I boarded the ferry and the two of them stood and watched as the ship drew away. I was a different man then. I was worried about her, yes, but I was sure that I could resolve things, certain that I left her behind to work on her behalf, on behalf of her whole generation. I remember standing at the railing of the boat for a long time after the ferry had set off, looking back at Kenzie and Mum, who kept waving as they became smaller and smaller, making it a game, I suppose, united in their stubbornness. I remember feeling such leaping joy at that sight, recall standing out there in the chill sea wind, as they were lost to the town behind and then the town in turn was lost to the great lump of the island and then the island melted into cloud and I was just out on deck alone at sea, set free to my mission.

I say, "I'm sorry. I can't do this." I step off my spot.

"What?" says Miles, incredulous.

We get a Bug back into the city. The vehicle trundles through the streets of Livingston, making little moans as it picks up speed, sighing where it comes to a stop. Miles has taken the backwards-facing seat. He's not prone to motion sickness as I am. An old joke of ours: as a campaign manager and former PR man, nothing turns his stomach.

Except he looks green now.

He makes calls at first, tuts and interjects. I recognise the names of those he speaks to. He sighs, says, "No. No. No. He's not going, of course. He's disappointed too." He exhales heavily, redials. "Alaine," he says. "Yes. Yes. He's horrified, of course. But his relationship with his daughter is his own business." We move into the traffic of the M8. I look at the people around me in other Bugs, eating or sleeping or watching screens in front of them. "No. No. I know," says Miles. "But you have to *trust* him." He slumps back, throws down his device. It vibrates a couple of times and he picks it up again. He types and swipes and replies to messages now. As we pass the airport, the traffic slows for the diversion, in place since the leaks and public outrage and the raised security alerts. They've checkpointed the routes leading to the terminals, and to accommodate these changes the whole motorway filters into a single lane. We move and stop and move and stop. The Bug's OS pings with little apologies for the delays. Then Miles looks up at me. He makes a shrugging motion and throws his device down on the seat again. It vibrates and vibrates. He shakes his head, but doesn't pick it up, leaves it to shudder there.

In the city, the Bug picks up speed again. The little engine fizzes beneath us. We pass blocks of offices now, the reflection of the vehicle squashed and then teased out in curving façades of mirrored glass, my own face a tiny spot within, looking grey. At Lothian Road, Miles slaps the Bug's control screen. The vehicle stops and the door gasps open. Miles steps out to the pavement. Though the day is overcast, the air here in the city is hot, humid. "I'm going home," he says. "I think there's not much I can do today. Unless you . . ."

"I understand," I say.

"Even then . . ." he says. He spits air, slaps the top of the Bug. He turns then, and I watch him shimmy into the crowd of commuters on the pavement.

The Bug, in its soft OS voice, asks, "Shall I continue to our destination?"

As I approach the flat, I think that there must be something going on. The traffic is backed up. A van pulls very slowly into my street, and—oh—a whole massed crowd is standing in the road.

There are lots of journalists, but ordinary people too. Protesters? Rubberneckers? Passersby drawn in by the commotion? I notice a neighbour, Siobhan, standing on the pavement where the crowd is sparser, holding her Labrador tightly leashed. It comes to me too belatedly that all this is for *me*. I feel what is almost déjà vu. The crowds are pressed around the Bug, and I think of the other journey which I have lain in bed and imagined. I've thought of riding in the old car to the Parliament to be sworn in as First Minister. I've visualised the car from above, as if from a drone, as I have watched when, on-screen, other men and women have been sworn in before me, imagined the newscaster whispering my life story over the footage. Yes. I have dreamt of that, wanted that.

I couldn't believe it possible until so recently.

My laggard heart pounds now for it. Too late.

A hand slaps the side of the Bug. The vehicle stops. "Hazards detected," the OS says. "I cannot complete your requested journey."

Oddly, when the door opens there is a space for me to step into. The crowd has drawn back as if taking a collective breath. Then come the voices, clamouring with questions, charges, slogans, and suddenly, above that, words that could have come from anyone, that carry: "Are you going too?"

I look back over the roof of the Bug at the people watching me. I say, "Of course not."

The mob absorbs that and then begins to churn, to call out again. Next to me, Sara, one of the police officers who has been guarding the flat since the campaign began, appears. She is pushing back photographers, men and women levelling microphones. Her colleague, Seamus, is beside her. They are trying to force a way through the crowd to the dark green front door of my tenement building. I see people straining to hold their place, looking panicked, angry.

"Have you spoken to her?" someone says, and I realise that they mean Kenzie. They no longer even need to say her name. The story is so clear to them, my whole life is torn out, exposed, like a bag of rubbish ripped open.

What do they want? Me to take her by the ear and punish her?

The police ahead of me keep pushing. Above Seamus's shoulder is Alan Mackie's face. Alan, of the *Evening News*, holds a microphone, inching it around the police officer, pointing its tip up at me. He says, "Andrew! Andrew!" and he has me for a moment.

I pause. Seamus stops pushing so hard against him. Alan says, "You said that Mars colonisation was, I quote, *the most selfish endeavour in human history.*"

"Right."

"And what do you think now?"

"The same," I say. "The same, of course."

I look at Alan's eyes, and yet they are not the eyes of the man I know, the man with whom I have had off-the-record drinks regularly, the man whose third wedding reception I was invited to. He has drawn that person out of himself. A stranger looks at me. The stranger says, "And I suppose your daughter is selfish?"

"Um . . ." I say. There is such hunger in the expressions of those watching. They've stopped shouting. They merely wait.

"Would you answer that question of your own daughter, Alan?"

Alan tuts his tongue. "I'm not running to be First Minister."

"Well . . . I still disagree with the idea of colonising another planet in preference to alleviating our crises here on Earth. None of my positions have changed."

"What about your position in relation to your daughter?"

"I don't have a *position* in relation to my daughter. I have a relationship."

"Which deeply concerns people . . ."

"I'm not sure . . ."

"Do you think she is despicable? That's another word you've used about Axel Faulk."

I turn then. Seamus and Sara are pushing hard again. Faces ahead of them are red and straining. Someone shouts, "Judas! Judas! Judas!" The chant is taken up. Then the glossy green door appears ahead of us, finally. I fumble my keys. I find the lock, and then we are through. The police force the door back closed. We stand in the dark coolness of the tenement hallway. I feel relief and then I doubt that relief, because what have I just done but taken another step towards failure?

I eat a sandwich and I sit in the living room, shocked to be still after so many months of rushing around. The room darkens by degrees. Occasionally I take up my device to reject calls and delete messages. Then a picture of Kenzie flashes up on the screen. I press accept.

"I'm sorry," she says.

"You could have warned me," I say.

"I know," Kenzie says. "I'm sorry."

I wait for something else. I don't know what. At the other end of the line, she moves. I hear her footsteps, a door opening. Is she in her flat? I cannot picture the space.

"Dad?"

"Yes?"

"Go on the news and tell them I'm a terrible person. I really don't mind."

"But I do."

"That's not fair, though."

I laugh. "Sorry? Not libelling you on the news is unfair . . . ?"

"This can't be my fault. You can't torpedo your career and your party because of my choices."

"I'm not making it your fault, Kenz."

She sighs. "You are, though, Dad. That's the thing. If you leave it like this, you are. You just needed to say that I'm a shit. You still could."

"You sound like Miles."

"I'd understand."

"I know you would."

"We have different lives."

"When you were a student, I'd always say that people would come around to what I was saying. That they could share and work together."

"Uh-huh."

"And you'd say, 'How does that happen, though? How do people change so fully?' "

"I remember that."

"You said once, at least you had a theory for your magic solution. Your fusion."

"Yes. I remember."

"Well, what if it's me who can't really change? What if I can't become the man who stands and rejects his only child?"

"You need to, though."

"They won't believe me."

"You're making excuses."

"They won't believe me, and meanwhile I will have said all of those things."

"But why not try, Dad? You're being a martyr. Taking the comfortable role of a principled failure."

I wait. She is trying to poke at me, to provoke me into an anger that will allow me to say all she thinks I should say about her. I won't accept that, though.

"I don't mind," she says again. "It doesn't matter what you say."

"But it does matter, Kenz," I say. "Of course it matters."

"But I'm going, Dad. I'm sorry. I'm barely going to be here to hear it."

A week later I stand in a nearly empty ballroom and call the First Minister to concede. Turnout is appalling nationally, less than thirty percent. Yet already, before one a.m., I've lost too many key seats. The only people moving with purpose in the room are press, seeking footage of my failure. Miles went home before midnight, so it is his two assistants who fend off the journalists. I sit on the rear of the podium facing the wall and hear the First Minister sucking his teeth. There is music playing in the room behind him, a celebration in progress. (Though who knows what pleasure they will take in dragging out their charade of government?) "You ran us close," the First Minister says eventually. "But I suppose people came to their senses."

13

ROBAN

2106

I *sit on the floor of the room and look at the food tray. It is a dimpled grey tray* of the kind used in the base cafeteria. There's a long depression in the centre for the cutlery. The fork and knife within are both blunt. To the left of that channel is the biggest dimple, filled with Rute noodles. Above that is a circular depression, in which sits a little glass of water. On the right of the cutlery channel are three oval spaces: one holding sliced boiled carrot, one—intended for dessert—empty, a final, smaller dimple containing three grey pills.

I look at the tray for a long time because there is nothing else to look at in the windowless room. The walls and floor are rubberised and coloured orange, the same colour as the boiled carrot. Behind a partition is a bathroom unit. I sit on a mattress on the floor.

I stare at the food for long enough that when I do begin to eat the noodles, they are cold. I swallow one disc of carrot, leave the rest.

I know that the room is deep underground. When they brought me here, we descended a spiralling corridor. They told me to remove my Interior Exo, took the suit away. They gave me a set of indoor clothes and shut the door.

The room *feels* like a space that is deeply buried: no echoes, no footsteps from above or below, no closing or opening doors.

The silence is like the silence of deep space travel. As it does on journeys, my body fills this quiet. First with its own noises—my breath, my stomach gurgling, even my pulse thumping in my own head—and then, secondly, with its own expectation. The tiniest sounds are extrapolated by my mind. The creak of my mattress causes me to imagine people coming to the door, or a craft taking off from the surface above conjures a voice speaking far off, saying things that I cannot make out.

I put my knife and fork in their space on the tray and pick up the three grey pills. I take them. I lie back on the mattress. The hue of the walls and ceiling seems to soften. When I wake again the tray is gone.

Previously, I have wished for the utter silence of a room like this. On a mission, you get tired of the noises of your partner, no matter how well you like them. On our first trip to prospect an asteroid, midway into the journey I found myself maddened by the way that Vishay would breathe when sleeping deeply. It was not a snore, exactly, but a rough, wheezing inhalation that made me feel suffocated myself. Doubtless, he had his own complaints. (I'd notice him looking at me when I slurped from my food pouch.) Still, I suspected that these irritations were better than the alternative. You are liable to lose yourself out there. Even the friction of living with close company keeps you grounded. You need to be busy. Command mandates checks be done daily on the craft, and I'm sure that this duty is prescribed for the welfare of us cadets, not a necessity. On that first trip, Vishay and I found that we liked to play old-fashioned word games on our devices, drifting, staring at the screens and taking turns and talking nonsense.

Otherwise, there was the view from the big convex window at the front of the craft to take in: such mad abstract beauty as risks undoing you if you stare at it too long. I recall the stars out there, the streaking asteroids, the far-off glimmer of galaxies.

Prospecting sounds exciting, but it is mostly killing time as you cover the distance to the destination. We'd rehearse the final approach until we knew the plan to the nearest second. We studied the remote topographical surveys. Yet now what is the drill? What should I be preparing for?

I sleep and wake and think for a moment that I have heard that strange not-snoring sound of Vishay's, but of course I haven't.

There is a new tray in the middle of the floor, however: noodles with a disc of white protein on the top. Three grey pills. No dessert. A single baby tomato in the vegetable dimple.

I eat and I take the pills and I sleep again. When I wake, I notice that the light has brightened. I sit up. There is a man, a Homer, sitting cross-legged in the middle of the room.

"Hello," he says.

"What time is it?" I say.

He flaps his hand as if fanning away a bad smell. His hair is close-cut. His eyes are green. His brows are heavy. He is the sort of man I think of as the last of a kind. He is young for a Homer, though the stripes on the arm of his sweatshirt suggest some progress through the ranks. His neck is thick and he has the strong jaw of someone who ate Home food once. He says, "Don't worry about the time."

"But I want to know," I say.

"We're letting you recover first. Then we'll debrief you."

"What are the pills?" I say.

Again this is a question that he chooses not to answer. "We really only get one shot at this debrief. One clear view. We don't want you trying to remember."

"You don't want me *trying*?"

"Straining, I should say. Inventing accidently. Becoming suggestible."

"I see," I say, though I am so tired that I'm not sure that I *do* see.

The man stands and then walks to the edge of the room and thumps the wall. The section that he thumps draws back slowly, becoming a doorway. He goes through this doorway. It seals behind him.

I travelled back from this last mission alone, and it did make me feel a little mad. When I came down to the base it looked small: a little white wheel amidst the endless red hills. I feathered the thrusters and descended towards the central hangar, and the circular portal of that hangar opened like an iris enlarging in the dark. I dropped the craft down through the hole, and slowly the scale of the location resolved in my mind. Two Homer attendants in work suits stood looking up at me. There was a cart waiting.

They made me stay in the craft while they took Vishay from the air lock. They put a blanket over him, as if it mattered then that I would see him like that.

After that, the attendants came back. They led me from the hangar down the main corridor to a door that I'd never noticed. We made the spiralling descent to this little room.

I stagger to my feet. I move to the middle of the floor. I am losing strength already, idle here. I should be training again, as I usually do when I have returned from missions. We have a routine, Vishay and I. *Had* a routine.

Previously, we were feted after returning to base. A month ago, Vishay and I stood in the central hangar with the other recruits and were called forward to receive our stripes of commendation. No one on the prospecting track had been given the honour quicker, I told Mum on a call that night. Contrary to her usual scepticism, I could sense her pride in the way that she asked about the ceremony, about the work that led to the prize. Vishay and I fitted together perfectly, I told her. "It's special when you find someone who complements you like that," said Mum. I told her that I flew the craft and Vishay took the lead when we touched down. Sometimes I would merely dock the craft, and he would go through the air lock and take a sample and return, and at others I would tether us and then follow him over the surface, trying to match the smooth way that he used his thrusters and grappled and made his way to the sampling point. We had started on the planet itself: the frigid poles, the plains, the rough mountain land. I had brought the craft down in deep gorges, amidst dust storms. We found deposits with greater regularity than our peers. "You have good impulses," Haley told us in the Command Centre when she rediverted our work to asteroid prospecting.

Command scanned the belt, seeking bodies that might contain the rare metals so necessary for Colony development, and when orbits were due to be aligned, Vishay and I would fly out. It was harder work, space flying: landing on these tiny bodies, which spun and twisted. But I realised that I loved it. The universe doesn't need us, is what I felt, and that was perversely fortifying. Each second out there is its own kind of improbable victory. It was an environment in which we First Gens, used to piloting machines, were more capable than Homers.

We came back and dropped our sample tubes into the hoppers in the landing bay, and inevitably Haley would call us in to debrief and tell as that we'd done well.

Then, after an M-year of this, they decided to send us to 109556.

The Baguette, Vishay called it. It's a type of bread, which I've had a few times when the Fauxlour supplies were plentiful. He called it this because a baguette is long and thin, and as filled with air holes as this rock was cavernous.

Command treated 109556 as significant. "We weren't alert to it at first," Haley admitted. "It's atypical." It had an unusual density when scanned from a distance. The specialists thought the presence of novel elements likely.

The body aligns every couple of M-years, so we planned to prospect and if we found anything Command would prepare and mount an extraction mission on the next pass.

Haley and her colleagues were jumpy giving us the mission, I supposed because the trajectory gave us just a small window in which to land.

"Tell us the samples you need," said Vishay, "and we'll get them." I remember the way Haley smiled at him when he said that. She admired his straightforwardness. Haley's colleagues grinned too, though I still felt an apprehension in the way that they looked at each other and spoke together. Homers are so often inattentive to the fact that we can follow them from within our Exos. They extrapolate their own experience of being in suits, of feeling cut off. But I registered tension in their words. I'm sure Vishay sensed this too.

We went on one last run together before we departed.

We stood in the swirl of a minor storm. "Are you worried?" I said to Vishay.

"Always and never," he said.

I thought of reminding him that he could speak clearly, but he knew that. I sometimes worried that there was a disconnect between us. He had told me of his trip to Home, and I had felt myself his close accomplice. Yet over our year of working together, I'd expected some *result* of the revelation: some action he would take, some idea he would explain further. We just lived, though. He'd shared with me a vision, an alternative to this life we lived in the pinch of the hourglass. It would be centuries before Mars could be terraformed or other habitable planets located. Our work drew this future minimally closer, I suppose, and I wondered whether this was enough for Vishay. Probably he didn't have an answer. It was only I, who seemed always to need to be led, who required a course of action to be spelled out.

"The plan looks fine," said Vishay on the plain.

"Sometimes it feels that they think we're machines," I said.

"Agreed. But I feel flattered, in a way."

"Yeah?"

"I mean, it works. We do the missions. We find their metals. Rather this than being trapped in the Colony."

"I suppose," I said.

"What else is there?" Vishay said.

We stood for a little longer, set to deleting the conversation. There was barely anything compromising in it. Yet between the words was an uncertainty, a weary doubt, that I understood we must hide from those above us.

More food, more pills. I eat a little. I swallow the small grey tablets. The orange dims.

I dreamed of Home on the trip to the Baguette. I told Vishay. He said, "It seems like a dream to me now, but I flew there in a craft like this."

We went to the front of the craft and looked out the big window, and he showed me on the dash how he initiated the flight program.

Why he did this, I don't know. Such information is classified, so we erased the logs. Maybe he just wanted to remind himself where he had been. Everything gets loose on a mission. Sometimes you'll do whatever you can to make a thought solid again.

I wake suddenly, and the walls around are vibrating. Someone is screaming, and I belatedly understand that person to be me. I know my dream, then: I was back in my suit, the systems off: darkness, cold, glinting rock.

I stand unsteadily and go to the wall where the door appeared for the Homer. I beat against the orange rubber. Nothing changes, however. I keep beating. I shout. I exhaust myself. I go back to the bed and collapse. The light in the room seems to seep over a gap between the tops of the walls and the ceiling. If light can be said to seep. I blink and it is behind my eyes.

I wonder what time it is. Maybe the Homer was right. Maybe the time doesn't matter. Not in the way that I have previously understood it, at least.

I realise that my hands are shaking. I push them between my thighs to still them.

I don't think I have slept, but when I look up there is a new tray: nothing in any of the food sections, merely three pills. I take them. The whole space flares out like I am in the epicentre of a slow explosion.

I open my eyes. The Homer is back. He sits cross-legged. He massages his stubbly scalp with a large hand. I sit up slowly. I shuffle back on the mattress and lean against the padded wall.

"You're ready," he says.

"I think so."

"That wasn't a question," he says.

He has a screen. I can see nothing from where I sit. It is just a black shiny thing in his hand. He stabs at it definitively. "Commenced," he says. He looks at me. "Talk," he says.

I feel sick. It feels impossible, what he is asking me. I don't know how to string words together. I feel as if he has commanded me to place each of my organs—my liver, my brain, my juddering heart—on the floor between us.

"Start with the landing," he says.

I take a breath. The Homer watches me with surprising patience. He nods curtly when I finally begin to speak.

I tell him about our first sight of the asteroid. It was as strange as had been promised: a spinning cylinder. Both Vishay and I gawped at it through the observation window. I tell the man that we were both nervous—I could feel this, though Vishay didn't confirm his apprehension. Yet, as we approached, our training took over. We followed the routines for landing. Things clicked.

The man asks me whether anything was unusual about the landing itself. I say, "You have the logs for this, right?"

He holds up his hand to stop me. "Did anything feel strange?" he says.

"If there was anything unusual, it was how easily it all went to plan."

We came upon the spinning cylinder and flew alongside. I began to rotate the craft around it, picking up speed until it no longer seemed the cylinder was spinning but the universe around it. When we had synchronised, I took us towards the docking point that we had established from the remote survey. Vishay sat at the second controls, but he didn't need to touch them. He watched the pitted surface moving closer. He said, "You're very good, you know."

I describe to the man the way that we came within five meters of the rock. I sent the legs down and used pitons to anchor us. The Homer looks at me calmly as I talk through these manoeuvres. We were aiming to quickly take samples and then move them back to the craft for analysis, from which we would determine the need for further exploration. Every movement on a mission like this is optimised. Each instant outside the craft is planned, because each second on a rock like this raises the chances of the unforeseen, the catastrophic. I don't say this. This is the background context in which we speak.

I say, "As per the mission itinerary, Corporal Simms went through the air lock first."

I had checks to do before I left the craft, but I paused to watch Vishay floating down towards the asteroid, feathering his thrusters. He was laying a line behind him, and he used a laser to burn open a crack in which he set the first cam.

"Was there anything notable about this descent?" the man asks.

"It went to plan. I clarified Corporal Simms's status. He confirmed that there were no issues."

Vishay had moved off, flying close to the surface. He was aiming for a large fissure in the rock that we suspected led into a cavernous space. The surveys had suggested that the asteroid was riven with caves, and we wanted a sample from as deep as we could get.

"And you?"

"I was doing a system check. I was running a scan of the environment using the instruments of the craft."

"And?"

"Everything was fine. The strong magnetic field that we had anticipated was present. The particulate readings confirmed a lot of ferrous ore. But there was also a trace of beryllium, as we had hoped."

The man nods. "Then you descended?"

"Then I suited up and descended."

"And corporal Simms at this point?"

"He had entered the cave."

"Had he communicated?"

"He remarked that the space he entered was large. He said that I could have piloted the craft right in."

"He was joking?"

"I suppose. But I imagine that I could have."

"What do you base this assessment on?"

"Seeing the space later. I'm getting ahead of myself."

"Go back, then."

"I reached the surface. I secured my cable. I used the laser to take a sample. The rock was very hard."

I recall setting that laser running, watching it cut slowly. The rock was greenish black and speckled with crystals that shimmered under my lights. Above me, the sky was churning around, each star dragging a tail like a comet.

"The sample took a while. I canned it, sent it back to the craft by drone."

"Meanwhile?"

"Vishay was in the cavern."

"Corporal Simms?"

"Sorry. Yes."

"And?"

"He'd mentioned the first strange thing."

"The first strange thing. Interesting."

"You'll have it in the log."

"Don't worry about the log. I want your recollection."

"Okay. Sorry. He said that his light was flickering."

"That's all?"

"He said that it was flickering, and then he said, *Not quite*."

"*Not quite?* Those words struck you?"

"I think he meant that he hadn't quite described the effect."

"I see."

"He was precise."

I don't like this past tense. The accuracy is necessary for the report, but I also feel that speaking like this is a betrayal, a gesture that makes space for his death to be real.

The Homer watches me with narrowed eyes. "Then?"

"Corporal Simms told me he was continuing into the cave."

"Did he say where he was?"

"He'd reached the back of the large space. He said he was choosing a route. The space forked into three tunnels, apparently."

"And you?"

"I was moving towards the cave at this point."

I floated over the surface, modulating the thrusters. The cave was a crack that spread at its bottom: a triangular hole which I moved down into. I felt watched, though maybe *watched* isn't quite the right term. It made me uneasy, the space. It seemed structural. My lights chased shadows up the walls, flattened the silhouettes of the rocks on the uneven floor. I don't mean that I thought it had been built, exactly, but it felt contingent, *necessary* in some way. I felt as if there were a purpose to the place I was not immediately aware of, as if I were an insect as they used to have on Home and had flown into a large human building. Yet if the place had been made, as the previous metaphor seems to suggest, it had not been made with a logic I could grasp.

I tell none of this to the man who sits ahead of me.

I tell him instead that when I moved into the cave my light beams began to behave strangely. The man asks me to define what I mean. I say, "The light went heavy and liquid suddenly. It pulsed, and then it was slow, laggy."

The man frowns. "Where were you at this point?"

"In the middle of the cave. I could see Corporal Simms's line running ahead of me. I fixed my own line, taking care not to tangle with his."

"Did you have communication from Corporal Simms?"

"He said that he had reached a dead end. He'd come into a larger cavern that terminated. Another tunnel, he said, led back, parallel to the one he had arrived by."

"What was the plan?"

"He was to take a sample."

"Did he?"

"He set the laser running."

"And then?"

"And then things got chaotic."

I try to do as the man wants, to talk him through the moments as I experienced them. First there was silence, darkness, and panic. Maybe there was a flash of light, or maybe not. Everything in the suit was suddenly out. My systems were down. On impulse, my fingers found the switch for the backups, but nothing happened. I was jolted forwards in my suit. I realised that this was my wire coming taut. I was floating in darkness in the cave, tethered by that cord. My world was quiet in a way that I had never known: no humming, no atmosphere, no temperature support. Then came a high uneven sound like shearing metal. It took me some time to realise that this sound was my frantic breath. I'm not sure how long that moment lasted. I started to black out. I had been seized by a sense of panic and then everything was very soft, almost fine. Yet at the end of what seemed like the longest instant—a warm, liquid span of time that I could have sunk into—the hum started again and my suit was on.

I do not narrate the moments in exactly this way to my interlocuter. I say that the suit was off and then the suit was on again. I say I was disorientated. I say that I was floating, anchored to the floor of the cave by my line.

He says, "And then?"

"The communication channel opened. Corporal Simms asked me my status."

"And?"

"I replied that my status was fine. I asked his."

"What was his status?"

"He said he was okay. His suit had turned off like mine. The laser hadn't cut the sample. He was interested in that."

"And then what happened?"

"I saw him, or what looked like him, floating right above me, near the apex of the cave roof."

"I thought you said Corporal Simms was farther into the tunnel."

"Exactly."

"A contradiction."

"A contradiction. Yes."

"What did you do then?"

"I asked where he was, over the channel."

"What was the reply?"

"He replied instantly that he was still at the end of the tunnel he had navigated. He was examining the laser."

"And what did you do?"

"I used my thrusters to move towards this floating body."

"Were you sure it was him?"

"Who else could it have been? It was an Exo. It had the stripes of commendation on the arm, I noticed."

"What happened when you approached?"

"It seemed to be floating dark, but then it powered, and a face briefly bloomed, then cut out. The opacity settings turned off and I saw Vishay's real face, not his Avi."

"Yes?"

"Sorry. Corporal Simms."

"What did he look like?"

"Bad. He gasped for air. He tried to talk, but there was no channel open between us. I moved closer. The power seemed to be failing. The light around his head was pulsing. I made a manual connection between our suits. I fed him power. He spoke over the connection. He made a great effort to do this."

"What did he say?"

"He wheezed and then he said, 'Go! Get out of here! Turn around!' "

"He said this to you?"

"He was in a bad way. His eyes were half-closed. His pupils didn't seem to focus."

"What happened then?"

"A voice came over the channel."

"Whose voice?"

"Corporal Simms's normal voice."

"What did it say?"

"He said, 'I'm wondering whether to run the laser again.' "

"What did you do?"

I've lost track of that memory. I was still floating, clasping the other Exo, yet I could hear Vishay's voice coming from elsewhere. Vishay's real face was ahead of me in the suit. Something struck my suit lower down. I saw that the right arm of Vishay's Exo was dangling, horribly mangled, twisted and melted, though I had been sure that this was impossible, that the material was impervious to the highest temperatures. For some reason, the sight incited a sudden vision of Vishay moving the right arm of his suit forward to touch something. I felt an immediate understanding that this body was ahead, was the consequence of what was about to happen. "You have to go!" said the Vishay I was clasped to. He knew something I did not. His eyes were still closed. His face was bluish. I slammed my thrusters. I dragged him behind me. I opened the channel and said, "Don't touch the laser!" The other Vishay's channel opened for just a second, and there was a single instant of static, a great warm fizz. I hoped for a moment. Yet, after that, behind me, there was a rippling from the back of the cave.

I tell this to the man. He says, "An explosion?"

"Not an explosion, exactly. A rolling pulse of energy."

"What happened to you?"

"I was thrown forwards, toward the mouth of the cave. I was still strapped to Corporal Simms and we were both still connected to our lines. Our wires were yanked and the cams they were connected to popped and failed."

There was a sound to it all in my mind. But of course there can't have been a sound.

"And what happened then?" The man rubs his hand over his stubbly head.

"I was floating outside the mouth of the cave. I was still strapped to the other Exo. I took a moment to ascertain my condition, then I used the cord connection to read the data of Corporal Simms."

"In the Exo you were connected to?"

"Yes. There were no life signs."

"Right."

"And also, something strange was that the systems of his suit were ahead."

"Yes?"

"The mission reading was ninety-five hours advanced. I couldn't understand it . . ."

"I see."

"Have you studied the logs?"

"This is about you. About what you experienced at the time."

I note unease in the man. He is squinting at me.

"What do you want?" I say.

"I want to know your conclusion at the time."

"I believed the reading, actually. I was certain that he'd been there floating at the top of the cave for days. The pulse had sent him back, and I found him."

"That's your interpretation? Okay. What did you do?"

"I returned to the craft. I rose into the air lock. I secured Corporal Simms's body."

"And then?"

I pause. "I went back. I thought I might be able to save Corporal Simms."

The man shakes his head. "But you'd just secured his body in the air lock . . ."

"As I said, I felt that something strange was happening. I'd clasped his nearly unconscious body and spoken to him in another location in the same moment."

"But you'd blacked out. Your equipment was malfunctioning."

"I'm trying to explain my reasoning."

The man raises his palms. "I understand. I shouldn't have interjected. Go on."

"I went back towards the cave. I stopped at the entrance. I set a cam."

"What did you see?"

"It looked like the cave had suddenly shortened. I thought at first that there had been a collapse."

"Why so?"

"My light only illuminated so far. It was as if there were a wall where there hadn't been one before. I floated forwards, though, and saw that something strange was happening. The cave did seem to go on, but the light was dying quite suddenly, not moving past a certain point."

I glided through the space, over the rounded boulders on the floor of the cave. It was like a strange curtain. My eyes couldn't really understand it.

"You approached?"

"I approached."

I still felt the possibility of Vishay back there. I still felt the urge to get to him.

"I came up to it. The beam of the light didn't pass through, yet I had a sense now that the space continued beyond. I could somehow glimpse the empty darkness ahead. I moved right up to this invisible barrier. It reflected nothing. It just killed the light."

"And?"

"I stepped through."

The Homer's strong jaw is set. He watches me silently. I feel sure that he is angry. I should not have gone back, I know.

I felt sure Vishay was alive somewhere that I could reach, though. There is a limit to the losses one person can take.

"What happened?" the man says.

"My suit went down again. Not with a snap like you might expect, but a sort of yawning diminishment."

"We're talking about complex electronic systems here . . ."

"It sounds strange, I know. I'm trying to say how it felt."

"Go on, please."

"My suit went dark. I heard my breath again, but this time I knew it. I was drifting. The moment seemed very long. I felt my weightlessness within the suit. I felt a weariness in my limbs. Then the line I had set behind me came taut, snapped me back somehow. I was through the dark curtain again. It was rippling next to me. I couldn't rightly see it, but I could sense it. My systems began to turn back on."

"And then?"

"I was near the roof of the cave. I made out the rippling curtain and saw movement. I saw a body passing through."

"A body?"

"Me in my suit."

"You think you saw yourself?"

"I did see myself."

"Describe it."

"Just a flicker: my suit . . . my lights . . . the slight glow of my thrusters. My past self moved below."

"What did you do?"

"I began to move as quickly as I could back towards the craft."

"Yes?"

"I don't remember it. I only remember having to clamber through the air lock past Corporal Simms's body. When it pressurised, I opened his suit. He was dead for sure. The strangest thing was that he had stubble, almost a beard."

"I see."

"You've seen the body?"

"We don't need to discuss that."

"Okay."

"Anything else you remember?"

"The time settings of my suit were strange too. I'd stepped just momentarily beyond the curtain, but my time log was out by a whole five minutes."

• • •

I go to Vishay's memorial. They put him in the ground as they did Miz. The same celebrant speaks in the same tones. Haley comes to the podium and says, "He made great discoveries, of benefit to all of us. He made the ultimate sacrifice on our behalf." Vishay's parents are there: his dad straight-backed and glazed, his mum hunched and shrinking from it all. His dad has his eyes, and his mum has his thin delicate hands (in motion, fidgeting when people come and speak sombrely to her after the ceremony). I don't know them. I'd like to tell them that their son saved me, to describe the way that Vishay held on until he could tell me to get away. But I cannot. They don't have the security clearance. Command made clear the need for secrecy on releasing me from my debriefing.

I hang back and watch. I think of that ragged stubble, that face I studied in the air lock. I wish I'd looked at it longer. I cannot unsee it, but I cannot fully remember it. I want to credit his remarkable persistence. He lasted only long enough to warn me, after all. He kept himself going. He was always ahead of me.

Command sent me back here on leave. I spent two weeks in the orange room, tranquilised and then debriefed, and then debriefed again and set loose. When I climbed back into an Exo my hands were unused to the controls.

They flew me to the Colony. Mum was at home in the unit again, waiting for me. I drank the tea Mum made for me. She looked at me with sad eyes. I sensed that she had a grasp of what had happened to me, though it was all classified. She had her privileges, I supposed, leeway to demand something of an explanation for why her son was on leave early, ashen.

She had even, it turned out, taken an unprecedented three days of leave herself.

It is on the third of these days that Vishay's memorial is happening.

Mum is lingering on the edge of the crowd. I stand at the glass and look out at the markers with the lights upon them gently winking. There are new graves since Miz, I notice. The dead move closer.

Mum and I walk away from the memorial window without speaking. They do something to the light here, make it dusky, tranquilising.

At the junction back to the transitways, a couple of very elderly Homers hobble along, arm in arm. A man walks with a strange, hitched stride. A woman totters with little steps next to him. They wear clothes—shirts with collars, open jackets—of the kind that people used to wear on Home. So unsteady is their way of walking that I wonder whether I should help them. I look to Mum, who has slowed, who watches them very carefully, smiling.

They reach a set of doors, push through into a bright space.

"The chapel," Mum says. "Do you want to go?"

The chapel is a narrow room, clad inside with bleached stone. At the threshold I must crouch to enter. Inside an aisle leads past rows of small, plain benches to an open space and a gold-coloured lectern. The ceiling arcs up in a high parabola. "A catenary arch," says Mum, who sees me turning the face of my suit upwards.

Behind the lectern is a man in a smock decorated with gold threading. There are four old Homers—the couple I saw coming in and two others—seated, slumped, in front of the smock-wearing man. I take a place on one of the rearmost benches, which is difficult. The space is not made for Exos. I cannot imagine that many First Gens have been here before me. Mum shuffles in next to me.

The man at the front is waiting for something, and for a moment I worry that he is going to address Mum and me, but he does not speak. From behind him, quite suddenly, comes a clear tone. It prickles my skin within my suit, before I comprehend that it is human voices, joined, rising together.

"It's a recording?" I message to Mum.

She receives it, taps back on her wrist input. "Yes. From back on Home."

The voices tumble together and then one high note rises above others.

"Latin?" I message.

"Yes."

I could have run a translation, of course, but I wanted to ask. The man at the front stares down the aisle, his eyes glassy, his head bowed, a slight smile on his lips.

"Did people used to sing like this?" I message Mum.

"In church," she taps.

"You went to church on Home?"

Mum looks at me and smiles. She types back on her wrist input: "I hated Christians on Home, actually. There were a lot of Christians just before I left when things were getting worse. They were always proselytising. If you know what that means."

"Of course," I write.

"But now I feel bad for being angry."

"Why?"

"I realise that they really believed in what they were saying, I suppose. They were really sure that I was going to hell. Why wouldn't you be pushy if that was what you thought?"

The voices change, falling away, and something somersaults in my chest.

Another song comes: a structure of sound built to fill the tall space in front of us. The man at the front keeps smiling patiently.

"Why don't people sing like this now?" I message Mum.

She thinks then taps. "It takes a lot of practice. Maybe people don't have time. Maybe the kind of people who would devote such time are not here."

I look up again. The place arcs around us. It feels as if we are inside a resonant body. I think of the tall dark cave on the asteroid. I think of Miz, as I always do when something surprises me. We came to the memorial wing together once, to see Other Mum, yet we would never have thought to come to the chapel.

My thoughts are interrupted by movement behind me. I turn to see two old men in smocks, their faces different from faces I have seen before. I look down and see the lights they hold, which illuminate their skin inconstantly.

I send the thought to Mum as soon as I have formed it: "Is that fire?"

"Yes," she taps. "They're called candles. The chapel has a special dispensation."

I know about candles. I have seen them in films, considered phrases featuring them when trying to make my dictionary in the past. To *snuff out* means to kill, and that comes from the way a candle would be turned off. I study the light at the top of the sticks that the men hold. It is unlike any light I have seen before. It moves in the air as if it has an inertia, trailing as the men carry the white sticks forwards. The light shimmers, opaque in places and translucent around the point at which it is anchored. A tiny curling line of dark vapour rises from the tip of the flame. The men stride to the front and place these candles in holders to either side of the lectern.

The robed man begins to speak in a creaking voice, and I don't register much of it because I am still looking at the candles to either side of him, using the magnification on my suit, watching them send their lines of smoke up towards the high bone-white dome above us.

Mum goes back to work, and I am left in the unit. I await clarification of my status from Command. Sometimes I go out in the Colony, walking the transitways, overtaken by people with surer purpose. More often I am in the unit, exercising, reading, preparing dinner for when Mum gets home.

We have been through the mirror, it feels, because I now ask her how work was, as she used to enquire about my school day.

She considers such enquiries more seriously than I did when I was a kid. One day, when we are eating dinner, she says, "I've been working a little outside of my area. I've been consulting on an internal investigation. A strange phenomenon, recorded by another branch."

I put down my fork. Her eyes are on me, steady. My pulse jumps in my neck. I nod to show her that I understand.

"I can't discuss the details, of course. Except to say that it's very odd."

"Yes."

"Important for the Corporation to investigate. Though it's outside of their key concentration, which—as it should be—is moving through the hourglass as expediently as possible." She is speaking for the OS, of course. We don't want our conversation flagged, especially as I wait out this strange period of leave.

I say, "Certainly." I swallow, wait.

"I tried to be of assistance, but really it's outside of our competencies. That means it's distinct from the Corporation's key objective, which is forward progress. They're reallocating their resources now, not planning to deepen the investigation."

"You're stopping, then?" I look at my left hand, palm down on the table. It shakes. I place my right hand on top of it. I try to breathe evenly.

She frowns. "Yes."

I recall Haley's words at the memorial. She spoke of Vishay having made discoveries, having died in the course of discoveries. *Of benefit to us all*, she said. Is the Corporation board not curious about the possibility of going back in time? Do they not wonder about what may be changed, recovered? Who may be saved?

It only really strikes me then that I hoped still that they might go back, pluck him out of that strange vortex into which he seemed to have been sucked.

But no. Of course. He is really gone.

Mum seems to know what I'm thinking. She says, "Our leaders

understand that they are implementing a plan. There is a lot ahead of us. The discovery suggested possibilities. But also risks." She raises her hand, gestures around us. "They feel that all of this should not be jeopardised." She keeps her eyes on me. There is a sadness in her gaze. I have the sense that she is wishing to apologise.

I stand and make my way to my room. I lie on the bed and think of the hourglass, that sense I had so clearly after Miz, of being trapped between what came before and what will come.

Two days later, midmorning, I get a message on my device. My prospecting work is to be suspended indefinitely. I am to be allocated to another work stream. I should await further details.

I do not feel the loss at first. I walk the transitways numbly, thinking that soon I will be taking one of these routes to another job, another life. Prospecting is all I wanted, and they have taken it from me. Yet the strange thing is that I am not hurt by the loss, or I do not yet *feel* hurt by the loss. The face of Vishay in the air lock is resolving in my mind now, remembered or invented: the stubble, the hair slicked to his forehead. He is there now, stuck in time. He looked very different in death, without motion. His face was like that of another person.

I return to the unit from a walk. I do my exercises. I cook a chili with M-beans. I place it steaming on the little table. When Mum comes home, she looks at it. She looks at me.

I say, "They're reassigning me."

"Oh yes?" Mum's tone is flat, though. She knows this already.

"Yes."

"Well, I think that's a poor choice on their part."

On impulse, I look at the OS microphone in the corner of the room.

Mum catches my eye. "They know I think this. I've communicated my views on the matter."

"Oh?"

"I have a proposal, in fact."

"Yes?"

"You did well in your algebra modules at school. We need an assistant in the labs, with the Stellar8Rs. It's work you can learn on the job. You just need a head for figures."

"I'll work with you?"

"Why not?"

We eat dinner. Afterwards, I agree to what Mum is suggesting. "I'll make it happen," she says, and she does.

We walk to her lab together. We talk about work at the dinner table. I educate myself on the reactors. It takes a lot of effort to understand. I feel awe that this is Mum's own design. I tell her so, but she shrugs it off. "Mine and others'," she says. "Other Mum helped. Granny started it all. Granny did so much. She was so close years before. She got most of the way to this design half a century earlier."

"Really?" I say.

"Yes," says Mum. "It could have been so useful on Home. But . . ." She sighs. I notice that she is looking at the strange old-style watch that she wears on her wrist. I've always been confused by this watch. Why would it be needed, when she has access to interfaces? When she has her interlinked wrist input to wear when she leaves the house? It's sentimental, she's always told me. Now she sees me looking at it. She undoes the buckle carefully. She holds it out.

"What?" I say.

"It was Granny's," Mum says. "Try it on."

Mum helps me put it around my own wrist, shows me how the buckle closes. She is gentle, careful. It is nice to feel such care, I must admit. I raise my hand, and the watch is loose. It slides down my forearm. I turn the face and watch the thin arm—barely wider than a hair—tracing its way around the dial.

Mum explains how the watch works. The screen is cracked, but I can still see through to the dial. I look at the hands and the notched figures around the circle and I try to understand the pattern. "How is it powered?" I say.

"By your movement," says Mum.

I shake my arm, exploring the idea.

"Isn't that clever?"

"This is old?"

"Maybe a hundred and fifty years."

"I didn't know people could make things like this then."

Mum smiles. "We weren't just banging rocks together back on Home."

I struggle to undo the clasp, to hook the small metal catch with my nail. Mum says, "Keep it. She'd like you to have it."

"I don't need it," I say. "I'm in my suit."

"*I'd* like you to have it. It's sentimental." Mum laughs. "Try being a little sentimental."

The watch is a pleasure, I must admit. I sit at the table in the unit and study it. I am still amazed that time can be kept manually, charted by a little mechanism ticking away, notching one second after another. What even is it at base, a second? It is like a riddle. How did they even begin to solve this riddle with metal?

I suppose that, yes, I did assume the people of the past cruder, mostly mistaken. I suppose I never really considered the continuity. There was the break, yes. But we are them.

At work, in the archive, I read my great-grandmother's papers and see that Mum was not exaggerating. Great-Granny sketched out the theory, but couldn't realise a machine in real life. In the archive, as I move my arm to touch the screen and scroll, I feel the weight of the watch. I like the sense of connection. I feel sad for Great-Granny, back there, mired, knowing but not quite able to speak that knowledge clearly.

I tell Mum of my research at dinner. I want to talk of the feeling I have of connection, but today Mum isn't so hopeful. She only smiles sadly. "It was a waste, wasn't it?" she says.

14

HANNAH

I *sometimes think myself like a certain kind of sports star, famous for one* single moment in a game far in the past. Or a singer who recorded only one good song.

My whole life, it sometimes seems, happened in less than three days. What had occurred before that was buildup, and what came after, consequence.

That morning Red kept speaking of the reactor he wished me to realise. It required no great conceptual leap from current reactor designs, yet it had been made functional through neat refinement, through the surmounting of countless little problems that currently plagued researchers. There was a balance to it, I sensed: a neat kind of natural mathematics, much like the patterns that shaped the shells on the window in the kitchen. It didn't seem like a design that one could *invent*. It was a pure form, a thing that needed instead to be *realised*. I could see that balance before I could truly describe it. But I get ahead of myself already.

I was at the window. The boy, the broken boy, who seemed half an old man, was out on the grass in the new sunlight.

I stepped away from the glass. It seemed important to give him privacy, to let him meet this world alone. I sat on the unmade bed. I felt happy, though this was an unreflective happiness. I was very present, and I had no sense of time passing at all.

Eventually, when the light seemed to have changed, I stood and went back to the window and looked down. The boy was gone. I could have dreamt it, I felt. I looked at that clear patch of grass, the old stone shed, with its ramshackle roof. In the dawn, it all appeared so neat, like part of a model village.

I dressed and went downstairs. I felt alert. Outside, the wind was fragrant. I could smell the sea and the spicy odour of the dry peatland.

Jasper padded into the long grass. A couple of birds, disturbed, rose and flew chattering towards the cottage, then up and over the roof and away.

I walked a little way across the field, towards the huge low shifting of the surf.

The day would be warm and clear again. It was so unlikely, this fineness, and I wondered whether the boy knew this. I felt that he needed to.

I was filled with gratitude that morning. He had come for me and I felt so grateful and behind that I felt a great sadness for the boy. I quaked again at the thought of his fate, the unaddressed question of where he would go after this. I wanted to give him something, I suppose.

When I went into the shed, he was sitting up in his suit. His glowing face watched me step across the uneven dirt floor towards him.

"Are you ready?" he said, and I nodded. I took a place at the desk. Jasper came in behind me, sniffing the air. He looked at Red without alarm. The boy in the suit was ordinary to him now. The dog flopped down next to me on the blanket that I had laid out the day before.

We worked through the morning. Red talked again of the reactor. It ran on deuterium and tritium, and he spent some hours explaining the process by which the latter element may be produced without the need for rare isotopes. I listened and wrote swiftly. “You’re following?” Red would say at intervals, and I would nod, still scribbling.

He forced a break on me for lunch. “You’ll tire yourself,” he said. “You need to be able to focus.” I looked up at him in that big kneeling suit in the shed, a tombstone looming over me. I thought of the boy inside, of the frail body, his pale skin. “How old are you?” I asked him.

“Twelve,” he said.

“Twelve?”

“In M-years.” He paused. “Twenty-four in your years.”

Yet it was he who was being the parent, caring for *me*, encouraging me to think of eating.

That felt wrong.

I rose from my little desk. Jasper raised himself from the floor and prepared to follow, shaking out his floppy ears. I walked through the glowing doorway of the shed into the light and the sound of breaking waves, out to the honeyish scent of midsummer heather.

I ate toast and a soft-boiled egg for lunch. From the kitchen window, I could see a long way, over the fields and cliffs and across a sea that shone like hammered copper.

I thought of Ruaraidh and Andrew in Edinburgh. I would soon need to call Ruaraidh because he would worry. Yet I would tell him none of what was happening. How could I?

I felt glad to have secrets, I realised, thrilled to be deep in something that I couldn’t articulate.

When I’d eaten, I walked to the beach with Jasper. He needed to run and maybe I also needed the time. The long grass between the house and cliffs was still, and this calmness was unusual, almost eerie. The sun was very high. I could feel it striking my shoulders, hitting my scalp where the hair parted.

I descended the steep path to the sand. In the winter, the path would be overtaken by a stream that emerged burbling from a bog in the meadow and trickled down to slick over the beach. Now, however, that stream was merely a thin, whispering thing, darkening the rocky gully next to the descending path, giving a mineral aroma to the air.

On the beach, Jasper dashed over the sand, running quickly, turning, arcing back towards me, then racing off again, leaving behind loops of prints that emanated from the point at which I stood; forming a pattern, I thought, that must look like a drawing of a flower from above.

I walked to the water. Jasper followed. I took off my espadrilles and stood on the soft wet sand. The waves washed around my ankles. The water was still cool. Jasper capered away from the waves as they came in, then turned to chase them back out, barking, seeming to think that he was repelling the water, forcing it back with his playful fierceness.

Hubris, I guess. I thought myself in control then. I felt things clicking, working.

I walked back up to the cottage quickly. When I came back into the dusty shed, I was panting. I said to Red, "You have to come outside tonight. Out of your suit."

The illuminated face looked at me steadily. I watched it and recalled his real face as I had seen it from far off in the early morning. He said, "I can't come out."

I said, "I saw you do just that this morning."

He paused for a long moment. "That was a mistake."

"No," I said. "It wasn't."

"That's not why I'm here."

I was full of it. Forgive me. "You want to save this world?" I said. "See it. Allow yourself to see it."

He argued that we had to work first of all, and I agreed with that. We went back to the lesson, yet I felt that we were both distracted. A vehicle moved down the road—the farmer going to the end of the track, I suspected—and we both stopped and listened. Red talked more haltingly. Perhaps this was because he was starting to speak of the more complex elements of the reactor design.

He explained the design of the magnetic containment. He talked of the components of the breeding blanket. I felt that he had rehearsed all of this. I tried to follow and just about clung on. At times I had to ask him to repeat himself, and as the day wore on I found myself more often confounded. Maybe it was me. Maybe it was him. Probably it was both of us. We were exhausted.

Evening came in and the sun was still so bright. The shafts of light that nosed through the roof had begun to climb up the wall, so that they seemed less like columns, more like slanted beams.

"I wish my mother was here," Red said.

"Sorry?"

"This is her field," he said. "She could explain it easily."

I nodded, but I felt that there was another meaning in the declaration. I could feel his loneliness. "Let's walk," I said. "Let's go outside together."

I was dogged. I convinced him in the end.

I was glad that when the suit clicked open, I felt tenderness. Red's appearance from a distance had elicited a stab of repulsion that shamed me. Yet now I felt a tenderness on seeing his uneven face. He looked like a long-exposure photograph, I thought, in which the subject has moved, blurred themselves. His forehead was long, his cheeks very thin, his mouth very small. His eyes were greyish blue and beautiful. His hair was red. That's why he had the nickname, of course. There are aspects of him that made me think of Andrew.

He sat hunched within the suit in a cockpit. There were buttons and joysticks and dials. There were tubes. The inside of the thing winked with lights like a night sky.

I went to him and put out my hand. He grasped it. His grip, I realised, was weaker than the grip of my octogenarian mother's. His tiny mouth was pursed with effort as I leaned back and tugged him up and out of his suit.

I caught him. He smelt a little yeasty; new, I thought, like a baby. The suit closed.

"Are you ready?" I said. I held him against me. I felt the effort he needed to speak, the way that his whole body tensed.

His voice was very quiet. He said, "Yes. I am."

I thought I was doing it for him and not myself. But maybe the walk was really, in a twisted way, about me. He braced against my shoulder. He was not heavy, but it was awkward to move like this. At the door, when the light off the sea hit us, I felt that it was not just him seeing the dusk for the first time, but me.

I was new to it too, vicariously.

He made tiny steps towards the grass, grunting a little with the effort. I said, "Are you okay?"

He said, "I'm good."

I ran into the house and rummaged in the closet until I found an old pair of my husband Ruaraidh's shoes. I returned to where Red stood unsteadily in the doorway. I lifted his feet, one after the other, slipping the light running shoes on and tying them.

Jasper seemed to understand Red's vulnerability. He didn't crowd the boy, but moved ahead, an advance guard.

The grass was dry, yellowed by the hot summer. I watched Red's feet shuffling. I looked at the sea ahead of us. I could smell the ocean water. Red's eyes were closed, perhaps in effort, perhaps in ecstasy.

The surf seemed suddenly very loud. The sky had darkened with the evening, gaining a purplish tinge. We came to the edge of my land, beyond which the path sloped down, curving through the meadow.

We stood for a long time, and then I felt Red summoning the resolve to speak. "Farther," he said.

"Farther?"

He said, "The sea."

It felt necessary, a task bigger than either of us. Though Red wheezed and strained to walk even so slowly, we were silently resolute in our aim to make the clifftop, the vantage of the beach, the breaking waves.

When we had made it some way down the winding path, Red stopped. He squeezed my arm limply. He made to turn, and I helped him shift around and look back at the cottage, pinkish in the evening light. I watched him staring at the hills behind. His eyes narrowed to take in the sheep milling on a far-off slope. Then something arced through the air, so quickly that I didn't catch what it was. I thought that it must be something to do with Red: a flying device summoned to assist him. I remembered the flash that preceded his arrival. But I saw that he too was looking up in confusion. Then another shape fluttered out of the shadow of the cottage, arcing, cutting, dipping over the long grass to the side of the path. "What was that?" said Red.

"A bat," I said, laughing as I came to know it. I could identify a tiny, high-pitched noise, like a wheel turning slowly on a rusty axle. Two more bats flew over us, tacking and shifting in the air, diving down to skim over the meadow in search of insects.

Red made a noise like a deflating tire, and I was readying to lower him to the ground and attend to his apparent distress, when that noise changed, broke into racking, spluttering laughter. His head rolled on his thin neck and he gripped my arm harder. I felt a throbbing happiness.

We walked on. The walk was like a meditation: one step, and then another. The last sliver of the sun descended into the sea. Our entwined shadows stretched back towards the house.

There was a whole lifetime in all of this: the time to reach the clifftop divided into endless steps, which themselves might be divided again. Red moved his small mouth as he walked, as if he needed to recruit the muscles of his face to do what his legs could not quite manage. I had worried that he would tire, but he seemed to have found a level at which he could keep going. His movements were puppet-like. But he walked still.

There is a before and after, as I said, to this night. The two of us stood at the edge of the cliff, above the gully that the path and trickling stream followed down to the sand. The tide was out. There was weed and crusty sea froth on the beach. The sun was gone. The sky at that point was pink, bleeding dark purple as it flowed over our heads. The water was glowing darkly.

The moment felt significant, even then. I have since considered all the speculation that surrounds time travel, and wondered stupidly whether the presence of Red was altering the moments we shared together, giving time a different consistency. Red's breath had been fast, but it slowed again as he rested, looking at the view, supported by me. Jasper dashed down to the sand, where he chewed on a tendril of weed.

I've had years to reflect on those moments, to replay Jasper padding back up the path from the beach towards us, and Red at the same time saying, "I want to sit," and starting to lower himself down towards the ground. He must have wanted to feel the grass beneath him, I have since thought, because that was probably what was most novel to him; not the sun, which still shone up there where he had been born, but dirt, plants, natural textures. Jasper meanwhile loped up the steep slope, and some small portion of my attention was snagged on the dog; enough that as Red began to initiate his movement my grasp of his forearm faltered. Still, there was so much time to rectify things. I had a chance to grasp him again before his weight truly shifted and before he began to stumble. There was the opportunity even as he stumbled to pull him back to solid ground, the chance to account for the lurch forward that happened as his weak legs sought to balance, as his foot found a declivity in the uneven grass that pitched him towards the edge. I wasn't thinking fast enough. I wasn't reacting as I should have. How many conjectures can I make about what could have happened? An unlimited number, I suppose. They are all useful to hold off recalling what did occur, which was Red falling forwards onto the sloping ground towards the gully and then tumbling headfirst, in a motion that was dreamlike until it wasn't, until there was a sound that made me clench my jaw, that I still hear sometimes in dreams.

He lay down there in the gully, where the water trickled towards the sand. I thought of birds and of the way they seem so light until they're not. I thought of the way one finds a seagull on a beach, dead, thrown up on the sand like an old coat. I was sure then that he was gone, though I was working to deny it to myself.

Jasper was next to Red almost immediately, his tail wagging placatingly.

I had to look away from Red to turn and make my way down, and tearing my gaze from him felt dangerous, as if holding my eyes on him could somehow keep Red in the state that I knew him, living; as if turning away would damn him to a new fate. I tried to be rational, however. If there was any hope at all, it lay in being down there, attending to his injuries.

I remember coming down the steep slope with a momentum that I could hardly control. I brushed Jasper aside. The time was terrible, but it was still better than the instants that would come after, because there was still a sliver of possibility that Red wasn't gone.

But he was, of course. I reached him, and that was when the second part of my life really started. He lay face down in the gully. I turned him to see a great cratered wound over his left eye, which was closed. His other eye was open yet seemed already sightless. The small amount of water coming down the stream ran around us. Red's clothes were wet, his hair was damp, stuck to his head in full curls. At first the blood in the water was sparse, running from his head in filaments and strings that made me think of the water I spat from my mouth after flossing. But then the flow of blood from his wound started to pulse more quickly through his hair, and suddenly the trickling water was overtaken by a billowing cloud of red.

His bones were soft and brittle. I tried CPR. I recalled what I could from a first-aid course I'd done at the university. I felt his ribs crack as I pumped his chest: another terrible sound, another terrible sensation. Yet there was no air in him, no getting air into him. I kept going for a long time, perhaps because I didn't want to stop, didn't want to really understand what had happened.

Eventually, I felt very cold. He was cold, of course. I was covered in his blood. Jasper was shivering next to me. It was dark now. The water still trickled around us. The sea kept coming and going.

I didn't know what I would do, but I had a strength that I couldn't have predicted, couldn't believe afterwards. I got him onto my back and carried him up that steep path out of the gully. I felt like I could smell the metal aroma of blood on us, but perhaps that was just my imagination. I needed to rest for a moment at the top of the gully. Then I hoisted Red's body onto my shoulders again and moved towards the cottage. It was fully dark, so I didn't worry about being seen by passersby (in the unlikely event that there were any). I felt that our presence in the landscape—one hunched figure carrying another limp body—fitted eerily.

I staggered into the shed and laid him down as gently as I could on the dusty floor next to his suit. I went to the kitchen to fetch a camping light, but when I came back I found that I couldn't bear to look at his face. The blood had begun to dry and turn black. I said, "Sorry," then said it again and again. The wind whispered through the building, and I spoke against this hissing.

There seemed to be a voice in my mind, instructing me. I followed this voice because it was the easiest thing. I found a shovel at the back of the shed.

I went to the west side of the cottage, facing the sea, where the builders who made the house had cast away the dirt dug up in constructing the foundations. I killed the lamp and began to dig.

My eyes grew accustomed to the darkness eventually. The moon rose. The earth came up more easily than I expected. I had an energy that surprised me. I stepped into the hole I was making and worked from there, digging and sinking. When the lip of the hole was above my chest, I told myself, *Enough*. I went back to the shed, where he still lay, of course, looking small next to that giant suit. Later, I would prise that suit apart, seeking to access the data stored on it, to no avail. I forced myself to look at Red's face once more to make sure that he was gone. I'd left the lamp by the hole, so I used the light on my phone. The lifeless eye—the one not closed by the wound—told me all I needed to know. I said, *Sorry*, again as I lifted him onto my back and staggered to my hole. I had to drop him, I'm afraid. The body landed in the hole with a dull thump. In the east, there was already a rising lightness. I needed to do this before the sun was up, the voice inside me said. I dropped the first shovelful of earth on top of him and felt terrible. But the next scoop was a little easier, and the next one after that more so.

I tumbled all the earth I had dug out of that hole back in, until I found that I was piling up a mound. It looked like a grave, of course. I told myself that I would do something about that in the morning.

I recalled the blood that must be left down in the gully, but then I thought that anyone finding it would imagine so many causes before the real one. They'd think of a deer or a sheep falling, wounding itself, limping away: an ordinary, natural cruelty.

When I got into the house, I looked at the time. It was a quarter past four in the morning. I realised that I had damaged my watch. The glass was cracked. At the top of the face, fine fissures spread like webbing from a single little chip in the surface. It seemed to fit, somehow. The search for this object had led me to him. I could still make out the time behind the cracked face, though. The hands still moved.

I went upstairs. I took off my filthy clothes in the shower stall. The dark dirt and blood ran off under the spray, and I thought again of Red's lifeless eye as I turned him in the gulley. Jasper was curled under the duvet when I came into the bedroom from the shower. I didn't shift him as I would have usually done. I slid into the bed next to him, pressing against the knobs of his spine, feeling the shiver of his body as his chest rose and fell. I told myself that I needed to think, that I needed to gain a real understanding of what had happened, but a self-protective impulse took me over, put me to sleep more deeply than I had slept in years. I didn't wake until much later, when the room was full of daylight. The world felt new and disorientating for a moment, before the events of the previous night returned to me, and the questions that I would come to know so well came into focus: What was lost out on the cliff? What had been held for me in that brain struck and ruined on those jagged rocks?

15

KENZIE

2079

I *have a therapist now, Clem, and sessions with them are wonderful. Yet, as* with so many beneficial new habits—new diets, new exercise regimens—my pleasure comes with a tinge of regret that I have come so late to living this way, speaking about myself, thinking about myself, allowing myself the leeway that I give others. Clem is *going* and I am *going* and the fraught division of this world into *going* and *not going* is the main reason the company mandates this therapy for its Mars Shareholders.

I speak to Clem in an office that is even nicer than my own. I have moved one block east along the river, from the start-up campus to the Tevat HQ proper. I have a similar view of the other bank. I still look across at Govan, where the blocks of flats have yet to be repaired after the flood three years ago. Residents of these towers were supposed to be rehoused, but they have not been, and so people have moved back into the buildings without electricity or heat or running water. When I work late at night, I look across the river at these flats to see the glimmers of headlamps, even the lights of candles and fires. Clem is on the very top floor, and so from their office one can see beyond these towers. Today, beneath packed cloudy skies, I can glimpse beyond the edge of the city a sliver of emerald fields. Their space is furnished pristinely with antique twentieth century pieces: a long teak dresser, a boxy green velvet sofa, wooden-framed armchairs upholstered in faded brown leather. Clem's position is that I have too long been inattentive to my own needs. Their story of my youth is that of a child pushed into a self-sufficiency that she wasn't ready for, first because of my parents' attention to their own work, then due to Mum's death. Today Clem tells me, "You don't always have to cope. You're allowed to need things. You're allowed to deserve things." Clem has amazing blue eyes that gleam like they are their own source of light. They wear the same kind of black trousers and navy shirt each session, as if already preparing for the sartorial uniformities of the expedition. "A lot of people struggle with this," they say. "We're going, and they're not. But just because they want to go too, that doesn't mean that we don't deserve to."

On the days—Mondays and Wednesdays—that I have a session with Clem, I must walk home quickly to beat the curfew, in place since the riots and looting of last summer. Today the city is hot. The year has turned. Until last week, I would find myself crossing the street into sun. This week, when I leave the main building, I seek shade. I can smell the thick stink of the city's clogged sewers.

HQ is defended like a military base in hostile territory. Between the front door and the new security cordon I pass three men in black Kevlar combat gear. They eye me through their yellow-tinted glasses. These men are SWs—Shareholders in Waiting—in company parlance. That's how the firm holds things together: a pyramid of promises regarding who should be allowed to ascend to the Colony. Why would people protect those of us due to depart if they thought we would yank the ladder up behind us?

Clem's brief acknowledgment of how many in this city want to be going sticks with me. That was not the point, I know. They sought to underline my own deservingness. But still I walk through the streets this evening feeling alert to the yearning and fear, though there is no clamour in this city but instead eerie quiet. Passing down a lane, I hear a screeching sound and look up to see a woman closing a sash window. I smile at her, but she doesn't seem to see me.

Justine wants me to hail a Bug back from work each evening, but the walk is short, and I have only so long on this planet. The activities of my days will soon transform into a succession of *lasts*, though no one outside the company's top management knows when the transports will be going. The train is run north to the launch site each day to prevent our departure date becoming a focal point of unrest. Still, I saw on the news feeds video of a man in a village up north who goes out to protest the passing of every train in the possibility that that train should be carrying those of us leaving the planet. He is one of Dad's people, I suppose, though Dad himself is past protest, working on his allotment, organising mutual aid. SHAME! the man's sign reads.

A siren indicates the ten-minute warning for the curfew. I am up the hill now, next to the nice flats like my own. A well-dressed man emerges from a Bug and hurries to his doorway, where he squats to align his face with the iris scanner. Down an alley, which serves as access to old garage buildings, I see a bearded man in a long army jacket: not someone rushing home to avoid the curfew, but a guy who will try to tough it out, hiding from the police. Our eyes meet. He turns and shuffles away, clanking because he is the kind of man who picks salvageable items from rubbish and packs them into the bulging, grease-stained hiking pack that he wears.

I watch his limping retreat and think that he and I probably foresee the future in similar terms. I am fleeing, and he is hunkering down. Those I don't understand are the people at stations between us—the police, for instance, waiting for the clock to hit the hour, when they will begin their patrols in pursuit of a civic order that trickles through their fingers like sand.

Just shy of a month later—a Tuesday like any other Tuesday—the alert comes through. It's evening, and Justine and I are in the kitchen.

We know that it is the alert as soon as both our devices pulse at once. We look at each other. We have the same impulse to share the moment before the confirmation: a little space where things are not yet real, a breath together before we go over the edge. Love, I guess, after all these years. We are still saving each other. She comes to me and holds me. The pasta pot is boiling on the stove.

We're going. Tomorrow. We are leaving all of this; all we have known, all any of our ancestors have known. We're forsaking this air, this light, this earth. We are giving up all of it for one thing: for the other body, pressed against our own.

That night, Justine, to my amazement, is able to sleep. She has wanted this for a long time, I suppose. She is tantalised by the thought of space, the implausibility of it all. And I take heart from that. I sit awake in an armchair in the living room. It's June, close to midsummer, and the light turns into a blazing dusk and hardly dies before it is back again as a dawn, the start of my last day down here.

Justine is readier than I am. Since I secured my transport place, she has come into the corporation as a Shareholder, my Designated Partner. She was interviewed at great length, underwent endless medical tests. She has been assigned a role as a technologist in the Mining Division, and I wonder if the straightforwardness of her colleagues in this division has helped her acclimatise. On the first day, she reported back to me the words of her new boss: "Some folk want to be working on the glamorous shite—the rockets and the space suits—but let me tell you, we're the main fucking game up there. Those things need material dug out of the rock, and for the first five hundred years we're going to be a mining enterprise with a few living quarters on the side."

Justine and I laugh at those words. *The main fucking game*, we repeat to each other. Justine seems galvanised by the possibilities of her new job and by the challenges of mining a whole new planet. I try to meet her in her enthusiasm, to hold off the darker conclusions that might be drawn by her boss's frank assessment.

We both leave behind only fathers. Justine's mum died a few years ago now, but not so long past that she didn't hear the news that her daughter was *going*. She was lucid in that moment, and the memory is a good one: the old lady pointing up at the panel ceiling in the small hospice room and saying "We're both heading up there in our own ways . . ."

Now we have notification of our departure, we're forbidden from contacting anyone before the takeoff. After we're gone, the company will message relatives, sell our property, convert what is realised to M-coins. Our train will pass within a couple of miles of Justine's dad's house, but he'll be oblivious. He'll be pottering around his garden as he does each day. He carries a little snub-nosed handgun now because there have been disturbances in that area of the city. My dad is still in Edinburgh. We talk weekly, though things haven't been the same since the election. We speak only of simple day-to-day things, try to avoid the terrain of past arguments. We barely touch upon the downward spiral of his career. Maybe we should thrash out our issues, but it seems too much: structural work for which we are no longer equipped.

Justine and I have a dog now, Larry: a brown dachshund with pretty caramel spots on his little face. I have been granted one of the limited pet places on the journey (perhaps because I didn't take up my full family allocation). We acquired Larry six months ago, in time to train him. At first I was shocked by all he expected from us. He wanted attention. He would wake us in the night, and we would take him to pee on a little disposable paper pad. The next step would usually be to teach him to pee outside, on grass, but we're training him for a spaceship and then a Martian base. I have taken him outside, though. He loves the stench of the city in the summer. Justine has focused on teaching him to be inside, throwing the ball around the living room, showing him how to run on our treadmill. I worry about what he'll miss, whether it will be fair to keep him in the sparseness of a base. "He'll be okay," Justine has replied to my concern. "It'll be a fine life if we do it right."

Larry comes from the bedroom with the new light. I lift him up. As the dawn blooms, he lies curled in my lap drinking in his rest. I place my hand on his side—his soft fur, his ribs—and feel the beating of his little fervent heart.

The morning is like a play. We dress as if we really are going to work. We call a Bug, descend the musty stairwell for the last time. Justine talks about a meeting she is due to have later in the day—too much of a pretence, maybe, but we want to do things right.

At Headquarters, we take the foot tunnel to the company station. There is a crowd in the big space before the platform gates. I see Clem in the press of bodies ahead of me, and I raise my hand, though they don't seem to notice. They are looking down at their device and it strikes me that they are just themselves now, not professional as they are up in that lovely room in Headquarters, but another body in this mass of people all ringing with nerves. The crowd moves forwards slowly. Someone trying to pass the gate to the platform is stopped and led away. "I didn't mean to tell her!" he is saying, and I assume that he must have leaked news of his departure and that that leak has been traced and that—as we have been warned in the contracts we signed—such breaking of the terms of travel will preclude him having a place on this transport or any other. Around me, people keep their gazes averted from this man. A guy behind me whispers, "Stupid fucking bastard."

His friend or partner next to him clucks her tongue and says, "He'll be okay. He'll take one of the nice houses that we'll leave behind. Move north later, farm his own vegetables. Self-sufficiency. I'd even try it myself if my back wasn't so bad."

We need to indulge contradictory notions, I suppose: a recognition of the urgent necessity for our departure from this planet and also the belief that there is hope for those who stay. We need to think that we are not merely rushing for the lifeboats.

At the gate, Justine's iris is scanned and then she is through. My heart jumps to see her past the barrier, released to this future she has coveted. I shiver as my own eyes are scanned. After what seems a very long time, a soft ping confirms my passage.

The train itself is hushed. Classical music plays. A man moves through the carriage with a breakfast buffet cart. I sit across a small table from Justine. She lays down a folded blanket for Larry at the foot of this table, and he lies quiet but still alert. In this, the little dog mimics the other passengers. I recognise a few people from work in the carriage, but I don't know most of the other travellers. Waiting to access the platform, I did see a couple of government ministers. Justine and I accept coffee from the buffet man. We take pastries. No one around us chooses the cooked breakfast that the man offers.

Then, quite suddenly, the train is moving. I look up to see the sky shifting behind the domed glass roof, the webbed beams that hold it up seeming to move now.

We follow the river at first, a high stone wall to our right. Then the track peels up and away from the water. We traverse the outskirts of the city above the street, at the level of second-floor windows of old tenement houses. Faces are sometimes visible from living rooms, kitchens. Scraggy trees line the railway banking, stroking sky. We cut past industrial units, flash through underpasses. I realise that we must be as near as we will ever be again to Justine's dad. Then we are out into fields. We move towards distant hills. The open sky does something to my heart. I haven't left the city in two years. Justine sits opposite, shadows passing over her face. She smiles at me tightly. I smile back.

I sit and try to master myself, seeking to halt these small farewells, to forestall the yearning occasioned by the threaded lanes and paths that I will now never walk. Larry sleeps stretched out on his blanket. Justine holds my hand across the table.

The train passes through the Cairngorms. I look at the rounded mountains, dry and patchy looking. I see a flash of red, then realise it is him: the man with his sign—SHAME!, in livid letters. I gasp a little at the sight, strangely glad for the fact that the man actually managed to come out for us. I feel a funny, almost welcome, ache in my chest. Justine is reading something on her device and no one else in the carriage seems to have noticed the small figure in the field now left behind.

We climb incrementally upwards until the Findhorn Viaduct, where for a moment we seem to be taking flight over the coiled river beneath. The train descends towards Inverness, through uneven forests of pine.

I have done this part of the route many times before. The viaduct we passed over is nearly two hundred years old. I know because Dad told me often. He worked with planners renovating it, making it safe for the passage of high-speed trains. This was the route that we'd take to the island house when I was a kid. At Inverness, however, we take a different branch of the line. We're heading directly north, to the spaceport. I can only fitfully hold to the thought that these are my last glimpses of the world.

At the Cromarty Firth I am struck by a pang because we are out on a bridge whirring over the water and I realise that I will never see the sea after today. It's such a fine day out here. A little wind blows west, lifting riffles of white froth in an expanse of blue that is light-shot, dappled, a great shield beneath us. Justine seems to understand the involuntary noise I make, because she says, "It looks nice, right? But even if we stay, that's gone one day . . ."

I nod.

She says, "Acidification. Ecosystem collapse . . ."

"Yes," I say. "I know. You're right. It's just . . ."

"Yes."

I will never swim in the sea again. Obvious. But still . . . Then we are back over land, a change in tone to the humming of the train. A village flashes past, fields, sheep. A narrow road rises to a crest and drops out of view.

Farther down the carriage, a woman's voice is speaking unsteadily, recording a message for someone left behind. It will be delivered later, via the Corporation's communication channel. The woman talks to her brother, from what I can ascertain. Everyone in the carriage is listening, I sense. "I'll be on my way when you hear this. I just wanted to say . . ." There's a long silence. The wind hums around the carriage. The suspension of the train creaks as we lean into a turn. "Well . . . I suppose, that I'm thinking of you. Yes. I will be thinking of you." The woman is all of us, I think. She speaks with the fear that we are all trying to control. I try to imagine her face. I think that she has come to the end of the message, but after another long silence she inhales and says ". . . if that's a comfort to you. If that is any kind of comfort at all."

A few months ago, I broke the unspoken agreement that Dad and I had reached not to talk of the future. I wanted to explain the way that he and I could exchange messages once Justine and I had departed. I said that we would be able to send and receive communications on a thirty-minute delay, subject to data limits and the Corporation's right to screen out viruses and misinformation. Dad had been so quiet on the line that I wondered whether the call had failed, but then he said, "Kenz, I'm sorry. But when you're gone, I have to think of you as gone." I asked what he meant, and he said, "I won't be able to keep writing to you." I let myself feel angry then. Maybe that was his intention. Perhaps that was best for us. Perhaps it *would* be easier if we allowed a rift to grow between us.

I said, "So I lose my family now?"

"No," Dad said. "I'll still send my love. I just can't . . ."

I sighed.

He said, "You've chosen to go there . . ." I think that he stopped because what he was readying to say was too stark. I had made my choice, and now I was to be cut off from him, compartmentalised. But now, on the train, I look at Justine ahead of me, her expression calm in a way it has seldom been in recent years, and I think that he was right. Of course I have chosen.

The carriage is utterly quiet now. We're going fast. We're far north, nearly at the tip of the country. The coast is to our right, and then quite abruptly we are peeling away from the water, losing sight of the bright blue to dunes, bunchgrass. I crane for a last view of the sea. The dunes fall away as we cross an estuary: clear water over braided patterns of silt. Out where the low waves break is a child running with a dog, a lithe silhouette against the bright sand and shining water. Then the train line wrenches away definitively, west over the mainland, across flat peat bogs, past low forests. It is still bright here, open. A murmur comes from elsewhere in the carriage as someone sees it. It takes me a moment. I catch it only as the train moves around a wide bend: a great white thing, standing in its dock like a huge silo. We begin to slow as we approach.

16

ANDREW

2087

The train hasn't been running for three years now, and so I travel to the island with the assistance of a network of friends: men and women with private vehicles charged off-grid by panels, windmills, hydroturbines. There is even one guy—James—who charges batteries by burning peat. At James's place, a shack in a secluded valley beneath Beinn Dearg, I watch him stoking this furnace, hefting squares of cake-like soil into the big metal drum, which will make the steam to spin a little turbine. James wears filthy overalls and swears as he works. He batters away midges from what little of his face is exposed between his thick beard and dreadlocked hair. James is a friend of an old university friend of mine. I have a memory of going to a party at James's student flat forty years ago. It was a little place off Cockburn Street, too good a location, really, to have been a student apartment. One climbed a winding stairway from the busy cobbled street, up to a bedroom with a window which gave onto a tiny piece of flat roof in a valley between sloping slate-clad gables. All the party guests sat out on this flat roof, from where we could hear the tourists on the street below and the vehicles coming and going from the station down the hill. It felt like the top of the city in that little hollow, leaning back against the slope of the slates, and I remember staying until the sun rose out by Portobello and the gulls arrived to swirl the sky and descend on takeaway scraps left behind by the post-pub crowd. It sounds like another world, of course; an era of plenty we didn't fully appreciate. James was studying English, I believe, though now, in this tepid October, neither of us speaks of this history. James works at the furnace, and I, at a loss as to how I might assist, drink a cup of the coffee that I brought with me to barter as I make my journey.

It's a long time since I've been near an open fire. The shack itself is murky, heated by more peat burnt in an ancient cast-iron stove. Everything is soiled with smoke. James must generate the emissions of a factory. None of it matters now, of course. People have been vocalising such a sentiment for years, and I've been resisting it, but now even I struggle to object. I experience only a sadness at the unsubtle symbolism of it all. The peat forked into the outdoor furnace is part of the very system that could have saved everything. People like Mum and Kenzie were obsessed with technology, with getting energy for nothing, or with finding a perfect solution for carbon storage. Yet this peat had been sucking in carbon for millennia, part of a system of balance that we could have striven to renew. As it is, the bogs are collapsing anyway, with the changing temperatures, droughts, and invasive shrubs sapping the land.

At dinnertime, we eat rabbit stew. I sleep fitfully. The next morning, James drives me in an old electric four-by-four to the coast. We cut up back roads before Loch Broom. The old train is parked along the water's edge, a couple of miles outside Ullapool. It's now the living quarters of a ragged community that James suggests is best avoided. The last of the police retreated to the Central Belt two years ago. "It'll get messy up here soon enough," says James as he drives, his eyes on the narrow road ahead.

At the bay, I hand over the last of my luxuries—coffee, chocolate, weed, and soap—to a contact of James's who owns a small boat. The man, Alasdair, throws the bounty into his living space: a shipping crate, dropped between dunes and furnished like a tiny apartment. He closes the crate and secures it with three big locks. He pounds the door and it clangs, the noise reverberating within the metal box, bouncing out over the dunes.

The sea is cold and choppy. We bump through the breakers. I look back to see James's Toyota climbing the narrow road that threads back towards his shack. Sitting at the stern, steering the outboard, Alasdair wears an ancient yellow fisherman's jacket and a baseball cap that says STAFF on it. Unlike James or myself, he seems to have found the means and resolution to shave regularly. He chews gum, or something like gum, and spits into the sea at intervals. There's some dilapidated-looking fishing equipment tucked under the gunwale. He sees me looking and says, "There's fuck-all to catch, but I try sometimes anyway."

"You've got to hope, I suppose," I say.

"Maybe."

"I used to fish mackerel when I was a kid, but I was never good at it. I didn't like having to kill the fish."

Alasdair levels a steady stare. "It's not a good time to be squeamish."

"I know that."

The man's goodwill is not assured. Out here on the boat, I'm at his mercy. But we do chug on, approaching the island, navigating the swells and waves as the little craft nears the beach.

I wrestle on my rucksack and jump into knee-high water. I wade through the breakers. I feel Alasdair watching me like a dog regarding a morsel he is unsure about eating. I spin to face this look then, taking it in, trying to stay calm. I turn back again towards the sand and pace as easily as I can up the beach, until I hear the revving of the propeller and then the sound of the boat's hull slapping over waves.

The prickling at the back of my neck gradually reduces to the more general crackling, ambient dread of these days. It's the background now: threat, encroachment. It has grown to this point over years. In the flat in the city, the new ways manifested first as ordinary selfishness: the neighbours who played music all night, the guy who turned the communal tenement garden into a private junk-trading business. The sentiment—sometimes vocalised, sometimes left unsaid—was, *What are you going to do about it?* The bits of government that were left had other objectives than policing relations between citizens. This insidious question floated about, spoken or implied. *Nothing*, is the most common answer, and one doesn't want to be the one having to cough it up. (Nor, in fact, do I ever want to be tempted into prompting it, seduced into taking a thing because I can.)

I walk west, sometimes following the shore, sometimes—where the water is too high, or the way is blocked by cliffs—trekking up and over rocky moorland. A few sick-looking sheep lope about. Some of the people are reverting to the old ways where circumstances allow: subsistence livestock farming, nursing up crops that can survive the changeable weather. On my first evening back on the island, at dusk, I look down from a ridgeline animal track to see figures with large baskets out on a beach harvesting seaweed. I cut inland farther. I'm not a libertarian, not so certain strangers should be hostile. People are more often kind than they are calculating. But I am so tired, unequipped to test the truth of my own logic.

I sleep that night without a fire, in a bivvy bag in a hollow beneath two large boulders. The bracken surrounding the mouth of the hollow crackles and whispers in the wind. When I wake, my old bones aching, the ground crunches under my step and there's a thin film of ice on the puddles.

I leave the coast as I cross the body of the island, avoiding people as much as possible. I break cover only to come through the village in which I used to shop when staying at the cottage. I walk down the street, feeling myself observed from curtained windows.

In the small village store, the watchful old proprietor takes an exorbitant sum for a bottle of milk.

I sleep in an abandoned shed next to a radio tower. I wake and walk towards the west coast of the island.

A little after midday, I glimpse the sea again. I see birds, far off, which I can't identify, but which lift my heart. They're still finding food, I suppose.

It starts to snow. When I finally come to the crest on the narrow lane where I can gain a vantage of the cottage, it is nearly lost in the whiteness blanketed around it. My fingers burn and my feet are blocks of ice, but I still linger at the top of the hill, feeling a leaping relief to be arriving at the house. From here, the place looks as it always has done and I savour the feeling that all is in order. Still, it will only be on entering the house that its soundness can be confirmed, my childish dream of refuge truly tested.

Yet, when I reach it, the house is as I left it a year before. The shutters are still closed over the downstairs windows. The old key, which I have worn on a cord around my neck like a totem, turns smoothly in the lock. Inside, I walk through the dim, dusty rooms. Upstairs, the unshuttered windows shine whitely as the damp snow keeps burying the land. There is no electricity, of course, but remarkably the windmill that I installed twenty years before is intact. I fold out the retractable blades and set it running. This should generate the power necessary to run the lights and to charge my device. I replaced the reserve batteries of the electrical system a few years previously, and I am very glad of this. I am even more thankful that I never got around to ripping out the woodstove after Mum died. In the shed I find a shelf, which I break up and carry back into the living room to pile onto the grate. I light a fire. With this heat, with the reawakening of my limbs, I really feel the pain of these days of travelling.

When I am able to raise myself from the fusty sofa, I find a few old tins of soup and beans in the kitchen. I open a can of potato-and-leek soup and let it heat on the top of the stove, starting on it when it is only lukewarm and abrading my knuckles on the rim of the tin as I dig in my spoon.

I sleep. I wake in the dark. The fire has gone out, but the room is still warmer than the places where I slept during previous nights. I put on my boots and tramp to the shed, where I find a child's school desk. I prise the top from the desk and snap it under my foot. I drag the pieces into the house and push them into the stove. I can't keep living this way—burning through furniture—but the room heats and I only wake again when there is light coming through the shutters.

I put the last of the wood in the fire and then eat another can of soup. When I go outside, the snow is turning to slush. Water pools in the footprints I leave behind. Down at the bay, the tide withdraws, leaving a crescent of biscuit-coloured sand that stands out from the white landscape and dark rocks around.

I go to the shed and locate a spade. I make a space on the concrete floor on which to dry chunks of peat. Outside, I clear a patch of snow and begin to dig, portioning the bits of earth like brownies, piling those neat squares into towers, which I then carry into the shed. As I'm working, I feel the prickling on my neck rise. I look up to see a vehicle approaching along the road from the rough track south. It is too late to flee or hide, I think. I watch the pickup swaying as it makes its way through the ruts. It stops next to the cottage. The man at the wheel is the farmer, Jim McHugh. Jim lowers the window. He's wearing khaki overalls. His beard is trimmed short as usual, his thinning grey hair cropped as it has always been. "You're here, then," he says.

"Yes," I say. I approach the pickup slowly, still holding the spade.

"Aye." Jim nods. "We were thinking you might come soon."

"Yes."

"The city is probably not . . ." Jim trails off.

"Yes."

"We watched this place," says Jim. He nods at the cottage.

"Thank you," I say. I feel like weeping, and for what? For the man's plain decency? I've barely spoken more than a few sentences with Jim McHugh before, but maybe that is the way with a man like Jim. I feel regretful of the way I skulked here.

"We'll keep an eye on each other, eh?" says Jim.

"We will."

"There's some fuckers about."

"Yes."

"Well," says Jim. "I'll see you around."

"You're going to the town?"

Jim nods. "Seeing if I can find painkillers for Miriam."

"Right."

"She's not well."

"I'm sorry to hear." The window rises before I can say anything more. The pickup pulls away and joins the tarmacked section of the lane, leaving behind parallel lines of slush, through which the surface of the road shows greyish blue.

When I've dug and stored a decent quantity of peat, I turn my attention to my other problem: food. I have some money, and I can travel to the village shop, perhaps even ask Jim to bring some things back for me in the pickup. But the shop's inventory will surely be too limited to rely on. There's the possibility of buying meat and what produce can be grown here from the farmers, though that supply will be changeable. I think of the men I saw harvesting seaweed. The time will come for that, and I'll need to know how to pick it and how to prepare it. I can try trapping rabbits, as James does in his little glen. Though I know I shouldn't, I eat another can of soup for late lunch. I chew the soft lumps of potato and carrot and I think that these thoughts of provisioning are hard because they prompt me to consider my objectives, my prospects. The game is not to survive forever, I suppose. The game is to survive as long as it's worth it.

For the first time, I really understand Mum's love for her dogs out here. Jasper's little memorial cairn still stands behind the house. With a dog, yes, feeding would be an issue, but I would have a companion, another set of eyes and ears.

I fall asleep on the sofa for a time. I rise and go outside. I look towards the sea. The snow has melted further, and patches of grass, bracken, and rock are reemerging. The day is dim now, dragging into evening. In the shed, water has seeped from the stacks of peat, dampening the concrete floor. Behind them are a pile of rusty tools, some odd bits of furniture, and a set of Land Rover tires, so ancient now that the rubber has cracked and crazed. At the rear of the shed is the trapdoor that accesses the basement steps. It's mad to have put a basement in this rocky land, but Mum did it at great cost when she first moved here full-time, employing a couple of island men long dead now. I haven't cleaned it out since Mum died, though Kenzie, as I recall, organised most of the notebooks. For now, the trapdoor is hidden by a twisted plastic sheet and a few bags of cement. I clear the things and I pull on the door. The hinges resist at first and then open with a whine. The air as I descend into it is icy, as if I am lowering myself into a pool. There is a smell of chill stone. At the bottom of the steps, my way is blocked by a stack of cardboard boxes. The cardboard is in perfect condition. Mum would have done things properly when making this space, damp-proofed it.

I carry the boxes back up the steps, breathing evenly, trying not to strain my back. When I look inside, I find they are packed with notebooks full of notations that I recognise as my mother's but have no chance of understanding. Kenzie did, though. Kenzie has copies of these pages,

I think, where she is. Up there. I can't sit with this thought, so instead I try to focus on the book in my shaking hand. There are diagrams, too abstract to really comprehend. There are also little sketches in the margins at different points in the books: tiny worked-over pictures that seem to have nothing to do with the jumble of text next to them. There is a fine sketch of a fern, a picture of a shell. I flick through another book and find a sketch of a gull standing on a rock. In another book is a strange drawing of a boy's face. I wonder whether it is my face, but though it looks a little like me the eyes are quite different. The drawings are all so carefully executed. She was serious, even in her doodling. I remember that she was very particular about the pens she'd use, would always order a special kind of fine-line made in Japan. I sit on the steps and think back more than half a century to being in the kitchen here, perched on the bench seat next to the window, my face barely higher than the surface of the table, which I gripped for balance as I looked across the expanse of wood at my mother writing something, her fingers squeezing the pen so that the tips of her forefinger and thumb are yellowish white. The light was flooding through the room, but she didn't look at the view or at me clinging to the table. She stared at the notebook in front of her. Perhaps she was sketching then. She loved the world, I think, but differently, not as I have. It has taken me a lifetime to allow her this.

I approach the door of the shed and draw it creakingly open. The sun is down and the sky is dark blue. The snow is half-melted, holding on in uneven patches that pattern the landscape like winter camouflage. I hear a vehicle on the road, which I can't see from the door of the shed. I make no effort to check who is approaching. It will be Jim, I think. And if it isn't Jim, then it will be a person I will have to face one day anyway.

I close the shed door, push the bolt across it from the inside. I should be lighting the fire in the living room again, but I'm drawn back to the cellar. I've cleared a space to move past the boxes now. The cellar is also lit by a single bulb. It's about a third of the floor space of the shed above, merely two or three meters in each direction. The ceiling is very low. The walls bulge where the workmen dug around immovable rocks. What a strange battle it must have been to make this place. But then, Mum was already regarded as odd when she began this work. The area is filled with yet more boxes. These hold old physics textbooks and bound academic journals, their pages yellow and as crisp as rice paper. My heart leaps to find a box of the Japanese pens, though when I take one out and draw it across the margin of a journal it makes nothing but a furrow on the dry page. An odd thought: *She has made herself a burial chamber*, furnished with her things. On a workbench against the wall are stacked bits of metal: joints and mechanical components which appear to be parts of the old Land Rover, but which on inspection seem to be something else entirely. There are sets of computer chips, wires, lengths of hydraulic hosing. Did she manufacture some machinery herself? An experimental apparatus? I was so sure in the end that her aims were chimerical, that she was chasing phantoms.

There's a stool, which I drag to the middle of the room and sit on. I feel exhausted. I should return to the house. It is all too much to take in. At the end of her life, she drifted. It was harder to follow what she said. Her hands shook. I moved her to a home on the mainland after her fall, and for that last year of her life she begged me to return here, though I wouldn't let her. I regret it. I see the value of choosing one's final place now.

This was where she wanted to be, and I didn't allow her that. The stool is wobbly and shakes as I sit slumped and as my chest begins to heave. I cry for regret—yes—but also for release: all the tension of my journey here, decisions, calculations.

I cry for a long time. I wipe my face with my sleeve.

There are yet more boxes at one end of the room that I haven't started on. They're more broken-down than the others. I set to opening one, and the tape on the top peels away easily. Inside are things I recognise instantly: battered old metal cars, which were once my grandfather's, then my father's, then mine. I move that box and open another beneath it, and here are childhood books of mine. Another holds a collage I once made of a house standing on a clifftop above the sea. They are all my things, the boxes, and I think—well—that this part is not *her* tomb. I shift more, find novels that I owned as a teenager, an old pair of my hiking boots, a set of printed photographs that I took of the tiny beach. She saved all this: For herself? For me to find one day? Behind the pile of boxes are a set of built-in cupboards. I shift the boxes until I am able to lever open one of the wooden doors. I feel an impulse to look behind me.

I feel observed. It is like a dream, in which everything is too fitted to my needs, in which what I see is just a projection of my desires, like a mirage. The cupboard is stacked with pallets of tinned food: soups, pulses, chopped vegetables, tomatoes, fruit in syrup, custard. I turn and look at the deserted cellar. This is for me, I'm sure. I put out a hand and touch a can and it is real. She knew somehow that I would end up here. I see a tin of the rice pudding that I used to love so much as a child, that I ate at that kitchen table in the cottage. The text on the labels is faded and outdated. She must have acquired this decades ago, put it here before I dragged her from this place to die amongst strangers. How did she predict my need, my hunger right now? I spent my life feeling that she wasn't my mother as she should have been, and yet here she is, parenting posthumously. To the side of the cans, I find two crates of whisky, and a box full of medications, soap, and toothpaste. The crates are stacked three-deep. This will last me years, if I last that long myself.

I pull out a bottle of whisky, a tin of pasta and meatballs in tomato sauce, a tin of peas, some rice pudding. I stumble back up the cellar stairs cradling the bounty. I turn off the light. In the house, I light the stove with the last of the wood from the school desk. I tear the labels from the tins and burn them as the flames get going. I heat the meatballs and peas. I put them into a shallow pasta bowl. I feel compelled to do things properly. I eat greedily. My stomach groans and turns at the plenty, but I open the rice pudding anyway. The taste—the gummy, bland sweetness—makes me a child again. I scrape the bowl, and only when I'm done do I feel myself once more a tired man in his sixties, persisting, cowering at the edge of a broken land.

I drink a lot of the whisky. I get drunk and tired, though this weariness is a strange kind which does not incline me to sleep. I lie on the sofa and look up at the ceiling of the living room: the cracked plaster, a patch of white paint flaked away to reveal a previous coat of creamy yellow.

My device is on the table, and I lift my chin to look at it. It sits inert, black and slick: a little stone I should just skim into the sea. I have had flashes of signal out here, but nothing reliable. On the home screen is the saved video I must have watched a hundred times at least: the little boy with livid pink skin in a white hospital ward, wailing at the shock of his own birth.

The video came a year and a half ago from Justine. I was in the flat, and the fighting on the Continent was further off. The migrant crises hadn't fully hit, and the militias had not mobilised. They were easy, slightly frivolous times, I now think. People still worried about the lack of toilet paper.

I remember watching the video for the first time on the ancient sofa that Lina and I once chose together, that had to be re-covered when Kenzie spilled a bowl of soy ramen over it. The subject of the message said only, "You're a grandfather." The content of the email was just the film of the boy, in this perfectly white place, and Kenzie there in bed, smiling groggily at her wife, who was taking the video.

I watched it until I knew every breath and word by heart: Justine saying, "How are you both?" Kenzie's whispered reply. The boy's grasp, and gurgle. The pause of a few seconds before the child would break into an earsplitting cry.

Yet I didn't write back. It was all happening in another place. A place I wasn't able to acknowledge. The video does something to my insides, but I don't let that overpower my resolve. I can't think of her and her wife and the boy up there, in their sterile little base on their huge desolate planet. Human life is here, only. I must believe that, because if I didn't I couldn't now keep going, couldn't understand my own position. I am at the end of history here, one of the last of the real humans, seeing things out.

I watch again and then again. Five times. I drink more whisky. I look at the cracked ceiling, making out patterns in the fissures.

I loved her so much, but it went wrong somewhere. I would love the boy too, I know. She will be a great parent. She is so serious, dedicated. But that is all a counterfactual.

In the morning, I walk along the lane to bring Jim and his wife some painkillers from the basement store. I carry a bottle of whisky too. The lane hugs the hillside, above the sea breaking and spluttering against rocks. Maybe it's a risk to give such gifts, such hints of the plenty I've found. I walk into the yard in front of the farmhouse. I note Jim watching from an upper window. At the door, he takes the pills and whisky with evident relish. He grips the bottle and looks at it and says, "I didn't used to drink, but it all helps." At the threshold, I feel the warm air of the house moving past me. The house has a specific smell, as strangers' houses do. I walk back along the lane. Jim's scrawny sheep, up on the hill above, bleat and cry over the pounding of the surf.

I dig peat. I walk to the beach. I eat my tinned meals. Jim brings me some cured lamb. The meat is salty and covered with foul grease, but I get through it.

The nights draw in and some days are overcast and the sun seems barely to rise at all. Snow comes and melts and comes and melts again.

Then there is a rain followed by a freeze and everywhere is black ice and I fall walking from the shed and the blow causes my wrist to swell to twice its size. I drink to fall asleep that first night, but after a few days the pain diminishes to manageable levels. I can move the arm stiffly. I plan to survive the winter, to see the turn in the year again. This simple goal is enough for now. I will choose another if I need it. Everything smells of burnt peat. I read old paper books. I watch the video. Sometimes the device gains signal and I'm able to get scraps of news.

On the shortest day, I put on two thick coats and walk down the snowy track to the beach. I look out at the water while sipping whisky from the bottle. I watch the sun descend, blessing it as it does. The next day will be longer, and even now there is hope to be found in this. The wind is high on the beach. The surface of the sea is chopped with waves and specked by the marks of icy drizzle. I wrap my coats tightly around me and huddle near the cliff next to the path up to the house. The rock here is crusted with ice and frozen snow. I can hear the faint trickle of the stream beneath this crust. Hoping to make a place to sit, I brush snow from a flat space with my glove. I knock a frozen piece of peaty earth away and in the dark revealed dirt is something glinting. I put down the whisky bottle and scrabble impulsively, prise a little disc of metal from the dirt. It is caked with earth. Fibres stick from it. I brush at the object and realise as the earth comes away that it is a watch, the parts sticking from it the remnants of a rotten leather strap.

It is shocking to find such a relic here, more so because it looks so like the watch that Mum used to have. I take off my gloves and use my nails to work the dirt away. I am frantic. The watch is gold just like Mum's. It's the same model, I am sure. I turn it over and my heart seems to halt completely as I see that it is cracked on the face just as Mum's watch was.

How? I ask myself then. Kenzie has the watch, has worn it since Mum's death. Could she have left it here, lost it here? Surely not?

The crack is exactly as it was on Mum's: a webbing of thin lines like mist at the top of the dial. I loved to study this damage to her watch as a child, remember doing so at the kitchen table in the cottage. "Why don't you fix it?" I would ask her. She would merely shake her head, inscrutable.

Something chimes within me. I take my device from my pocket and run the video. I watch Kenzie mouthing the words I know, catch a flash of gold behind the right hand she holds up to support the head of her child. I slow the footage, pinch, and zoom. My breath fogs the screen of the device, held too close. It is unmistakable: the watch, the strap. Up there. Not *here*. I look at the watch, the *same* watch, that I have placed down on the sand, dirty and burnished.

I feel what now? The great yawn of my own ignorance, I suppose. *How?* I think again. I think that maybe I have only understood half of anything, known life only in glimpses. I think of the food in the basement of the shed, locked away for me. My limbs feel very heavy.

Maybe there is a way to work this out as a coincidence—the same model of watch . . . a crack in the same place made in different circumstances . . . But I don't believe this. I was *supposed* to find this watch, I think. I feel a stuckness, an animal bafflement. It is all beyond me. Was this always going to happen? My presence here? My failure here? Have I blundered through my life in vain?

I think of Lina then, though. I remember those last days with her: her living eyes in her dying face, her soft voice filling the bright, quiet flat. We chose to live in days then, and the days were good in their way. Was it so bad to be blinkered? What could we have done but what we thought best at the time? I turn and the sea is suddenly bright with the last of the sun, which has slipped from the cover of the clouds now, which scuds its glow low over the waves. I was content in my resolve, I tell myself. Fulfilled. I have lived this way because I chose to, felt I must.

Just as Mum did, I think.

In the days after the solstice, I feel the presence of my mother. The drawers and cupboards are still organised as she used them. The scissors swing on the nail that she tapped in, the shoe rack waits by the kitchen door where she would put on her boots to walk the dog. I feel a love I didn't have access to before. She was doing what she thought necessary out here. I understand that better. I feel benevolently haunted by her. If we have been lost, we were lost in a similar way, I think. A life is not an equation, I tell myself; not a thing made or broken by its end.

Jim comes and raps on the door. I can tell before he says so that Miriam has died. I visit the spot where he has buried her, on the slope above the house. There are rocks piled over the mound of earth. "It's a mercy, I suppose," Jim says.

Signal comes and goes on the device. From the news I get, it sounds like the capital is collapsing. I hear from Jim that the shop in town has stopped accepting cash, becoming instead a location in which people barter what they have. It can't be long, I think, until the communication networks fail.

Spring still breaks, though. I'm walking to the beach and I feel the sun warm on my face. The snow retreats, until it merely caps the peaks. The days lengthen. I don't write to Kenzie.

I count the days since I last had signal on the device and realise that it has been a month. I haven't seen Jim for nearly as long either. Each evening I tell myself that tomorrow I will go to the farm. But I don't.

Often I'm happy; standing in the sun, walking near the water, clambering over rocks.

One morning, I wake and look out the window and it appears to have snowed again. I put on a coat and go outside, but the air is not cold, and the white on the landscape is not snow, but a dusting of ash. There is a foul, burning chemical smell on the air. I rub the ash in my hands and it turns my fingers grey. I go back into the house and the ash falls for four days, and on the fifth day I walk down to the sea with the ash still falling, because what else is there to do? When I reach the beach, I look over the water and I see out beyond the islands a giant old ship. I return to the cottage and periodically use binoculars to look from the bedroom window at the boat. The next day, a smaller boat is lowered from this big one. It begins to make its way towards the coast. The ash has stopped falling, and the sky is now a colour—an oily greenish blue—that I've never seen before.

The boat is approaching the beach below the house, and I can make out figures aboard. I put the binoculars down before it gets too close, though, before I can study these people, the implements they carry. I look at my device, on impulse, but of course there is no signal. It is just me, now, just this.

17

ROBAN

2110

Things return, circle back. I ruminate on language as I did when I was a child and was making my dictionary. One word in particular. I am on *indefinite* leave and I turn that adjective around like a puzzle piece: a simple way to say unspecified, or, on the other hand, an empty echoing silo, containing *until tomorrow*, containing also *forever.*

Today Mum comes over to my desk at work. Normally she moves through the lab without acknowledging me. That is Mum in all her conscientiousness: so keen to avoid treating me preferentially that she usually blanks me. Yet this afternoon she leans across my bench and says, "Shall we go to OldTownSquare this evening?"

This is a gesture on her part, an attempt to connect, to drag me to the light. I came past the preparations in the morning: technicians fitting a new illumination module to the Simi-Sky and setting out a rectangle in the middle of the node. Our information feeds have been clogged with notifications about the event. It's the Colony's first lawn, the first purely recreational green space. I don't really want to attend, but watching the way that Mum smiles firmly, with too much effort, I decide that I will go for her.

We reach the OldTownSquare twenty minutes before the lawn will be unveiled. The space is as busy as I've ever seen it. The crowd stretches up the lanes of EatTown and into the connecting transitways. Mum and I nudge forwards until we can at least glimpse the rectangle in the middle of the square, covered with a thin white cloth. The spectators, mostly Homers, stand shoulder to shoulder. I wonder whether this is what Home was like in Terrestrial History, when people struggled and fought and rubbed together. There is a raised podium behind the sheeted lawn. Homers in the colours of the Corporation Administration move around the base of that small stage. A few other First Gens stand out in their Exos. There is a giddiness rising from those unsuited: happy chatter, smiles cast around. This is nostalgia for them, I guess. At the podium, Myers M, the Corporation's acting CEO, climbs the steps and clasps the lectern. He clears his throat in an odd mewling way and then begins to speak of the next stage of development here, of the transformation of the place into a world of plenty and beauty. His amplified voice echoes from the walls of EatTown. He is a pale man, bald but for patches of white hair above his ears, and beneath the new light for the lawn he looks washed-out. Yet his translucence seems appropriate. He is like a hologram of himself already, speaking prophetically of the future. The faces of the Homers around me are beatific, thrilled to hear the comfortable myths repeated, the dreams they were sold reaffirmed. Mum stands ahead of me, so I cannot see her expression, but I notice that her left hand is clasped across her body, grasping the cloth of her sweatshirt at the shoulder and pulling it into a little knot as she listens.

After Myers, it is the turn of Virginia Faulk to speak. I recall the medal this woman once gave me. I think of the space out in the plain where it is buried. Vishay, my witness to that moment, is gone. It could almost be a dream now. Virginia Faulk speaks haltingly in her strange elderly voice. "A new stage," she croaks. "The future. What is to come. A pleasure."

She rings a little bell. The white sheet is pulled back, revealing the lawn in the glare of the spotlights.

We catch only glimpses. The crowd jostles. We wait for a long time, shuffle forwards as others who have seen the lawn depart. I stand behind Mum, shielding her. People shout at those behind them to stop pushing, and those they address say that they too are being pushed in turn.

It is a shock when we finally reach the barrier and see the green just metres away. I glance at Mum, who is sniffing the air. I can't smell much in my suit. "I remember that smell," says Mum. I'm about to ask her to say more when I see that the man to my left is holding up his wrist input in an odd posture, trying to disguise the fact that he is directing its lens towards me. I turn to look at him, and he moves too quickly, gives himself away in the guilty manner in which he draws back his arm. He is short. He has long grey hair, a big reddish nose with a mole on the side. A retired Homer. Maybe back on Home he was a businessman, a politician. He has the look of someone who scraped here, the kind of man in retirement from the apocalypse. He knits his grey eyebrows, pretending to concentrate on the grass ahead. He was filming me to have a video to send out to his friends. I can imagine the caption already, something along the lines of "First Gen Sees Grass for the First Time." I look behind him, to a Homer woman, who smiles back at me. *They think that they are giving us the greatest gift*. I turn to the grass: a square of green like a rug but rougher. I can imagine Vishay's voice in my mind, speaking of the terrestrial grasslands as he floated over them, the shadows of clouds on the green surface. So much. I look at the green and cannot help but ask myself, *How does this become a world?* Mum says, "I wish we could walk on it."

"Yes," I say.

Mum appears to read my mood. She says, "Shall we go?"

"That would be nice."

We turn to fight our way out of the crowd, and suddenly it is almost unbearable: the crush of them around us, the way that they grin condescendingly. I push people away from Mum as we move, and I must check myself to not do so with violence. Then we are out in the clear transitway and I feel my hands twitching and I think that I just want to run in my Exterior Exo as I used to while training on the base.

In the night, I wake to the dream: darkness and the sound of my breath, the giddy feeling that I am drifting. Of course, the dream is the dream of the asteroid, the cave, the systems failure. I half know this in the dream itself. My body recognises this panic now, yet the recursion exacerbates the terror, as in a room of mirrors. It's a nauseating sort of infinity. I have had night upon night of this. I come to in my dark room. A solemn line of light from the living area breaks through the gap between my door and its frame: a single stripe that lays itself over the floor, my desk, and the wall.

What is this life? I think.

I used to dream of Home—borrowed visions from Vishay—and now I just dream of that lurch to darkness. Once it made the hairs on my forearms rise to imagine Earth rolling beneath me. I recall the lawn again and find myself sickened once more to imagine that the Board members think their square of hemmed-in green recompense for all our loss. I recall Virginia Faulk's strange croaky voice. Do they never doubt? Never regret?

I get up. I stagger to the main living area. Often Mum is still up at this time, writing in her journal. Yet today the room is empty, the light low. I approach the table, bracing myself against the wall as I move. There is a damp ring on the surface where Mum's cup of tea stood recently. Her journal will be packed away where she keeps it in the drawer beneath the chiller unit.

We don't talk of this journal. Even for a Homer, writing by hand is perverse, interpretable as a ploy to keep what is written from the OS. There are five books, and she has filled four of them in both directions. She completes a journal and then turns it over and works the other way, writing in the spaces between the lines. She told me this was how people used to save paper far back in Terrestrial History. Now she is working on a second pass through book number five. I don't know what she will do when she is finished.

My throat is dry. I go to the kitchen for a glass of water. I drink braced against the counter and the cold water makes my throat clench and throb. I stand until the feeling passes. I look at the drawer, the *journal drawer*, as I think of it.

I have always felt the tug of it, I suppose. Previously, I've been wary. It seems too much to take on: all that was, all that I've missed. Maybe I once thought Mum's old stories irrelevant, indulgent nostalgia even. But this lack of interest was self-protection. I'm not sure I could have managed to understand her losses.

I feel regretful of the times I doubted her attitude. I haven't been fair. I should have tried to know her better. Is it a desire to compensate for this failing that I balance against the trespass of reading these journals in the night? Is that reasonable? I don't know. The drawer whispers open easily. The journals are stacked. I pick them up. I take the bottom one, which I assume to be the oldest, replace the rest. I slide to the floor of the kitchen. I take a breath, open the book.

But then nothing. I can't read it. I can just about make out the numbers at the top: the date in Terrestrial calendar. Then just tortured scribbles, lines. I study it for a long time. I can make out *t*'s, maybe. *A*'s. Not much more.

I go to bed. I sleep eventually. I wake and go to work. I return and eat and go to sleep and wake with the panic of the dream again.

I go to the kitchen, which is quiet once more. I open the journal. The first word is *The*. I try the next word. I run out of momentum. I go to sleep, repeat the routine. The next word begins with a *w*, I realise. The word is *water.* The night after, I realise that the word after that, which seems a single letter, is actually two: *is*.

"The water is at the steps," the journal says. I am learning. I can scan the cluttered page and make out most of the text. The page is an account of a flood back in a city in which Mums lived, Glasgow.

I read nightly, improving my comprehension. There is water all around the buildings, and still the rain falls. Mum's concern is that the river will rise right up into her lab. Other Mum is in the background, working steadily. This is the real world as it once was. I always thought that Home was terrible in the Terminal Years, but there is doubt in this account. Mum isn't sure she wants to leave.

I flick pages. I read about the house by the sea to which Mum took Other Mum. It belonged to Mum's family, grandfather, and great-grandmother before. She writes of the flowers and bushes, of the sand and what she finds washed up on the sand. She writes of the quiet, of the little cottage on the cliff and just the noise of the sea washing into the cove. It makes my chest ache to read it all, and so I flick and read about the hot foul summer after the flood, about the election in which Grandad was apparently involved.

I worry about her coming out of her room and catching me, but she doesn't.

I open another journal at random and there is an account of Larry the dog, padding around the flat in Glasgow. "This waiting is unbearable," Mum writes.

Home is different to me now: not the flat place of my former history lessons, but a city, two women huddling together in a flat, their dog.

I want to read it all but, forgive me, I skip. I open the top journal, scan through the pages doing the maths to recalculate M-years to the Terrestrial dates Mum still uses.

Then, just when I think I won't find it, the page is in front of me.

My hand shakes. I'm conscious of the dryness of my mouth. "Investigation:" it says on the page. "Incident on 109556. Roban involved. Cprl. Simms (deceased). Anomaly in systems readings."

The strange thing is that after reading the investigation entry of the diary I miss four nights of my routine. I do not have the dream. I don't wake and go out into the living area.

When I put on my suit, my health ratings are better. My OS tells me that I am making progress on well-being indicators.

I read that Mum thinks, as I do, that a glitch in the flow of time was at play, that Vishay and myself both travelled backwards. I felt such relief to read Mum's words, to know that I'm not the only one to have perceived the strangeness of the event. Still, despite Mum's firm belief, the Corporation board decided against investigating the phenomenon. She writes, "Cmd. wary of future engagements. Sceptical of validity of data. Cite danger and loss of Simms. Told that investigation does not align with objectives."

Maybe they really do think that there is nothing worthy of alteration in our collective past. "Failure is only a route to accelerated growth," Axel F once said.

I think of the slogan on the medal: *The future belongs to us.*

Mum has calculated the relationship between the backwards travel registered in our suits and the real time outside the cave. It multiplies, she thinks. I was in there for a second of outside time and travelled back five minutes. Vishay, in moments, travelled back a week. Mum surmises from the data that the relationship is linear, on the scale of 18000:1. "Provisional," she has written next to her figures. Still, it seems to align with what I experienced. It took Vishay two minutes of outside time to live days of agony and starvation and death.

And then I was there to meet that face. He had waited to warn me.

Mum thinks the phenomena was set off by the laser, by the power channelled into the rock by the burst of light. It opened a space, a sort of portal. You cross that barrier, and time flows differently, against you.

Now I have a different dream, of being in water. Mum used to swim in the sea on Home, she has told me. I have only been in the shallow pools we have here. Yet in my dream I float within a great expanse of dark liquid. Light shimmers through it. I'm not sure whether light really moves this way in water. I am unsure of where I am, in this dream, but my body seems to know.

I realise that it has been a long time since I first read the diary entry, because now when I walk to work there is no longer a crowd around the lawn. Alone, I can gain a scent of the grass now. But it smells like the plants in the crop wing, nothing more.

At work, I do less. I read the research archive. I reread Great-Granny's writings. The general history is restricted, classified Unnecessarily Distressing, but the papers themselves contain hints of their times. Great-Granny writes in a tone that speaks of urgency, loss, desperation.

Then there is a message on my screen when I wake: they want me back at the base for reconditioning. My leave is over. *Indefinite* means 631 days, I suppose. I feel an aching relief.

I have a week before I leave.

I go to work still. Mum tells me that I don't need to, but I must take in all that I can. I can't explain. I stay in the archive until late.

We go to the memorial wing before I depart. Miz's and Vishay's markers wink out on the plain, amidst a mild dust storm. Other Mum's is far in the distance, visible intermittently.

I ask Mum about Home, and she talks more freely than she did before about the little house in which Great-Granny lived next to the sea. "I'd give a lot to be back there," she says. "Everything, some days."

I go into the chapel. I sit in the white space and listen to the raised, beautiful voices from the past.

Mum takes a day off on my leaving date. She would never have done this previously, but I am grateful now. I ask that she doesn't walk with me to the transport bay. It would be too much for me. Instead, we part in the unit. I cry. She cries. She says, "I'm so sorry, R."

"I'm sorry," I say.

"No," she says. "Don't say that. What can you be sorry for?"

I walk to the transport bay with my belongings. Hours later, when I sit at the window of the transport and I see the round base beneath us, something loosens in my chest.

They give me a new partner, two years younger than I am: Sali. She's nice, skilled enough. I am the veteran now. We do a planetary mission and it goes without a hitch.

When I meet with Command, it is as if nothing has changed. They tell me that I flew well, beat the estimates.

"You've been missed," says Haley. She looks down. "Yourself and Corporal Simms."

We go out to the asteroid belt. I read. I keep to myself. I don't talk much to Sali. We get the samples. We return without incident.

Eventually things feel routine (appear routine, at least). I study the dynamic map of the belt. It is coming back around. It'll be aligned in a couple of months. I feel its approach.

There are moments when I wonder whether I could just prospect for years, sink into it. I could forget Vishay and Miz, take small victories, nurture hope as others do.

But that would be my fear winning, I tell myself.

I think of Mum carrying her regrets and I think I am not as strong as her, not able to bear as much as she has borne.

And my weakness will put further burdens upon her, I suppose. I cannot take the thought. It's too much.

I spend nights not sleeping. I hold Great-Granny's watch in my hand and feel it tick. I run my mind back over the work I did with Mum, the words I read in the archive. I felt amazed then by all she had worked out. I had always thought of all the machines in the Colony as *our* technology, manifestations of the ingenuity that separated us from all those left behind after the Great Collapse. *We took this from the past*, was my strange revelation. And then stranger, *We could give it back*.

Taking off for another mission, I fly up, and then, when some way from the base, I descend. It takes a moment for Sali to understand. I tell myself to stay strong. I feel outside my own body.

I bring us down in the plain. "You take a survival module," I say. "A couple of days, at most, until they find you."

She says, "What the fuck?"

"I'm not going to explain."

She looks at me. I open the door to the air lock. I release a survival kit from the bay. It drops, raising a little thump of dust on the surface. She stares at me. There must be something in the way that I return her gaze that makes her leave. She doesn't need to, but she does. Is it a kindness or an act of self-preservation? I don't know.

But now it feels easier. There is no stepping back from this point.

The air lock closes. She stands in her Exo next to the survival kit. I run the thrusters up. She steps back as I rise. I watch her until she becomes a speck and then is lost, indistinguishable against the dry fractured landscape.

On the journey, I am alone as I was when returning from the accident. They will not be able to catch me. I am at maximum speed.

I float at the front window and look out. Sometimes I trace letters with my fingers, writing manually like Mum, marklessly on the panels of the glass.

I sleep on missions as I can never sleep at home, weightless and tethered loosely to my bed.

At first I am unsure whether I mistake it for a mark on the window. But as I approach, I am more certain that I see it. It winks, the light from it changing as it rotates.

I guide the craft in, and as I do so I can hear Vishay's voice congratulating me. "You're skilled, my friend," I imagine him saying in a breathy whisper as I nudge the flight stick and align the craft with the spinning asteroid.

Then I am above the cratered surface, the whole universe going around and around.

I don't tether as I did when Vishay and I came. I modulate the thrusters. I come in low over the pockmarked surface, moving parallel with the long shape. The rock is gullied, broken up. I am about to consult my instruments to check that I'm on course, when I see quite surely that I am. The cave is suddenly ahead, a yawning void. I have dreamt of that triangle of darkness. My palms are slick on the controls. I hit the lights to full, and I fly the craft in.

I am so intent on guiding the craft into the tiny space that the weirdness of what happens to the light ahead of me does not, at first, really register.

In the closeness of the cave, the thrusters blow back, causing the craft to lurch and chatter. I manage to hold steady, however. I ease in. I see that the light ahead of me is falling away. The curtain of darkness is still there. I can hear a crackling sound from the instruments.

I bring down the craft and the first leg contacts. I tip the flight stick a hairsbreadth forward and the other two legs come down. I lock. I grip the controls for a couple more seconds. I release and breathe. Ahead of me the headlights die against the divide. It is not without its own illumination, though. A faint red glow seems to move beyond.

I turn the heaters to maximum. While the cab gets warmer, I open the other survival module. I tug out the bedding and rations, pull out my personal drawer. I take out the watch. I take out the six candles that I have smuggled from the chapel, and the matches—phosphorus-topped sticks—that the priests use to light these candles.

When the heat in the cabin is unbearable, I cut it off. I toggle a dial to raise the oxygen level as far as it will go. If I fill the cab, I've calculated, it should do me for the time I need.

Then I go back to the controls. I run the thrusters. The craft rises. I feel my pulse in the back of my hand. My clothes are soaked in sweat. I tell myself, *Now*, and give the flight stick a single forward nudge to take me through the curtain, which opens liquidly and which swallows the craft, killing the systems as it does so. In the last moments of power, I send a tethering line to the floor of the cave. The controls go down with a sigh. I am floating in the blackness. The tethering line comes taut. I grope for a match. I light it and transfer the fire to the candle. I look at the watch, which, needing no electricity, ticks on. *Two days, now*, I tell myself.

I am through and I am alive, for now.

In the first hour I talk to Vishay, as we used to speak on expeditions. It's calming. I eat a bar from the ration pack. "Your favourite flavour," I say to him.

At one point, I manage to say, "I'm sorry, by the way." I am going past him, past the end of his life in this cave. I could try to save just him, but I want more. Perhaps I will save him, differently. His fate is just a symptom. The result of a larger failure.

I speak into the silence. "You understand, right?"

The craft creaks and ticks. I feel his presence, imagine him saying that it is okay.

The watch clicks on. I am back far enough that he doesn't exist, that I don't exist. Yet here I am.

I do not sleep. I don't want to lose track of that watch, the progress of time here. Mostly, I preserve my candles. I float in the pure darkness. I can feel the tiniest things. I can sense the vibration of the little clockwork mechanism on my wrist.

I think of Miz and Mum and Other Mum. I imagine Larry the dog loping through the unit. Am I erasing them all? My own world? Myself?

Maybe it is the oxygen lowering, but I have vivid visions: distorted faces I do not recognise, saying things that I can't comprehend.

I think of Mum again and feel very sad. "I'm so sorry," I say to her. I am another loss for her.

But maybe I am a cure, too.

I must believe that I can save more than I will destroy.

She would do the same, I am sure.

Where even is she in relation to me now? Behind? Ahead?

I light another candle to look at the watch. It feels like a ritual. Not long now, I tell myself.

The candle burns up oxygen, I suppose. It leaves a tickling, scented smoke when it burns. It makes me cough. I didn't anticipate that.

I have a splitting headache.

Minutes now, ticking down.

The question of how I would power the craft back out of here stumped me for a long time, but I think that I have worked it out. There is a spare survival module. It can be triggered manually, with a lever. It will shoot from the bottom of the craft with a supply of compressed air. This should be enough to send the craft moving back the other way, as long as I undo the tether manually first.

I prise off the manual hatch with difficulty in the uneven candlelight. I toss it and it floats away from me.

I look at my watch. About a minute now.

My fingers are very cold.

About thirty seconds.

I count down from ten. I release the tether at five. I wait a couple more seconds. I pull the survival module. I have never exerted myself so much. I am pulling for my life, and I think for a long instant that my effort will never be enough. Then a sound of movement echoes out of the bay. Nothing happens for a moment, for too long. Then everything jolts. The candle flame brightens. There is a whirring. An alarm bleats. The systems come back up. The lights go on. The mouth of the cave is ahead of the front window, churning sky beyond. I have made it.

I take off shakily. I rise away from the asteroid.

I am back, my systems indicate, just about where I intended.

I go to the controls, think of Vishay, recall his hands touching the buttons to retrieve the stored flight program to travel to Home.

I do the same.

18

KENZIE

2110

I *sit at the round table by the window and think that the unit is changed by his* departure. This is different from when I lost Justine, though. Then there were things to pack away: her mum's faux-ivory hairbrush, her gold chain necklace, her clothes folded next to my own in the bedroom. Roban had little beyond his suit, left nearly nothing before departing for his base. He often mocked my love for what he saw as clutter.

It is only now, so late at night, after I have sat for a long time in the quiet unit, that I look back into the room and notice the ghosted marks on the walls that speak of his presence here. The decoration is tired, as it is in so much of the Colony, and in the dimness I see that the walls are glossed by the contact of my son's hands as he held himself up. I look towards the door to his bedroom and see the shiny mark made by the many times he placed his right palm against the wall to steady himself as he crossed the threshold. I can even make out dappled prints lower on the wall, from when he was a small boy. I sit and I look at the other blemishes—by the kitchen counter, next to the front door, on the wall between the bathroom and the sofa—and I build a little choreography for our child, imagine him moving in his clever way—a compensation that broke in time to grace. I picture him passing in and out of this room whisperingly, like he is the subject of a time-lapse video.

It is a comfort to envision all this. I have been thinking about time, trying to conceptualise it; testing out the notion that he survives somewhere else, before me, or beyond me.

The board called me to Headquarters, and I knew before they spoke that he had gone. We were in the main meeting room with all the most important people: the acting CEO, Myers M, Virginia Faulk, the other board members and department heads. Myers said, "According to mission logs, as of 14.25, three days ago, we lost contact . . ."

I could have stopped Myers then and guessed all that he told me. The orbit of the asteroid was favourable. Roban would have made the calculations carefully, arrived at a plan.

But I didn't say a thing. I sat and tried to master myself, to hold the shock of it all within. *He has actually gone*, I thought, but I kept the terror of that realisation to myself. I have given them so much already. I didn't want to allow them even a hint of my grief. (Though perhaps it would have made things easier to offer them a display.)

It took them a while to reveal their hand. They wanted me to state where I thought Roban was going, but I wouldn't. They knew and I knew, yet to say so might have caused them to suspect that I helped him. From the calculations I made in the moment I guessed that he would still be travelling to the asteroid. They have no ships faster than the one he is in, though, so catching him was out of the question. Pushing for information, Myers revealed that the corporation's calculations matched my own. He is beyond us, but not yet gone, due to reach his destination in the coming hours.

After they had made their reveal and waited for the reaction that I would not give them, they tried to find out whether I'd known of his plans. They suspected that I'd helped him.

"Check the OS logs," I told them. "Check the data from our unit."

"There are things we can't pick up, regrettably," said Virginia Faulk.

She looked at me with her head tilted. She knitted her fingers in a way that recalled her father. I thought of the old man in that glassy penthouse back on Home. "Did you have an inkling?" she said. "A hunch?"

"He was sad. He'd lost two friends. He was changed by that last mission. I'd never presume to know the extent of someone else's grief."

"Even your own son's?"

"Especially."

We sat at a large stone table in a room quarried from a cliff above the Inner Plain. Justine's division—mining—had made the place, though not while she was still around. The window looked out at the lighted colony beneath us, the threaded walkways and nodes amidst the dust and rubble. They'd had me in the room before, after Roban's first visit to the asteroid. Then, they'd wanted rid of me. I'd been excited by the data. I couldn't explain exactly how, but I felt sure enough that Corporal Simms had shifted back in time, had opened a wormhole accidentally. It wasn't my speciality, but expertise in this kind of physics—previously highly theoretical—was not what Tevat was seeking when decisions about uplifts were being made years before. There were no such experts in the Colony, so I'd been the one to take on the investigation. I assembled a team, read the data, and studied the theory, and then in that meeting I spoke about the readings from the craft and the suits, the curious results of the postmortem examination. They didn't want to know what I had found, though. They sought to close the case. "But it might be a way to change things," I said. "Have you really considered it?"

"Change things?" said Myers. He grinned indulgently, as if I were being naïve.

"Speaking very theoretically," I said, "what if there were a way to travel back in time? What if it were possible to go back and intervene? What if we could prevent the Terrestrial Collapse?"

"Come on," Myers said. "Your readings are just anomalies. And even if they are significant, you know it's not so simple."

"But why not just explore the possibility? I'm not saying you should be rash."

"But perhaps even that consideration would be rash," said Myers. He sighed. "This board's first duty is to the Shareholders. To you, in fact. To others like you. We have come this far, despite hostility on Home from governments and politicians. Our Shareholders invested their faith in us, and with their help and their faith we have made all of this. I appreciate that you want to . . ." He stopped, seemed to think. "Ameliorate greater losses. But my duty is to the people who have invested me with power, the people who are *here*, who Axel F in his foresight managed to save. We are delivering for those people currently. We have a plan." He frowned. "If we tinker and anything changes for the worse, if a single Shareholder is disadvantaged, I am not doing my duty. You know this. I am sorry. We are all sorry. The past is so sad. But our project and our priority is the Colony. We made this all ourselves and we must preserve it."

I'd seethed as I had walked out of the room, down the tunnel carved roughly through the rock. I didn't fully understand my own anger. Myers's flat denial seemed a travesty. But maybe, yes, it was consistent with their approach. I thought of Axel Faulk's face, of a kind of smile—faint, amused, superior—that he would flash at me across his penthouse room.

The second time—today—I stayed much longer. The questions circled. There was one thing I was keeping from them. I suspect that Roban had read my journal about the investigation of the event. I felt he was owed that, though. He was falling apart with guilt, with the repercussions of a tragedy he couldn't understand. I'd always felt he should be allowed to learn of Home and of all we didn't speak of regarding Home. I'd made no efforts to hide that journal. I'd been glad he'd read it. At the least, he deserved to understand all he could. I had no intention to provoke this flight, though. This reaction of his was a risk. I tell myself I am allowed no guilt, no regret.

He was tantalised, I suppose. We are alike, more so than I used to think. I wish he hadn't left, but I understand his urge to do so.

As the conversation went on, it became clear that the Corporation were flailing. They were scared. Eventually Myers came out and vocalised their terror. He said, "Is he going to erase us?"

"Sorry?"

"When he goes through . . ." He looked at a screen on the table in front of him, checking the time, I think. It was the middle of the day, still twelve hours or so before Roban was due to arrive and, presumably, to push into the glitch that he had found with his friend.

I paused. Even feeling such loss as I did then, there was a small satisfaction to be gained from Myers's discomfort. "So it's not just an anomalous phenomena?" I asked. "You do believe that it's a sort of wormhole?"

Myers cleared his throat. "I believe that is *possible*," he conceded. "Have you told the boy of your desire to travel into the past and visit Home?"

"I've told him nothing," I said. I stared at Myers for a moment. "And that wasn't my desire. I suggested it was something to investigate as a possibility."

"Okay. But if he has reached your conclusion, tries to alter things on Earth, in *our* past. Do we just . . ." He snapped his fingers.

I said, "That's not impossible." I waited. "But I doubt it."

"Why?" said Virginia Faulk sharply.

"The way I've understood it, we're either here or we're not. We either always were or never were."

"Yes?"

"And we're here. He came from here." I slapped the table. "I don't understand the causal mechanism by which this suddenly . . . turns off."

"I don't like it," said Virginia Faulk. "I never liked this stuff."

"What do you believe?" said Myers.

"I think time splinters," I said. "He's heading for another timeline.

Or he can't really change things. He thought Corporal Simms changed the timeline and saved him, but I'm not totally convinced of that."

"He spoke to you of these things?"

"I read the interview you did with him when you kept him captive on the base."

"I see."

Eventually I said, "Are you going to keep me here too?" That was the right question, it turned out. It affronted them.

"We're not a *government*," said Virginia Faulk. "We're not imprisoning you."

"No?"

"We'll request your cooperation again, but . . ."

"I'll be glad to give it."

She nodded swiftly then, and I stood, moved before anything could change. I walked out of the room and down the corridor. No one stopped me, and now I'm here back in the unit at midnight or after midnight. (I'm too far from the clock to see and my wrist input is on the kitchen counter.)

I haven't heard the shuttle in a while, which must mean that it's late. Out the window, in the far distance, I can see the lights from harvesters toiling over the plains.

Has he gone through yet? I wonder. I'm sitting up, as I have so often sat up, but I am also waiting.

I wept for a long time when I returned to the unit, and now I am temporarily on the other side of that grief, possessed of a tired lucidity.

A strange thought: Presuming I am not erased, today will be another anniversary in time. It will join Justine's death—seventeen years in a month and four days from now—and Dad's birthday. Mum's passing too. One more charged day to negotiate each year. I've become adept at keeping track of these things. Were I to say this to someone, I would sound self-pitying, but that is not the case. It is the privilege of the survivor to be able to remember, after all. At times I do feel lonely. But still, life goes on and I am glad of that, despite the wounds. I am a scientist, eager to know, to see an experiment taken to its conclusion. It saves no one to rue my own survival.

If I stood and went to the clock in the kitchen I would know. On course, Roban will arrive just before one. He'll likely try to enter the strange cave soon after. I'm staying up to test Myers's fear that Roban's crossing through this wormhole will erase us all. Then again, could such a thing even be confirmed from my perspective? What does it feel like to be flicked instantly out of existence? To never have been?

But I am here. I am still here. And still . . . and still . . .

I sit listening to the humming of the climate systems and the ticking of the cooler pipes in the kitchen. I look out the window, at the plain washed a dim yellow by the light that leaks from the base. My own face is reflected in the window. The eyes I know—they are the eyes I had as a child, as I knew myself best—but the face around them—the older face—is strange.

I look at myself and think of Isaac Newton, actually: an odd connection that comes to me in a rush.

He was interested in the way light bounces back from glass. He wondered what determined how much light was reflected back by a pane. The key factor, it turns out, is the depth of the pane. The deeper the pane is, the more reflective it becomes. And yet here is the strange thing: the light somehow knows this depth the moment it hits the glass. There is not some instant of delay as the rays travel through the pane to fathom its thickness. It just reflects in the right proportions instantly.

It all sounds trivial, until you really think about it and realise that this must mean that information is travelling faster than the speed of light. The light has charted the depth of the glass before negotiating it. But how? Has it moved ahead of itself prospectively? When I have pondered this, I've imagined the light making a phantom journey through the glass; outside of time, ahead of time. I wonder now—loose and weary—what if time doesn't move so cleanly forward, but jumps and jerks, blooms and shudders? It is late and I am tired and liable to half-formed thoughts.

The world seems not to have changed. I am not gone, but neither is Roban back, nor Vishay saved, nor Miz and Justine living once more. He will be attempting such miracles, I expect, but I also believe that they'll happen elsewhere, on a different track. Maybe I live in a little loop: the place from which the change—my son—comes and does not return. I want to believe that, actually.

What if there's a little provisional space before what is truly real? What if that is the mechanism by which the light bounces cleanly from the glass? Could you live in that space? What if I do? What if this life is the phantom light, as it were? Maybe Roban is returning to the main flow of events. Is he the correction, the data, the depth? I think of playing football with Dad as a child. It was never his thing, and I'd always score against him quickly, and he'd say, "That one was just a practice." His reaction was exasperating, but the memory pleases me now. It's comforting to think that I might be living in the *practice*. What if *this* is just a stretching out, a reaching, a whorl that eddies and goes nowhere? Could there be another time in which they're okay—Roban, Dad, Justine, and Mum? I'd be happy for this life to be a dream if it meant them all prospering elsewhere.

I'm half-mad with tiredness. I look at my reflection and see that my cheeks are damp, my eyes red.

What if I just chose to believe it? Decided that my son has jumped back to a reality deeper than my own?

And what am I doing then? Living in a counterfactual. A might. A maybe.

All I know is that he is gone from here and that I hope he prospers, and that meanwhile I will live a life that I'd be glad to know was a dead end, in this small station clasped to the cold red earth, this world ahead of time.

I hear a new noise then: a ringing so high that I seem to sense it in my teeth first.

The shuttle is starting again.

Which means that it is three. Which means that he has passed through.

I am still here, persisting; alone in my blunted timeline.

Maybe I will sleep, or maybe I will just sit here and then return to Headquarters as the board have asked me to. They are not happy with me still, and they want a better explanation, a fuller story, an apology. What would it cost me to give them that? I believe that he has skipped beyond their reach. I remember watching Dad on the news after I was selected to come here, asking why he wouldn't give me up, absolve himself. Yet now, at the point that someone might ask the same of me, I think I understand him. There is a sense of myself that I need to hold to, a principle. I have my own story.

What does my story mean here, though? Alone. What is the point of all the pain and wasted work?

I look at the glass again, at my face, traced in highlights against it.

Maybe the point is to have tried, I think? To be like the light. To try and then to turn around, knowing that this way is not the way.

19

ROBAN

2025

The sea catches my attention first. The suit lifts open and I look up as the front of the Exo rises to reveal the twisted beams, the rust-eaten roof. The sound of the water is all around me, heavy and abrasive and plosive and tinkling. It comes at me on every frequency. (Just as the light here, though it is whitish light like the light of the Colony, is so much *fuller* than any light I have known.) I can feel the noise on my lips, my skin. The suit, intended for use in locations without atmosphere, is not engineered to receive sound, and so to unseal it is a revelation.

I prop myself up on my elbows, experiencing the fuller gravity of the planet with this effort. I gasp air. I glance down, half expecting, so full is the sound of it, to see water crashing around the Exo, but no, that drama is a few hundred meters away, and the shed is as it was when I laid the suit down to sleep: the uneven floor, the crooked stone walls, the rising and diving of particles of dust.

I have a plan for this place, and this plan does not involve what I am doing now. When I made my calculations in the final days before my return to prospecting, I didn't countenance the risk of clambering out of my suit. But today, on my third morning here, I woke and something stirred in me, and I pressed the button.

It is very early, still. My great-grandmother will be asleep in the house. Why have I not told her that I am her relation? That I know how things are ahead of her, or *could* be ahead of her (without me here, that is)?

I wanted things to be smooth, frictionless. The important thing is teaching her, showing her. Not the other stuff. Not all this.

But still . . . Am I only here for the plan? These lessons with my ancestor? For this great long-shot attempt? I flail. I improvise. I have travelled such a long way alone, half-maddened by my journey. I have no strategy for my return. Am I not due, at least, acquaintance with this planet?

The air is so much. I feel a bit sick with it. It tickles my throat. I cough. It has a taste—dry and sour—and behind that a rich organic bouquet. I think of the grass, the bushes that I moved past in the dusk when I came here, the rubbery sea plants between which I strode underwater as I came from my craft. I think that I can smell all these things, and I try to overcome the unfamiliarity of the sensation. If anything, the air smells like the compactor in the unit sink—clogged with rotting organic waste—but I try not to let my disgust grow. This is the *real* world, I tell myself, the world as I should have known it.

I think far back to the Colony, to one time when I was a teen, and when my pain was bad. Mum gave me this look I knew: her *planning look*, as I thought of it. She brought me a thick metal disc. "What's that?" I asked her.

"Tuna," she said. "A type of fish."

She opened it right there: these chunks of flesh that had once been part of a living thing. She had carried it all the way from home and saved it so many years for me to try.

Yet I looked at it and felt ill. I knew that eating this stuff used to be normal, but I couldn't do it. I said, "I don't want to eat something that lived."

Mum laughed. "Believe me, the fish doesn't mind at this stage."

I put it in my mouth and managed to swallow. Mum watched. I wanted to please her.

Oh, Mum.

She would be glad to see me here, I tell myself.

I feel the pressure of the future or the past, or whatever it is.

Waking in the cramped space of the Exo, I thought of Vishay. I recalled Vishay describing circling the planet, speaking of looking down at the new growth on the ruined land.

But he is gone, or maybe he is not come yet, or perhaps my presence here means that he will never be.

But he *is* with me, in a sense. He is here through me.

I think of Vishay coaching me to run in my Exo, showing me how to move as fluently as he did: "Let yourself go," he said. He would have willed me out of my suit now.

I put a hand on the edge of the Exo. I haul myself up into a sitting position.

I catch my breath. My pulse throbs in the wrist of my grasping hand.

I bring my legs under me. I come to kneel. I feel stabbing pains in my back. But I manage to drag myself up to a kneeling posture. I stop and rest. Above the sounds of the sea and wind, I can hear a repetitive squeaking. It's a piece of machinery, I conclude at first, confused. Then the sound changes from this looping squeak to a twittering chatter. *Bird-song*, I realise. There must be birds outside, moving between the bushes, rising from the grasses.

I choose to take the song as a sign. I lean forwards. I drag up my left knee. I get a foot down, planted in the padded body of the Exo. I push up. My stomach aches. I draw something taut within myself. I raise myself too quickly. I tumble forwards, over the side of the Exo. I hit the dirt. I roll. I am lying on my back. Dust rises around me. The wind pushes through the cracks in the stone walls of the shed. I am unused to air like this: unconditioned, free, warm in places, cool in others, always in motion. It's like a living thing, plucking at me, trying to rouse me.

I rise. I push myself up. My head hangs forwards, my chin against my chest. There is so much that must be coordinated. Somehow, I get myself onto my knees and shuffle over the floor, enduring the pain of this abrasion until I am able to brace my weight against the wall and stand.

There's a coolness to the stone that I didn't expect, a texture under my touch that I couldn't imagine. I rest my face against the wall. There's a mineral taste in my mouth, whether from the stone or from blood, I don't know. I breathe. I walk my hands over the stone. I let my feet follow my hands towards the light. I close the distance to the doorway minutely, a single step at a time. I lunge into the sun, half believing as I do so that it will dissolve me.

At first there is just the sheer blinding force of the light, the furred heat of it on my cheeks.

It is so bright. I close my eyes and there is still light behind my eyelids. The wind gusts. I steady myself against the doorway.

The sea crashes. The birds still sing. The roof of the shed makes a sound like old music. I place one foot forward, then the other. I am beyond the threshold of the shed now. I look down and I see the grass. I step onto it, and it is cool. I feel the damp strands compressing beneath my feet, sliding over each other, giving, springing back to caress my arches. I have a hand against the wall to my left, supporting myself. I move forwards parallel to the shed, and then, when I am truly exhausted, I lean back against the stonework.

I close my eyes, for a long time because the brightness is almost too much. When I open them again, I can see the lawn that stretches away from my feet: so different from the lawn of the Colony, uneven and pockmarked. At the edge of the lawn, where the land slopes down, the grass gets longer, waving in the wind. Farther off, beyond, the island falls away completely, leaving air, rising birds, a great shimmering, shuddering, rolling sea beneath. It is unlike anything I have ever seen, all this water.

Then I hear a shaking in the air. I move my head very slowly, but I cannot make out the source.

I close my eyes. I listen. A buzzing moves past me. An insect, of course. Yes.

It returns. The sea breaks and shatters and groans. I feel a prickling on my skin.

The buzzing has stopped.

I look down at my bare forearm, and my heart leaps. It is *on* me: a fly.

I hold my breath. I try to stay still.

It makes a tiny, prickly stutter step, but it stays.

It seems content. It's a furry black thing. It has a head that shifts in a strange mechanical way, ticktocking back and forth, gyroscopic. It has big, strange eyes, like crystals, reddish, bulging.

The fly lifts its front legs, seems to brush them together. Its wings, veined, transparent, vibrate at great frequency.

A living thing, I think, on my skin as if my skin is a planet.

The fly's legs are bristly. It has a strange trunk-like mouth, which it seems to use to spit upon its legs as it rubs them. Its back, between its wings, is a shiny greenish blue, like metal.

I have seen animals on my entertainment feed as a child. I know of flies from people swatting them in dramas, and from nature footage focused on larger creatures—horses and herds of wildebeest in Africa, for instance—around which insects orbited.

Yet this knowledge is nothing against the actual moment of encounter. The fly is not a thing that I look at recorded. It is a thing that I see *now*, a being that is with me in this moment. It sees *me*, I think. There is a reality mapped inside that tiny brain of which I am now a part. It's the monarch of its own little world, a centre, a point in space, sucking stimuli. It makes its tiny steps. Its head turns and turns in that odd metronomic way. What does it make of me? I wonder. Am I a giant to it? Am I terrain?

Then as I watch its whole being shimmers. I realise that it knew before I did that a gust was coming in, because as I feel the wind, the fly has already sprung from my arm, rising forwards and then pulling back and up, ascending as if drawn on an invisible string towards the overhanging roof above me.

The breeze moves through the fabric of my shirt, hits chill against my skin. I look at the sea again: metallic, dark and light at once.

That ocean will die, I know. I did well in Terrestrial History at school, learnt all of this. The water will acidify. The currents will turn. Life within it will perish, compounding the destruction. The land around me will expire too, drying, burning. Too much rain will fall in the wrong places, and too little where it is needed. Yet it doesn't feel like the start of an apocalypse out here. I cannot help but forget myself.

I step forwards onto the grass, and step again, and again and once more, and then I am in the sun. I let myself go down, in a twisting motion that comes to me as I make it. I lie back, my arms thrown out, my legs spread. I don't tense a single muscle. I can hear the waves breaking and I can hear the bird still and I think that I can hear the moving grass too, and maybe the brittle bushes with their little flowers that I passed on my way here in the night. My eyes are closed because it is too bright. But I am okay. I feel the sun on my lids.

I should move, but I pause just a little longer. I am so glad that I came out now. It feels wonderful to be out of the suit. I allow myself just a moment, and then another moment. I should have known this place. This instant has been waiting for me, I feel. The wind plucks at my hair and the turf is cool beneath my shoulder blades. I open my hands and run my fingers across the stalks of grass, feel the moisture on them, the cracked lumpy earth between the strands. I must get up, and yet I stay lying, feeling myself alert to everything. *Now*, I tell myself. *Now. Now.*

ACKNOWLEDGMENTS

Thank you to my agent Molly Atlas, for the belief you held in early versions of this book, for your kind guidance as it was redrafted, and for your advocacy when it was completed. Thank you to my editor Nneoma Amadi-obi, for your vision and for your deft suggestions, which have immeasurably improved this novel. I'm hugely grateful to my students and colleagues at the University of Cambridge, for your creative fellowship. Thanks to Nick Bradley, for listening to my early ideas for this project, and to Alycia Pirmohamed, for reading and offering such encouragement at a crucial stage. Thank you to my mother, Nicola Bennett. As ever, special gratitude for the twin guarantors of my happiness, and humility: Jenny Reed and our dog, Cromarty.

Parts of this novel were inspired by Mark O'Connell's *Notes from an Apocalypse*. I recommend the book to anyone looking to read more about the perils and weirdness of Mars colonisation projects.